PROVOST

The Unfinished Manuscript

Gordon Kay

"PROVOST – THE UNFINISHED MANUSCRIPT"

Cover design by Emma Kay
Printed by CreateSpace, an Amazon.com Company, Charleston SC
Available from Amazon.com, CreateSpace.com, and other retail outlets
Available on Kindle and other devices as well as other retail outlets

ISBN 13: 978-1481110501
ISBN-10:1481110500

DISCLAIMER
Although based on happenings in the life of the author, most names, identifying details, characters, businesses, places, events and incidents are either the products of the author's imagination or used in a fictitious manner so as to protect the individuals' privacy. The author has tried to recreate events, locales and conversations from memories and used these in their context as a work of fiction.

PROVOST

For Emm

Many of the events in the following pages
take place long before I met Emm,
but
this book is dedicated to her,
because
for more than thirty years she ran
interference on my life
and
kept me safe.

For Emm,
with love,
G.
Semper ibi

Author's note

This book is based on true events in the life of the author.
It is, however, fiction.
To quote Stephen King:

"Fiction is the truth inside the lie."

Since making a conscious decision to rejoin society I have been fortunate to re-establish contact with friends of yesteryear. Friends that I thought had been lost forever. It has turned out to be extremely rewarding for all of us.

So, if you ever wore a white hat - or indeed if you wear one today - do yourself a huge favour and visit the site http://www.rafpa.com/.

More specific information regarding membership, fees, etc. can be found here – just copy the link, sign up and become a member – http://www.rafpa.com/organisation.htm
Make the effort; you won't regret it!

Also, regardless of your age and nationality, if you, or indeed a relative, ever served at Royal Air Force Duxford in the United Kingdom, I urge you to visit The Old Dux Association's website and sign up, www.olddux.org. We are a dying breed, we need your help and interest. And, oh, the Newsletters are a blast - just say Alex sent you.

Back in December 1959 Pete, who is mentioned in this book, went to the UK on leave. He handed over his married quarter to me on the condition that, when he returned in January, he could move into one of the spare bedrooms as a lodger. This we did, until someone snitched to officialdom. They were not amused; we lost our happy, but illegal, accommodation.
I would like to find Pete.

So, if any reader has any knowledge of Pete Hilman out of Eastbourne, ex No. 1 P&SS Detachment, RAF Sundern, BFPO 39, Germany, please contact me at gk@provostthebook.com.

Upon being evicted, a very kind person came to my assistance. Bill had just been allocated a new married quarter in Munster; he and his wife unreservedly offered to accommodate me. With gratitude I accepted and spent a very happy few weeks there until my departure for the UK in March 1960. I would like to find Bill.

His full name is Bill Mountain, ex Traffic, No. 1 P&SS Detachment, RAF Sundern, BFPO 39, Germany.
Again, please contact me at gk@provostthebook.com.

Gordon Kay

Snowdrops

Snowdrops
This is the nickname given to the Royal Air Force Police Non-Commissioned Officers who, unlike the rest of their Royal Air Force colleagues who wear blue headgear, stand out uniquely with their white-topped caps, which became standard issue in 1945, following the end of WWII.

Introduction

The idea for this manuscript was first planted in my head one sunny Spring day back in 1999. I was sitting on the balcony of our apartment in Athens trying to enjoy a pot of green tea, read a book and carry on a meaningful conversation with Son-Number-Two.

Impossible.

I closed the book; the conversation was more important.

At 14 life can be difficult; particularly for the parent!

The conversation ranged through many family topics – nothing of any great importance – until he suddenly asked me if I would tell him some stories with regard to some of the happenings in my life, just as I'd done when he was younger.

I hesitated.

'You know there are things in my life that I can't talk about,' I said.

He looked at me and nodded. I suddenly felt awkward. 'You do know I've done many things that I will never talk about, don't you?'

He nodded again.

Then, 'Why don't you write it all down, put it away somewhere, and only let us read it when you're dead.'

Such simplicity!

When I'm dead? And I'd always thought I was immortal!

But, the seed had been planted … I thought about it regularly – and rejected the idea with equal regularity.

Less than 6 months previously, Emm and I had spent days sifting files and destroying papers when we learned there was a high probability that visitors from abroad would come a-calling. Some files had also been moved to safer ground while the rest was firmly planted in my brain, forever.

Over the months and years that followed the seed had sprouted, and began to grow, watered no doubt by events that still had a part to play in my life.

The boys grew up, went to university, and then Son-Number-One departed for the UK to complete his Masters. While they were at university we'd kept an apartment for them in Thessaloniki. First, our youngest left and then, on his return from the UK, his brother followed suit. This was early autumn 2008.

With just under six months still to run on the rental contract I decided, for some still unfathomable reason, to move into the apartment and write, and I wrote for five solid months, reliving those events of fifty years ago with tremendous clarity. I didn't just see them again; I was actually there! It was wonderful …

The book you are now holding is part of those writings. I say part, because this book, which contains some 90,000 words, is roughly two thirds of what I produced. The remainder, which was on a USB flash drive and ready for printing, went missing in January 2010 when Emm's handbag was stolen on the car park of a supermarket in Sofia, Bulgaria. The person responsible was caught but only a solitary mobile phone was recovered. The case is ongoing, but at 4:57 pm on Tuesday 26th June 2012 in the Criminal Division of Sofia Regional Court, Vladimir Blagoev Ganchev, married, age 35, was found guilty on all four charges brought against him relating to the robbery. He was sentenced to four years' probation with the proviso that, if within the next two years any other criminal charges are brought against him, the four year probation term will immediately convert to a four year custodial sentence. Compensation and all legal fees were granted in Emm's favour. The sentence is in appeal.

So, where was I to start? Obviously at the beginning – but just where was the beginning? I sat and talked with Emm. We decided the events of the preceding 50 years – God, am I really that old? – could, quite easily, be divided into 5 separate books.

- Book 1: covering the first four defining years, 1956-1960. Royal Air Force Police, Provost and Security Services.
- Book 2: Europe, East and West.
- Book 3: Africa-1980 onwards. Ivory Coast, Congo, Burundi, Rwanda plus the changing of the guard in Sierra Leone.
- Book 4: Bulgaria 1992-1996. This is already partly written but would need to be extended with details from *those files.* Working title: Bulgarian Interlude. It would also include the possibly only one hundred per cent true account of the Plutonium 239 affair (Atomic Weapons for Sadam Hussein) that hit the news on Sunday 1st November 1992. Apart from perhaps the Bulgarian Security Services, I believe I may be the only person to have discovered all the facts behind the published stories that exploded around the world that Sunday morning in November 1992. After all, I was there, just two doors down the corridor from "the happenings". Once more, truth is stranger than fiction purporting to be truth.
- Book 5: Last, but by no means least, Suriname. The military coup of 1980 and the rise and rise of Sergeant Major – now Colonel – Desi Bouterse who, once again, is president of his country.

This would have been the most difficult book to write simply because Bouterse is still alive and once more running

Suriname. A convicted drug trafficker (Holland, in absentia, 1999), gun runner and still-to-be-convicted murderer.

Now, the farther your residence is from Suriname does not necessarily equate to a longer and healthier life span. But, back in December 1982 I was due to travel to Paramaribo, the capital of Suriname, to meet up with a group of people we shall simply call The Opposition. My trip was scheduled for the second week in December. On 8th December 1982, 15 Surinamers, 13 civilians and 2 military personnel were arrested, tortured and finally shot. My trip was aborted. Had I journeyed out earlier, then 15 would have undoubtedly become 16.

Two years previously and immediately following the successful military coup, Bouterse had sent a hit squad to Europe to eliminate any potential leaders of opposition to his regime. These were primarily Surinamers who lived in Holland and Belgium. He failed, but he hasn't forgotten. Desi Bouterse has a son Dino, who eagerly and energetically follows in his father's footsteps. Dino, also a convicted gun runner and drug trafficker, was recently appointed by his father to head up the State Anti-Terrorist Unit.

All the above is true.

Finally, there was the ingenious plan to kidnap the president, which had everyone running for cover.

Welcome.

This, then, is The Other World.

And so, with a plan in mind I began to write, and, as I've said, I wrote continuously for the next five months. It became obvious early on in the game that even then, way back in the late Fifties, I frequently did things in a fairly unconventional way. On reflection, I decided that, when viewed from several different perspectives, this manuscript needed to be fictionalized. So, that is exactly what I did and, as I've previously mentioned, what you are now reading is a work of fiction.

I thought about it for a long time but I simply have no heart to rewrite the missing parts of the manuscript. What's done is done. I can't go back again. Instead, I thought, if Beethoven can do it, so can I. Hence the title: *Provost - The Unfinished Manuscript.*

I feel I should just mention that parts of the manuscript are written in different ways. Some parts are done in interview format, written by an author of children's books who was brought out of East Germany back in the Sixties and went to live in America. His partner died in 2008 and he subsequently visited Greece to talk with Alex.

At Emm's request he conducted a series of interviews to which Alex reluctantly consented. Although very different in style to the main body of work it was decided to leave both the interviews and author comments untouched. Unfortunately, many of the interviews were on the stolen USB flash drive. Only a few survived.

One last thing: the name Alex Gordon. It is one of several names under which I worked. It is also my favourite working name and, to avoid confusion, will be used throughout all books.

Let Justice be done

The Provost

In 1629, the Articles of War of Charles I of England contained the following comment concerning the position of Provost and his responsibility:

> *"The Provost must have a horse allowed him and some soldiers to attend him and all the rest commanded to obey and assist or else the Service will suffer, for he is but one man and must correct many and therefore he cannot be beloved.*
>
> *And he must be riding from one garrison to another to see the soldiers do not outrage nor scathe the country."*

In 1662 Francis Markham compiled the ideal requirements of the Provost Marshal. These were:

> *"A man with great judgment and experience of martial discipline . . . well versed in all laws and ordinances of a military camp and in all matters essential to the smooth running of an army . . ."*
>
> *"The Provost Marshal should love justice, be impartial in his dealings and have an eye that could gaze on all objects without winking and while having a heart filled with discreet compassion was not touched by foolish or melting pity."*

Charles II in 1672 said of the duties of the Provost Marshal:

> *"The Provost Marshal, either regimental or general, was to apprehend and hold offenders for trial, to punish them according to the sentence of the court. No one was to hinder the provost except on pain of death and all officers and soldiers were to aid him or suffer court martial."*

Fast-forward almost 300 years:

> *Senior Aircraftman Geoffrey Irvine, Royal Air Force Regiment, 23:50, Saturday 13th December 1958, RAF Sundern, West Germany, upon being subdued and subsequently arrested for causing an Affray and attempted GBH (using broken beer bottle as a weapon) and then being propelled rather unceremoniously into cell no. 3 by Alex: 'All Provost are fucking arseholes!'*

For some, no doubt, a truism.

The realities, however, lie somewhere in the pages that follow.

Glossary

1250	RAF identity card
Amis	German nickname for Americans
Beata	pronounce Bee-AR-te
AOC	Air Officer Commanding
Brixmis	British Military Mission to the Soviets
Carpe diem	Seize the day (Latin)
Champ	Military vehicle used by army (made by Austin)
Colditz	A castle in the German town of Colditz that served as a high security POW (prisoner-of-war) camp during WWII. Built on a rock, the Germans believed it to be escape-proof.
DI	Drill Instructor
DP camp	Displaced Persons camp
DIE	*Departamentul de Informatii Externe*; Romania's foreign intelligence service
Dear John	A letter received from a girlfriend, fiancée or wife back home to advise the recipient that he had been dumped.
Dig	a reprimand (on your military record)
Dolmetscher	Interpreter (in German)
Dose of clap	Gonorrhoeic infection; a sexually transmitted disease
GD	General Duty (General Dogsbody)
Geordie	A person from NE England, i.e. Newcastle, Tyneside

Groschen	A *10-Pfennig* coin (10 *Groschen* to 1 Deutsch Mark)
Halton	Royal Air Force Hospital Halton
Jock	Slang for a Scotsman
Kraut	Slang for a German person, (short for *Sauerkraut*, the pickled cabbage eaten by Germans)
Kripo	short for *Kriminal Polizei*. Criminal Police, i.e. CID (Criminal Investigations Department)
LAC	RAF rank: Leading Aircraftman
Lolly stick	Carried by traffic police. Roundel on handle, red centre, white edging, black STOP printed across centre
MO	Medical Officer
MT	Motor Transport
Meat wagon	Ambulance
NAAFI	Navy, Army, & Air Force Institutes
NVA	*Nationale Volksarmee* – National People's Army, i.e. the armed forces of the former German Democratic Republic
ORs	Other ranks (below rank of corporal)
Paddy	Slang for an Irishman
PBX	Military telephone exchange
Pongoes	Army, soldiers
R&R	Rest and Relaxation
Rat-house	Pun on *Rathaus*, the German for Town Hall
Redcap	Army military policeman
Rosenmontag	Highlight of German carnival on Shrove Monday

RTU	Return to Unit
SAC	RAF rank: Senior Aircraftman
Securitate	Romania's secret political police
Senior Man	He is in charge of the billet, acting under instruction of the DI
Sludge	Nickname for draught German beer
Smudger	Nickname for Smith (Old Smudger)
Snowdrop	RAF police, referring to the white cap they wear
Soxmis	Soviet Military Mission
Spetsnaz	Russian Special Forces
Stammkunden	German for 'regular customers'
STASI	*Staatssicherheit*, i.e. State Security, the common name of the former East German Ministry of State Security
Taff or Taffy	Slang for a Welshman
U/S	Unserviceable
Vanguard	Standard Vanguard car used by plainclothes CIS
VOPO	Nickname for East German *Volkspolizei*, i.e. national police.
WAAF	Women's Auxiliary Air Force (1939-1949). Although later renamed Women's Royal Air Force (WRAF), the term WAAF is still used
Wegburg	Military hospital in the town of Wegburg
Wo-man	Pronounced 'woe-man'. Slang for Warrant Officer

BOOK I

GREAT BRITAIN

Alex enlists into Her Majesty's Royal Air Force Police

1- Flying the Nest: Welcome to Cardington
2- West Kirby: There's always a Bully
3- AWOL
4- RAF Police Training School Netheravon
5- No.4 Police District Duxford
6- Guardroom Duty, Attempted Murder and a Trip to the Asylum
7- Ginger
8- On the Move

Chapter 1

Flying the Nest: Welcome to Cardington

Monday 12th March 1956 was Alex's 18th birthday. Ahead lay the unknown; but also the right to choose for yourself, the right to plan your own future, the right to make your own decisions. These things were important to Alex. He made his first decision: to fly the nest.

Monday 19th March 1956. Alex collected a travel warrant from the RAF recruiting office, headed to the main railway station and exchanged it for a one way ticket to Bedford. Exciting stuff! The future – *his* future; a future chosen by *him* – was about to begin…

In the beginning, Cardington turned out to be a bit like school – three days of lectures, things like history of the Royal Air Force, learning ranks of all the armed services – and then a couple of days of tests. After this it was time for individual assessment.

Alex was greeted with, 'Come in, come in! And grab a pew,' followed by an extremely hearty handshake. 'OK, now this is confidential.' He paused until Alex nodded. 'You came out top in all the tests. Now, what do you think of that?' He paused again, while Alex thought of something constructive to say. Instead, he just shrugged, 'It was easy.'

'Yes, well, look, I see you got your GCEs and can speak French and German.'

Silence.

Alex shrugged again. 'Yes.'

‘Look, don’t you think you’d be better off going for officer training? I can certainly get you to sit the basic tests.’ He paused and looked across at Alex. Nothing; no reaction.

‘Don’t you think you’d be happier if you could make officer grade?’

‘Not necessarily. I know what I want to do. RAF Police, Provost, nothing else.’

‘Oh.’

‘I want to make this my career. If I like it, I’ll stay in and I can always apply for officer training if it takes my fancy somewhere along the line. I can, can’t I?’

‘Well, yes of course,’ said the Flight Lieutenant, ‘and education-wise you are already exempt from testing up to, and including, the rank of Warrant Officer. So, you seem to know what you want. You want to make this your career? How long would you like to sign on for: nine, twelve or the twenty two?’

‘Four,’ replied Alex.

‘Pardon?’

‘Four.’

‘I’m afraid you can’t just sign on for four years if you want to be Provost. It involves an awful lot of training. It’s a very specialized job. Just think of the cost. The RAF has to get its money’s worth. Surely you can see that?’

‘Four. I don’t want to make a mistake. I can do four years, even if it turns out not to be what I want in the end. I’ll make a decision, say, after three years and hopefully I’ll then sign on for the lot. I can’t risk it going wrong, though. After all, it is my life.’

‘Yes, quite,’ mumbled the Flight Lieutenant. ‘Look, I’ll tell you what I can do. I’ll talk to some people, and you come back here, shall we say same time tomorrow, and we’ll have another chat.’ He stood up. Interview over.

Alex wandered back to the billet. He got soaked; it was absolutely throwing it down.

During the night it snowed. Alex picked his way gingerly across the ice from a baking, fume-filled billet with two wood burning stoves, to the interview room. The door was half open. He knocked and entered. The Flight Lieutenant was seated behind his desk. 'Do come in, old chap, and take a pew. Terrible weather and I'm afraid the heating has rather packed up here. Probably best to keep your coat on.' He pointed to the chair in front of the desk, 'Do take a seat, old chap, do take a seat.' Alex sat.

'Now then,' said the Flight Lieutenant, 'I've had a word with some chaps as I promised, and I've got some rather good news for you. They considered your education, your test results here, your wanting to make a career in the service, and they've offered five years. There, what do you think of that then?'

'No. Four,' replied Alex.

'Oh? Look, as I said yesterday, there's an awful lot of specialised training involved, and four years doesn't quite cut it. Surely you can see that? After all, if it's going to be for life in the end, what's one year?'

'Well, if we look at it that way, and they say five, then why not four?'

'It's not quite the same thing, is it, old chap? You must remember all the training and investment being poured into you. Surely you can see that?'

'Sorry,' Alex replied, 'I'm not prepared to take the risk.'

'Then I'm sorry old chap, but under the circumstances, I don't think we'll be able to help you with your preferred trade. What will you do?'

'I go home, go to the army recruiting office, sign on as a Redcap for four years, and take it from there.'

'You seem to have thought it all out.'

'I have. I've spent nearly two years thinking about nothing else.'

'Right, let's see now, why don't you go away and come back here again tomorrow, about this time. In the meantime, we'll all have a bit of a think. How does that feel?'

'Fine,' said Alex, 'I'll see you tomorrow.'

Outside, the skies were heavy and dark. Snow was coming down by the bucketful and Alex went arse over tip on the ice.

Next morning, after a night spent trying to avoid being choked to death by the wood fumes that escaped from a cracked cast-iron stove, Alex again skated over to the interview room, ready to do battle. The door was open, and the Flight Lieutenant sat behind his desk, huddled in a greatcoat, staring into space. Alex walked in unbidden and sat down.

'Ah, yes, my dear chap. Do sit.' He stared at Alex. Alex stared back. Slowly, a smile lit up his face. He got up, came around the desk, stopped by Alex's side, grabbed him by the right shoulder and alternately slapped him on the back and shook him, saying, 'My dear fellow, my dear fellow. Congratulations. We've done it!'

Alex tried to remain upright on the chair. Again, 'We've done it, we've done it! The powers that be have agreed. Four years it is, dear chap. We've done it!'

Alex couldn't quite see where the "we" bit came in, but he smiled anyway. He'd done it; he was in - on *his* terms!

The rest of the week passed in a bit of a blur. Standing in line with another dozen or so recruits to swear allegiance to the Queen and take her shilling. Shaking hands with the Wing Commander, who kept repeating, "Well done, chaps, well done", and finally, two days before the end of induction week, best blues and battle dress were issued. He finally belonged. The motley crew were called together and first postings were read out.

For Alex, home for the next eight weeks would be Churchill Squadron, RAF West Kirby, Liverpool.

Chapter 2

West Kirby: There's always a Bully

For Alex, the lasting memory of West Kirby in April 1956 was the freezing, icy wind that came hurtling in from the Atlantic directly onto the parade ground, freezing your eyeballs somewhere deep inside your skull, and your other balls somewhere up under your heart where they desperately tried to keep warm. Becoming an involuntary eunuch was a distinct possibility. He also learned the real use for the "Saturday-night-finger".

For the uninitiated: Saturday-night-finger is the middle finger of the right hand shown to all and sundry by the driver of the car in the fast lane after you have unavoidably held him back from overtaking for the past twenty seconds. The real purpose of the Saturday-night-finger has, perhaps surprisingly, nothing whatsoever to do with carnal pleasures. Its true purpose is to keep the rifle in the perpendicular. One sticks one's Saturday-night-finger through the trigger guard of one's rifle while supporting the rifle barrel with the right shoulder and trying to march along with the other twenty nine members of the squadron in three very crooked lines across the parade ground, straight into the teeth of this sodding Atlantic storm. They say practice makes perfect. In these conditions, it doesn't.

Strangely, Alex enjoyed West Kirby. Much of it entailed being screamed at on the parade ground, and one recruit continually broke down in tears every time the DI stuck his nose in his face and screamed that he was a stupid bastard. The reason? After eight weeks of putting one foot in front of the other, the poor sod still didn't know which was his left and which was his right foot. More interesting bits included the classes which taught Royal Air Force history and the rifle range where Alex almost succeeded in taking off the top of his right thumb when the rifle blew back.

Oh, and he was involved in two fights and went AWOL once.

First fight took place when the barrack room bully reduced one of the more timid recruits to tears. Alex told him to pack it in. The bully then turned on Alex who hit him not once, but many times in rapid succession in the same place: the nose, reducing it to a flat bloody mess. He then grabbed the bully by the hair, dragged him across the width of the room, opened a window, leaned the bully's back against the sill and very slowly tipped him backward, head first, out of the window. He then closed the window and walked back to his bed to resume bulling his boots.

The second fight occurred a few seconds later, when the bully's henchman hit Alex across the back with a broom handle while he was looking the other way. It laid him across the bed. He lay there for a minute in agony, then turned over and slowly got up. He wrapped one end of his webbing belt around his right hand and swung, hard. The metal clasp caught Broom Swinger across the left cheek and opened it up in a big gash. Alex dropped the belt on his bed and hammered Broom Swinger repeatedly in the face, driving him the length of the billet and out onto the grass. He then returned to his bed and carried on bulling his equipment as if nothing had happened.

The room was deathly quiet, nobody said a thing. Bully and Broom Swinger failed to reappear and next day both were transferred to other lodgings. The hut DI asked Alex if he'd like to be Senior Man.

Alex declined.

Chapter 3

AWOL

The usual practice at that time was that after the first four weeks of torture, the recruits were shown mercy in the form of a 48-hour pass. One whole weekend free in which to go home and cry to Mummy and Daddy what beastly people these DIs were. Mummy and Daddy would make sympathetic noises and say they understood – a miracle really, since they probably hadn't understood you from about the age of twelve. Anyway, passes were handed out, signed and then handed back for the DI to keep until Saturday morning. Freedom from 08:00 Saturday until midnight Sunday, which of course is not 48hrs, but it pays not to argue! Time to laugh, cry, screw, and find once more a better use for your Saturday-night-finger.

The week passed normally enough; shouts, screams, tears, *fucking-this, fucking-that* with a few *stupid bastards* thrown in – you know, the normal shit: life in square bashing.

Friday afternoon came. Rifle range finished, lectures finished, billet floor bumpered and gleaming, everyone sliding about on pads rather than walking like normal human beings, which of course they weren't. Until …

'You! Come here! Stand to attention, you little turd. Don't look at me. Eyes front. What are you?'

'Don't know, Corp!'

'You're a turd. You're not a man, you're a turd. What are you?'

'A turd, Corporal.'

'The whole squadron would like to know what you are! What are you?'

'A turd, Corporal.'

'We can't hear you, can we squadron?'

Silence.

'WE CAN'T HEAR HIM! CAN WE, SQUADRON?'

'NO, CORPORAL!' they all roared.

'So, and at the top of your voice, so that even the Almighty knows – YOU – YOU ARE A FUCKING TURD! Ready?'

'Yes, Corp.'

'NOW!'

The voice screamed out, 'YOU – YOU ARE A FUCKING TURD, CORPORAL!'

Silence.

Absolute silence.

Then first one titter, and another one, until finally everyone fell about laughing, and Alex was marched off to the cookhouse in double quick time where he spent the next four days washing dishes and peeling ever increasing mounds of potatoes.

And so life continued. More shouts, more screams, more tears, more blasphemy, until at week six the squadron was deemed sufficiently advanced to, once more, be let loose on the civilian population: another 48-hour pass.

Alex slid his way to the washroom, stripped and climbed under the shower. Heaven, pure heaven. In the background he could vaguely hear the noise in the billet – laughing, shouting and then, one god almighty crash and clatter. It sounded like the roof had fallen in. Silence. Then, 'And just what the fucking hell is going on in here! Jee-zus, fucking Christ! You!

Don't stand there, get the fucking sand bucket and put that fire out. Who's responsible here?'

Silence.

'I said, who's fucking responsible here? Never mind! All of you confined to camp. All of you! Fucking 48-hour passes cancelled. You're all confined to camp. Tomorrow morning stand by your beds at 08:00, full kit inspection. Now get that fucking mess cleared up!'

Alex dried himself, put on fresh clothes and walked back into the billet. The place was a mess. Everything covered in dust and soot. Apparently two of the guys had been horsing around; one pushed the other who retaliated, sending his opponent flying back into the stove and chimney. The stove moved, the chimney collapsed, the soot slowly spread throughout the room, which brought about the DIs intervention and everyone's confinement to camp. Alex moved to his bed, opened his cupboard and pulled out a duffel bag. Everyone watched.

'What you doing, Alex?' squeaked Little Jimmy.

'I'm off!' replied Alex.

'You can't do that, they'll sling you inside!' exclaimed Geordie.

'Sod'em,' said Alex. 'Dave, come here. Now listen, I'm off. I'll be back midnight Sunday. When the shit hits the fan in the morning, you tell that prick in there that I phoned my parents to try and stop them coming to Liverpool. They'd already left. They're on their way. I had to go and meet them. Tell him I'll be back Sunday, and tell him specifically "Alex said, he hoped you'd understand", you tell him that exactly, OK?'

'OK. Alex, are your parents really coming to Liverpool?'

'Are they hell. Just tell him, OK? Exactly as I told you.'

'What you doing now?'

'Look, Dave. There's a bus that stops inside the camp at five o'clock to take the civvies into Liverpool. I'm on that bus.'

'But you'll be in uniform. They'll never let you on.'

'You want to bet? Look, Dave, stop being a wanker and tell old pisspot in there what I told you, OK?'

'OK, Alex, see you Sunday.'

Alex put a few things in the duffel bag, put on his uniform and then his greatcoat over it. He stuffed his beret in his pocket and walked out of the door.

The bus was parked directly in front of the guardroom, blocking the view of anyone inside who wanted to look out. The civvies were walking towards the bus in dribs and drabs. Alex walked closely behind a group of three and climbed onboard with them. Ten minutes later the bus departed and headed for Liverpool. Alex hopped off in the city centre, bought a train ticket and headed south. West Kirby it might be, Colditz it wasn't!

Weekend over. Back on the train heading north. Off at Liverpool and onto a bus. The nearest bus stop to the camp was two miles away.

Alex walked. His fingers were cold; he'd forgotten his gloves. He trudged on. A minor point, he thought, was how was he going to get back into camp. He couldn't just stroll in via the front main gate; they'd want to see his pass, and of course he hadn't got one. Hadn't thought about that at the time, had he? *A bit late now. I suppose I'll have to climb over the fence,* he thought to himself. He looked. The fence was at least ten feet high and topped with barbed wire. *Forget it!* He'd have to think of something else. He plodded on. Another mile and he'd be there.

Gradually he was aware of a car slowing down and driving alongside him. The driver wound down the window.

'Going to camp?'

'Course, I'm going to camp, there's nothing else for miles around, he thought. 'Yes, I'm going to Kirby.'

'Hop in. I'll give you a lift.'

'Thanks.'

The internal light came on as the driver leaned across and opened the passenger door. Alex climbed in and the light caught the insignia; three bars on the shoulder, two thick, one thin. *Oh, Jeezus; a bloody Squadron Leader! Now what!*

'Been on a 48?'

'Yes, Sir.'

'Enjoying the Service so far?'

'Yes, Sir. I'm going to stay in.'

'Oh, what trade?'

'Provost, Sir.'

The Squadron Leader turned and looked at Alex. 'Good man, good man.'

Do all officers say everything at least twice?

They turned into the main entrance, the barrier was down. The Squadron Leader beeped twice and wound his window down. The duty erk came running from the guardroom, saw who it was, sprang to attention and saluted. The Squadron Leader returned the salute. The erk hadn't moved from the rigid.

'Airman, would you mind lifting the barrier so we can come in?'

The erk moved at the double and lifted the barrier, never even looking at Alex.

The car stopped and let Alex out in front of the mess hall.

'Goodnight, Airman.'

'Goodnight, Sir. Thank you.'

With a wave the car drove away.

Alex slowly exhaled. He looked at his watch; 23:55. Then he started to shake; finally he started to laugh. His own Squadron Commander had actually brought him home. How about that!

Alex crept into his billet to the sound of gentle snoring. He laid his duffel bag on the bed.

'You're in the shit.' It was Dave. Dave had six fingers on each hand instead of five. Alex had idly wondered in the past how he coped on Saturday night. He'd have to look how he balanced his rifle.

'Go back to sleep.'

'Can't.'

'What happened? Did you tell shit-head what I told you?'

'Yes, word for word.'

'What did he say?'

'Nothing.'

'Nothing?'

'No, he just went purple and veins stood out on his forehead. I'll tell you, Alex, I thought he was going mental. He stood there for a minute, he was actually shaking. Then he turned round and walked out the door he'd just come in. We stood to attention for five minutes, nobody came back, so we just sort of broke up, you know, sat down and started nattering. Then the door flew open and arsehole came back in. "Did I dismiss you fuckers?" he screamed. We all stood to attention. "You will all stay like that until I dismiss you", he yelled. Then he stormed out. The fucker kept us like that for twenty minutes, then he came back in and dismissed us. Nice as pie. Told us we could take the rest of the day off. Guy's a fucking nutter. Needs locking up.'

'But he didn't mention me?'

'No. But I bet he will in the morning. You're in the shit, Alex, with a guy like that you're always in the shit.'

08:30 Monday morning. Breakfast over and everybody stood by their bed for the usual Monday kit inspection.

The door opened, Senior Man screaming *'OFFICER PRESENT!'* and in walked the Squadron Commander, followed by a Flight Sergeant, a Sergeant and the Corporal DI.

Alex wanted the floor to swallow him up. The Squadron Leader examined the kit laid out on the beds one by one. He used his swagger stick to turf things onto the floor – a shirt here, a pair of socks there. He finally arrived at Alex's bed, looked at the kit and then at Alex. Alex wanted to die. The Squadron Leader smiled.

'Good morning, Airman. No ill effects from the weekend, I trust?'

'No, Sir.'

'Good.'

The Squadron Leader nodded and moved on. Alex could see the vein throbbing in the DI's forehead. The inspection continued and then the billet stood down and the recruits picked their things up from the floor to put back in the lockers. They all looked. The only kit left untouched belonged to Alex.

The remaining two weeks passed quickly. The weather got warmer, the screaming died down, and Alex walked on air. He'd achieved God-like status in the billet; after all the Squadron Leader had stopped to speak to him – unheard of! And his bed hadn't been tipped up; don't forget that! The DI never shouted at Alex again; in fact he hardly ever shouted at anybody. Well, he still shouted at "Fucking Useless", but you could understand that. If you still didn't know which one was your left foot after eight weeks, then you really were fucking useless!

Passing out parade, photographs, handshakes, two weeks leave and then to Police School, Netheravon, Wiltshire.

Chapter 4

Royal Air Force Police Training School Netheravon

The best Police Basic Training School in the world, is how Alex once described it, and he should know. He's seen them all. Belgian, Dutch, German, Canadian, American. Oh, I forgot. When you're around Alex, it's best not to mention American police - military or otherwise. He is not a fan . . .

_

This is the only part of a fairly extensive interview relating to Netheravon that remains. Unfortunately, the write-up relating to the very intensive 16 week police training course was on the USB stick that went walkabout in Sofia.

_

Alex loved every minute of it.

Corporal Kendal, the course instructor, went absent without leave in week 14. A woman, of course – isn't it always! – but he was a brilliant instructor. They caught him and stuck him in the cells. That must have been a first!

Alex remembers his lectures to this day. He also remembers the self defence instructor who seemed to have a thing about trying to dislocate your shoulder or inflict other types of bodily harm on the quaking recruits. And then there was Jock who played a prank on Alex, which misfired badly. In the ensuing kerfuffle Jock received a burst eardrum which was to leave him permanently deaf in his left ear. This nearly cost him his career but he still didn't snitch. Something Alex isn't proud of.

At the end of the course promotions were handed out, and postings were allocated. Alex was hoping for anywhere overseas; instead, his home for the unforeseeable future was to be HQ, Number 4 Police District, Royal Air Force Duxford, Cambridgeshire.

He hated it.

Chapter 5

No. 4 Police District Duxford

Since the recorded happenings of Winter 1956-Spring 1957 are missing, courtesy of the previously mentioned gentleman who nicked Emm's bag, let's jump right into Summer-Winter 1957.

_

Bored stiff with doing nothing, Alex managed to wangle a posting to Horsham St Faith, near Norwich. Still boring. Temporary job as bodyguard to Prince Philip; no comment - might be dispatched to *The Tower*! Visited and saw USAF Police in action for first time - not impressed: drink-happy, weapon-sloppy, us-and-them attitude. Said so. Boss appalled. Alex not surprised; for him it was always 'Happy Hour' with the Yanks . . .

Two weeks following his return posting from Horsham St. Faith to No. 4 Police District, Duxford, Alex was beginning to feel right pissed off. There was nothing to do – again!

Each morning following breakfast, six police NCOs stood around talking in the duty NCO's room until it was time for NAAFI break. Following NAAFI break they would return to the duty NCO's room where they would stand and talk about nothing until lunch. After lunch they would return and continue to talk about nothing until approximately 15:00 when they would all troop off 200 yards down the road to Betty's Café where they would drink tea and eat biscuits for an hour. They would then return to the detachment until 17:00 when they would all wander back to the billet, pick up their eating irons and go to tea. 19:30 would see them all head off for the NAAFI until bed at about 23:00.

This was life as a Royal Air Force policeman? This was what he'd left home for? This was his future? *No way*, thought Alex.

Next morning he presented himself at the orderly room and obtained a form requesting an overseas posting.

Where to?

First choice: Germany.

Second choice: Far East.

Third choice: Middle East.

He then presented himself to Squadron Leader Rawlings and laid the form on his desk.

'So, you want to leave us then, do you? Why?'

Alex told him.

The Squadron Leader sighed. 'I sympathise. I really do. But your mother was recently widowed and it is your responsibility, at least in the short term, to remain close at hand. Therefore I must reject your application.' He handed the form back to Alex.

Alex didn't even bother returning to the duty NCO's room. He headed back to the billet and lay on his bed thinking. When it was time he wandered over for an early lunch, then back to the billet where he changed into civvies and walked down the road to catch an afternoon bus into Cambridge. He returned in the evening, happy. He had devised a plan.

The following week on Friday, Squadron Leader Rawlings departed on two weeks leave.

The following Monday morning Alex waited for the Detachment CO, Wing Commander Harry Henderson to arrive.

The duty driver always delivered him to the detachment at exactly 09:00. The Wing Commander would retire to his office and at 12 noon the duty driver would take him home again – drunk. This happened day in, day out, without any alteration in timetable. The man was an alcoholic. Squadron Leader Rawlings ran the Detachment.

Alex waited for him to close his office door, then counted to twenty and knocked.

'Come.'

Alex entered the room, stood before the Wing Commander's desk, saluted and laid the form in front of him.

'Morning, young man.' He looked at the form. 'Just arriving, are we?'

'No, Sir, been here for nearly a year. Out on detachment at Horsham St Faith, though.'

'Ah. I see. What is this then?' He tapped the form.

'An application form for overseas posting, Sir.'

'And where would you like to go?'

'I thought Germany might be interesting, Sir.'

'Yes, indeed. And what would you like me to do?'

'Sign the form, if you would, Sir.' Alex leaned forward and pointed. 'Just here, Sir.'

The Wing Commander unscrewed his pen and signed his name with a flourish. 'Would you like me to stamp it?'

'If you have a stamp, that would be nice, Sir.'

'Of course I have a stamp. Want to make it all legal, don't we?' and he applied the stamp delicately below his signature. "Wing Commander, CO 4 Police District, Duxford". 'There we are, how's that?' He handed the form back to Alex.

'Thank you very much, Sir, most kind.' Alex swung a salute and headed for the door. As he closed it he heard a chuckle, 'Good luck, young man, good luck.'

Alex headed directly for the orderly room and handed the form over.

One week later the detachment duty clerk pinned a note to the notice board. Alex was on standby for overseas posting.

Squadron Leader Rawlings had been back from leave less than fifteen minutes when he opened the door to the duty NCO's room, saw Alex, and beckoned him out. He walked across to the notice board and pointed.

'What's that?'

'I'm on standby for overseas posting, Sir.'

He looked at Alex. 'I could stop it, you know'.

Alex didn't speak. He waited.

Suddenly the Squadron leader stuck his hand out and grinned. Alex took it – amazed.

'Well done, son. Look after yourself over there; it's not all fun and games,' and with that he turned on his heel and walked back to his office.

Things seemed to buck up a bit after that; Alex even managed a few motorcycle runs: Wittering, Marham, Cottesmore and even back to Horsham. They were giving him work. Alex appeared to be the flavour of the month.

Chapter 6

Guardroom duty, Attempted Murder and A Trip to the Asylum

Alex knocked on the door, entered and saluted.

'Stand at ease son. Now then, how'd you like to work in the guardroom?' Alex's face dropped. 'I wouldn't. I joined Provost to avoid exactly that. Checking vehicles in and out of camp isn't exactly my idea of fun.'

The Squadron Leader smiled. 'I realize that and I know that you've put in for overseas, but I was thinking more in terms of experience. Can't hurt, you know. Shall we say two weeks? See how it goes, a month maximum. What do you say?'

What can I say, thought Alex. *If I say no, I'll probably get a bollocking and be sent anyway. So it's really Hobson's choice.* 'Put like that, how can I possibly refuse, Sir?'

'Quite. Tomorrow morning, report to Corporal Goodie at the guardroom. You'll be shadowing him for the next two weeks, then come back here and we'll have another chat.'

Next morning Alex reported to Cpl. George Goodie, a dark-haired lad with the remains of acne still showing. He also wore chains with lead weights inside each trouser leg down by his ankle. They held the trousers level above his pristinely blancoed white gaiters, but every time he took a step he chinked. Chink, chink, chink, chink, chink. The crease in his blouse and trousers were as sharp as razors and you could see your face in the shine on his toecaps.

Jeezes, groaned Alex inwardly, *what a prick!*

Alex, though, was one hundred percent wrong.

George was the life and soul of the party; he took nothing seriously – unless his Sergeant was around – and life for him was one long laugh. Alex and George got along together big time.

After two weeks he reported back to the boss. 'Well, how'd you like it?'

Alex grinned. 'I enjoyed it. I also learned a lot.'

'Thought you would. Particularly with Corporal Goodie. Now, I've got a job for you. Tomorrow morning you're going to Newmarket with Corporal Coleman. You'll dress in civvies and take one of the unmarked Vanguards. You're going to arrest a chappie who demobbed himself one year too soon. Seems he worked in movements, national service, missed his girlfriend and didn't like his job – didn't like the Air Force – so he filled in the appropriate forms, stamped them, filed them and discharged himself. It took us two years to find out. Pathetic, isn't it?' Alex didn't answer; he took it to be a rhetorical question. Squadron Leader Rawlings continued, 'YOU will arrest him, YOU will charge him and if necessary, YOU will cuff him. Understood?'

Alex nodded.

'Now then, when you've put him in a cell over the road, YOU will look after him until something happens. YOU will write up the report, YOU will handle everything. Then at the end of two weeks you'll report back here, guardroom duties complete. OK?'

'Yes, Sir.'

Squadron Leader Rawlings handed Alex a file.

Alex saluted and left.

'And don't make a balls-up!' was the boss's parting remark as Alex closed the door.

They arrived in Newmarket just after noon. The first thing they did was take a run past the soon-to-be-arrested LAC McGovern's address and then head off for lunch. According to the file McGovern worked in a local bank and returned home a few minutes after 5 p.m. every day. The girlfriend he'd left the Air Force early for was now his wife. She was pregnant. She also had a boyfriend. The baby wasn't McGovern's. McGovern didn't know about the baby, nor did he know about the boyfriend. His wife had turned him in to clear the pitch for the new arrival.

Alex suddenly didn't feel much like arresting the poor sod.

They watched McGovern let himself in through the front door, then sat and waited for ten minutes. Pete Coleman went to the garden gate in the lane at the back of the house. Alex rapped the front door. The wife let him in.

Alex walked through to the living room where McGovern was standing in front of the fireplace drinking a cup of tea. He looked at Alex, puzzled. Then he saw Pete walking up the garden path. He went deathly white; the cup and saucer fell to the ground, spilling tea over the pristine beige carpet. McGovern followed it, out cold.

A cool flannel brought him round. They sat him in a chair and Alex slapped the handcuffs on. Pete raised his eyebrows as if to ask "Why?" Alex ignored him. He charged McGovern, read him his rights and led him out to the car, placing him behind the empty front passenger seat. He climbed in the back behind Pete, the driver, and next to McGovern, who didn't utter a word all the way back to Duxford. McGovern's arrival was processed, the MO visited him and his coat, belt, tie and shoe laces were removed. He was led to cell number 1. The door was locked. McGovern still hadn't said a word. The time was exactly 19:30.

George was working until 22:00; that meant Alex was as well. He walked across to the billet and changed into uniform, then walked over to the NAAFI and picked up a couple of bacon rolls for George and himself to nibble on. Alex was starving and, most uncharacteristically, he felt worn out, drained. It's all in the head, he told himself, let's crack on. A meal in the Mess when he was finished and a couple of vodkas in the Club would soon put the world to rights. 20:00; only two hours to go.

Alex walked back into the guardroom and tossed George his roll. 'Supper'.

'Alex, can you watch the shop a minute? I need the pot.'

'Why didn't you go?'

'Well, it's the sit-down type of operation, if you follow me. Might be a while.'

'Take the roll and that newspaper with you. Be comfortable!'

George gave him the birdie and headed out back.

Alex sat behind the desk and bit into the bacon buttie; delicious. He devoured it ravenously. Roll on dinner! Then he thought he heard a sound back in the cells. The only occupant was McGovern. Alex decided to take a look through the spyhole. Stretched out on his back, arms akimbo, left leg straight, right leg bent and head just missing the corner of the on-the-floor type bed lay McGovern. Something didn't seem quite right to Alex. To fall and land like that somehow looked unnatural. Alex unlocked the cell door and went in.

First big mistake!

He bent over McGovern who appeared to be out for the count. Alex knelt beside him and looked down to see if there was any sign of life.

Second mistake!

McGovern's arms suddenly shot upwards and both hands grabbed Alex around the neck. McGovern squeezed – hard. Alex hit him repeatedly in the stomach; it had no effect. McGovern seemed to possess superhuman strength.

Alex was losing this one and he knew it. Stars appeared to be shooting around in his head. He tried to call out for George, but the sound he emitted was more like a screech. He pummelled McGovern again. Nothing. In fact McGovern was beginning to lift himself from the floor, using Alex's neck as a support. McGovern's eyes were staring as if he couldn't focus, and saliva was running down his chin. Alex tried to call out for George again. Nothing. He simply had no strength.

Suddenly there was an almighty THWACK and the hands around Alex's neck fell away.

Alex rolled to the ground beside McGovern, gasping for breath and retching. He was vaguely aware of George standing there, left hand desperately trying to hold his trousers up above his knees while in his right hand he held the large, grey guardroom torch: the source of the THWACK. He looked at McGovern lying next to him. Still, and totally out of it.

George helped Alex to his feet. He gestured towards McGovern, 'Do you think I killed him? He's not moving.'

'Frankly, George, I don't give a shit,' croaked Alex, 'the bastard nearly killed me. He would have if you hadn't come. I owe you another bacon buttie.' He tried to laugh but failed. He was gasping. The words seemed to come out in unconnected batches.

George pulled up his trousers and put the cuffs on McGovern, while Alex put his head under the ice cold water tap and tried to drink it dry. Swallowing hurt.

McGovern still wasn't moving.

The MO arrived. 'Where is he?'

George pointed, 'Number 1'.

They all trooped into the cell. With McGovern taking up much of the floor space there was very little room.

He MO felt his pulse.

'Hmm …' He lifted the left eye lid and shone a pencil torch in it. That was the very moment McGovern struck again. Both legs up together and across, catching the MO in his side. He flew across the room, banging his head against the wall.

'Fuck, fuck, fuck! ... Oh, Shit! ... Restrain that prisoner!' He looked comical, sitting up against the wall, holding his head with one hand and rubbing his side with the other.

Alex held back from laughing.

'George, get his belt from the drawer.' George came back with the belt. McGovern was lying there, watching them, eyes darting from side to side, spittle running down his right cheek.

Alex spoke to the prisoner. 'McGovern, I know you can hear me. Now, my friend here is going to put this belt around your ankles to stop you kicking. If you kick him while he's doing it, I'm going to bring my foot down in your face and break your nose. Understand?'

He raised his right foot and held it over McGovern's face, who still didn't move. But he started to whimper. The MO's mouth was wide open as he sat against the wall and watched.

'Do it George!'

George looped the belt over McGovern's ankles and twisted it tight. Not a single kick. Then they hauled him onto the mattress.

'All yours, Sir,' Alex said to the MO. Again the MO examined the prisoner's pupils. Then, instead of feeling the pulse, he used a stethoscope on the chest. Finally he took a long needle from his bag, pulled up the left leg of the prisoner's trousers and stuck the needle in his calf. McGovern didn't even flinch. He was muttering and mumbling incoherently to himself. The MO stood up.

'Quite frankly, I have never seen anything like it. He needs hospitalisation so he can be examined properly. Halton, I think. Who's in charge?'

With a big grin on his face George pointed at Alex, 'He is!'

The MO nodded. 'Right. You'll have to go with him as escort. I'll prepare the paperwork for you to take, and the ambulance will be over shortly. Now let's take a look at you. Open.'

He pressed Alex's tongue down with a spatula, made him say "Ah" several times, stuck a torch halfway down his throat, felt either side of his neck – that hurt! – and pronounced that Alex would live. Bruised, swollen, but essentially OK.

'Tell me, Corporal,' he said looking up at Alex, who was a good six inches taller, 'Would you really have brought your foot down on his face? The truth now!'

'Yes, Sir, I would. And I'd have been justified. It's called using the minimum amount of force to overcome the maximum amount of resistance. There's even an equation for it.'

George burst out laughing; he just couldn't help it. 'Sorry, Sir,' and then promptly burst out laughing again.

The MO looked at Alex, sure that somehow the piss was being taken, he just wasn't sure how. "Mmphh," and with that he turned on his heel and left the guardroom.

He arrived back with the ambulance forty minutes later. Two medics entered McGovern's cell with a stretcher. McGovern screamed and screamed, and although firmly secured with cuffs and belt, somehow managed to throw himself about and project his body a good two feet off the ground. Four heads turned and looked at the MO. 'My, oh my, I've never seen anything like this before!'

Talk about instilling confidence, Alex thought to himself.

'I'm going to give him an injection to calm him down. Would you secure him please?'

The MO filled a syringe while Alex held McGovern's head and George his feet. The MO stuck the needle in his left leg and pressed the plunger. 'Right. Let's give it a few minutes to take effect.'

They went back in to pick him up and the whole performance started again. McGovern was somehow still able to throw himself about.

'I don't understand it,' muttered the MO 'I've given him enough to knock out a horse. I can't give him any more.'

'OK,' said Alex, 'you two medics, one to each shoulder, George and I will do the legs.' They literally threw him onto the stretcher and secured him with restraining straps. Then he was loaded into the ambulance. The MO handed an envelope to Alex. 'Everything you need is in here. Halton are aware and are expecting you.'

Alex climbed in the back with the prisoner, the doors were closed. The two medics were up front. Alex was in the back alone with this nutter; he felt more than a little apprehensive. McGovern did not stop screaming obscenities at the top of his voice and trying to throw himself off the stretcher for the whole 90 minutes trip. For Alex it was a nightmare alone in the back. They finally arrived at Halton, the ambulance doors were opened and Alex staggered out, shaking inside and bathing in sweat. After five minutes of – once more – creating hell, McGovern promptly fell into a deep sleep. He was wheeled into a secluded reception area and Alex went with him.

A doctor carried out a perfunctory examination: pupils, blood pressure and pulse, and then turned to Alex. 'He's out cold. No telling how long this will last, so there's not much we can do now. We'll put him in a side room and try again in the morning. In the meantime, I suggest you get some sleep, the Corporal here will find you somewhere.' And with that he promptly departed.

The Corporal stuck out his hand, 'Nigel's the name.'

'Alex.'

'Let me show you to your quarters.' He led Alex away and into the labyrinths of the hospital. Finally he stopped and pointed at a room, 'All yours. Make yourself comfortable.'

Alex stared. A padded cell. Rubber walls, rubber floor.

'At least you'll have a quiet night,' said Nigel grinning. 'It's soundproof. I'll send blankets and pillows. OK?'

'Wonderful!' replied Alex. *Now, who's taking the piss!* He couldn't help thinking he was being set up, but once the door closed and his head hit the pillow, he was oblivious to the world.

Morning arrived in the shape of a matronly nurse bearing a cup of tea, a Penguin biscuit, a towel and a toothbrush. 'Thought you might be in need of sustenance, dear. Shower's down the hall to the right and someone will fetch you for breakfast at eight. That gives you an hour to freshen up.'

Alex grunted his thanks.

The someone turned out to be Jock, a Corporal medic from Aberdeen. He led Alex to the small dining room. Immediately inside the door he stopped and clapped his hands. 'Right. Attention everybody. We've got a guest for breakfast this morning. This,' he pointed, 'is Alex. And Alex is a policeman. So we'd best be on our good behaviour, hadn't we?'

He turned to Alex and in a voice that everyone could hear he went on, 'Most of the boys here don't like policemen, since it was often a policeman that put them here. Now, as you can see, I've given you the position of honour.' He pointed to a seat on the far side of the table.

Alex counted. Four nutters to the left of him, and four to the right. Opposite were nine and at either end there were two.

He knew he was being set up here.

With a calmness he didn't feel he took his seat on the far side of the table.

'Now, let me introduce some of your fellow diners. Immediately to your right is Brian. Now, Brian was caught dismembering his mother-in-law. The only problem was, she was alive at the time. To your left is Cyril. Now, Cyril's specialty is necrophilia. In other words, he likes fucking the dead. Don't you Cyril?' Cyril had gone bright red and was staring down hard at the table top.

'And this handsome young man here…,' he patted a rather grotesque figure in front of him on the shoulder, 'is Jimmy. Now, Jimmy's girlfriend sent him a *Dear-John*. Dumped you, didn't she, Jimmy? So Jimmy wanted to end it all, didn't you Jimmy?' He patted Jimmy's shoulder again. Jimmy nodded.

'So, Jimmy got himself a can of petrol and poured it over his head. Then he lit a match and this is the result.' He patted Jimmy's shoulder again. 'He's doing well, though, is our Jim. Off for a spot of leave in a couple of days. Aren't you, son?' Jimmy didn't move.

Alex looked.

Jimmy's face was mottled, red, brown and shiny. He had neither eyebrows nor eyelashes. Little tufts of hair sprouted here and there from his head and the rest was covered in scabby lumps.

'Oh, and Alex, you will notice that the cutlery is plastic. As are the plates and beakers. When we laid out the best silver the gentlemen here used to amuse themselves by sticking knives and forks in each other. Enjoy your breakfast.' And with that he left the room. Everyone was looking at Alex.

He felt sick inside.

Forcing a smile he did not feel, he clapped his hands, 'OK, fellas. Let's eat.'

As one they picked up their cutlery and attacked their food. Pavlov's dogs!

Brian leaned over to Alex. 'He's a nutter, that one. Should be in here instead of us. Malicious bastard. One day we'll fix him.'

Alex turned. 'Did you really cut up your mother-in-law?'

'Oh, yes. The old bitch deserved it. And Cyril did stick it to corpses. And Jimmy did set fire to himself. All the stories are true. Trouble is, that sadistic bastard really gets off on the humiliation bit. His turn's coming.'

He looked back at Alex. 'Best not do it while you're in here, eh?' he chuckled into his half-cold porridge.

After breakfast an MO sent for Alex. McGovern was apparently speaking to them, but had said that from the moment he first saw Alex he could remember nothing. The hospital needed to carry out a series of tests and until the results were in they couldn't officially accept the prisoner. The earliest they could take him off Alex's hands would be the next day.

'So, make yourself comfortable in the dayroom and relax. We'll be in touch again in the morning. And, oh, by the way, Duxford has been informed.'

Alex did just that, and by the time he turned in that night – again the padded cell – he was convinced that some of the inmates at Halton were saner than some members of the hospital staff.

Next morning, when he appeared for breakfast, the inmates at the table all stood up together and as one turned to Alex and offered a "Good Morning, Corporal!" Then they returned to their seats. Brian patted the seat next to him, indicating that Alex should again sit there. Since it was the only empty place, Alex had little choice.

Yesterday he'd spent a couple of hours with Brian in the dayroom and apart from the mother-in-law episode he seemed perfectly normal. He'd been a butcher in civvy street, then enlisted and became a butcher in the Air Force and had been caught honing his skills on the mother-in-law. It was only when she was mentioned that he became agitated. Apart from that, nice guy.

After breakfast Alex wandered off to the dayroom where an MO found him half an hour later. 'Right, Corporal, you'll be relieved to hear that we can now take Mr. McGovern off your hands. He wants to see you by the way. Wants to apologise.'

'I thought he didn't remember anything?'

'A bit more complicated than that, I'm afraid. You do as you wish, but it might be helpful if you went along. Always supposing you're not going to thump him, of course.'

Alex grinned. 'No. Already done that. Didn't help a lot at the time.'

'Yes, I've seen his ribs. They're black and blue and quite painful apparently.'

He raised an eyebrow and looked at Alex, 'Any satisfaction?'

'I guess. He damn near strangled me, though.'

'But he didn't. You survived. I suggest that you just let it flow away. No good holding grudges. Bad for one.'

Alex nodded, thinking, *but it wasn't you that was being strangled.* Then he went to see McGovern. McGovern lay propped up in a single bed. *No restraints*, Alex noted. And he also had a large square bandage on top of his head.

Alex pointed, 'What's that?' McGovern felt it. 'Somebody hit me with something. Two stitches.' – *Well done, George!* – 'I'm sorry; it's all very vague, as though it wasn't me. I know I hurt you, but I don't really remember it. I really am very sorry.' He held out his hand, looking at Alex.

Oh, what the hell! ... Alex took his hand. *Two mistakes to learn from. Could have been worse. Could've been dead!*

He went over to Administration to sort out a travel warrant back to Duxford. Jock the Medic was there. 'Alex, we were wondering if you could do us a small favour. You travel back via London, so we would like to ask if you would consider acting as a chaperone to young Jimmy. He's being let out for a couple of weeks leave to see how he responds to the outside world again. If somebody could shepherd him into London, I think it would be helpful to him.'

Alex nodded, 'Sure, no problem.'

An ambulance took them to the station. As they climbed out several people turned to stare. Alex felt Jimmy hesitate. 'It's OK, Jim. No problem. Just stay with me.'

Jimmy climbed back into the ambulance and sat down. 'Did you see how they looked at me? They think I'm a freak.'

'Bollocks. They're just nosy.'

Jimmy looked up at Alex. 'Alex, do you still have your handcuffs with you?'

Alex nodded. 'Why?'

'Would you handcuff me to you?'

'What on earth for? Are you mad?' The moment he said it, Alex regretted it.

But Jimmy grinned. 'Jock thinks I am. Go on, Alex, stick the handcuffs on, then they'll think I'm a prisoner. I'd rather everyone thinks I'm a prisoner than a freak.' Alex thought about it for a moment and then cuffed Jimmy to his left wrist.

As they climbed out of the ambulance Jimmy had a huge grin on his face. He looked at Alex. 'Thanks, Corp! You're OK for a Snowdrop. I'm good now.'

After changing their travel warrants for tickets they climbed aboard the train and found an empty compartment towards the rear. Twenty minutes to departure. Several people made to enter the compartment before the train left, but on seeing Jimmy handcuffed to Alex, they muttered their excuses and left. Jimmy couldn't stop laughing, which in reality was a pretty gruesome sight.

*

Next morning Alex reported to Squadron Leader Rawlings. 'Hectic few days, eh, son? How do you feel? How's the neck?'

'Neck's still very sore, Sir, but I feel fine. Thinking about it now that it's over, I enjoyed it.' The Squadron Leader's eyebrows went up. 'Well, let's put it this way, Sir. I'd rather do what I've been doing recently than bumper that corridor out there every day.'

'Point taken, son. Anything else?'

Alex told him about the treatment of the psychiatric patients at Halton and the threat to Jock the medic.

Rawlings nodded, 'OK, leave it with me. Can you use a 72-hour pass?'

Alex nodded, bemused.

'Right. Get one made out and bring it to me. After duty you can vanish. I don't want to see you for the next three days.'

'Thank you, Sir.'

Rawlings waved Alex away.

*

Alex was just leaving the building that evening when the Squadron Leader spotted him and called him back. 'Spoke to Halton this afternoon. Thought you'd like to know. Yesterday, after you left, a group of patients jumped your medic pal. They dragged him off to the Laundry, wrapped him in a sheet and stuffed him in one of those industrial washing machines. They set it on boil and scarpered. Fortunately for him they didn't know that you have to physically turn the water on to those machines in the hospital as a safety measure. He's had a terrifying experience, but at least he's alive. Do you know what the ring leader said? He's the guy that apparently butchered his mother-in-law.'

Alex shook his head, 'No idea.'

'He said – and get this – he said, we'd have done it before. But we decided to wait until old Alex had left. Didn't want to drag him into it. For a cop, he's OK.' He looked at Alex as though waiting for a reply. Alex shrugged. 'We spent a couple of hours talking together. Apart from killing his mother-in-law he seemed quite normal.'

The Squadron Leader's eyes opened wide. 'Apart from…?!' He stopped. 'Go home, son. You need a rest.' He turned and walked back to his office.

* *

On a sidenote

McGovern underwent treatment for the next twelve months at Halton. In November 1958 he was released and formerly discharged from the Royal Air Force. He was referred to a civilian hospital where he would receive counselling as an outpatient.

On Christmas Eve the same year, Newmarket police were called by neighbours to investigate an incident at McGovern's old home. The front door was ajar and on entering the house, they found a man lying in the front room in a pool of blood. He was dead, killed by repeated blows to the head. In the living room they found McGovern's wife, also in a pool of blood. She too, was quite dead and practically unrecognizable. In a pram in a corner of the room lay a small baby girl, unharmed and happily gurgling away. McGovern sat in an armchair, holding a long bloodstained brass poker. He was also covered in blood and offered no resistance as officers led him away.

At the Old Bailey, McGovern was found guilty but was also found to be of unsound mind. He was sentenced to Broadmore to be detained at Her Majesty's pleasure.

The Court was told he hadn't uttered a single word to anyone since his arrest.

Chapter 7
Ginger

In October 1957 Ginger arrived back from Cyprus for a bit of R&R. Ginger had been in Cyprus for just over a year, when on 1st April 1955 the first bombs went off, targeting police, military and various government installations in Nicosia, Famagusta and Limassol. These bombings signalled the start of a four-year campaign of violence orchestrated by Colonel George Grivas, a Greek Cypriot and leader of EOKA (National Organisation of Cypriot Fighters) who was seeking to bring about the expulsion of all British troops from the island, together with self-determination and union with Greece (ENOSIS) for Cyprus.

The campaign was to tie down some 30,000 British troops in the UK government's attempt to destroy EOKA. 104 servicemen were killed and several hundred more were injured

Avoiding bombings, shootings and ambushes became a way of life for British personnel in Cyprus. Ledra Street in Nicosia became known to all Brits as Murder Mile.

Four months previously, on 16th June, EOKA had bombed a restaurant and killed William Botelar, the American Consul. Botelar was actually a CIA operative, working under diplomatic cover. Colonel Grivas immediately put out a statement saying this was an accident and American citizens were not being targeted, but he warned the Americans, for their own safety they should stay away from any establishments known to be frequented by "our British enemy".

Ginger's explosion was deliberate.

Ginger and two colleagues were driving on patrol outside Nicosia when they passed over a concealed landmine which detonated on impact and blew the Landrover apart.

Ginger's two colleagues died instantly, while he spent the next 3 months in hospital recovering after extensive surgery to his legs, stomach and chest. The remaining scars were horrendous. Ginger had been sent to Duxford to slowly recuperate and reengage with service life.

One week after his arrival three quarters of all staff at 4 Police District HQ, Alex included, received orders that they were now on 24 hour emergency standby for Cyprus.

One week later the standby was cancelled.

Chapter 8

On the move

December 7 would have been Alex's father's 56th birthday had he lived to see it. At 10:15 the previous day Sgt. Short stuck his nose round the door of the duty NCO's room. 'Alex. Boss wants you.'

Alex knocked on the door and entered.

'Stand easy, son.'

He picked up a large brown envelope from the desk and waved it at Alex. 'You're on the move, these are your marching orders. You got what you wanted. Don't know where, you'll be told that at RAF Wildenrath, that's the distribution centre and, oh, you'll love this: you sail on New Year's Eve. 31st December you'll be at sea and 1st January you'll be in Germany. Couldn't be better, could it? New Year's Day, new job, new country. You're now due 14 days embarkation leave, so get yourself over to the orderly room and collect all the bumf. Make sure you get a travel warrant from your hometown to Harwich. Pack your kit, clear the station and then come to see me.'

He stood up, leaned across the desk and offered his hand. 'Good luck, son, I hope it works out. In the meantime, go and have a nice Christmas with your Mum. My best wishes – she's had a difficult time.'

BOOK II

WEST GERMANY

New horizons - New life

---

9. Off to Germany

10 - 16 Geilenkirchen

17 – 23 Sundern

24 - 26 Sylt

27 - 31 Back at Sundern

Chapter 9

Off to Germany: Troopship – The Perils of being a Policeman

In 1958 NASA was founded. The United States and the Soviet Union decided to halt atmospheric atomic tests. The U.S. launched Explorer 1 in response to the Soviet Union's Sputnik of the previous October. Dwight D. Eisenhower was halfway through his second term as President of the Unites States and the Queen gave her first televised Christmas address.

_

In the early hours of 1st January of that year, Alex stepped from a troopship onto a snow-covered dock at the Hook of Holland en route to a still as yet undecided base in West Germany. Heavy snow was falling and he stamped his feet and swung his arms in an unsuccessful effort to keep warm. Alex was probably colder than most, and with good reason.

The previous night, New Year's Eve 1957, several hundred troops had climbed the ship's gangway from the dockside at Harwich, all en route to postings in Western Europe. Outside it was freezing, but inside a thick fog soon developed as more and more troops were jammed in. The tannoy came to life: 'Will all service police, that means Military Police and Royal Air Force Police, report immediately to Warrant Officer Clark in the main lounge.'

A lone figure stood on a chair at the far end of the lounge and waved a piece of paper. 'OK chaps, stand aside everybody and let them through'. One or two people started pushing themselves through the crowd towards the WO-man. Alex didn't like the sound of this; he was going to be press-ganged into playing at ship's police. No way! He surreptitiously unhooked his whistle chain from the top button of his greatcoat and slipped the whistle into his pocket. Displaying a whistle chain when you're out and about had distinct advantages, but not now. This was a mug's game. He had no wish to help supervise a mass of vomiting humanity and he slowly edged his way back towards the entrance and stepped out onto the deck. Empty. He removed his whistle from his left pocket and hooked it up again, in plain view. From his right greatcoat pocket he removed his black and red RAF Police armband, pulled it up over his left arm and clicked the hook into the pin worked into the greatcoat behind the V of his stripes. *Right! On duty, but not on duty. Time to disappear!,* he thought to himself.

He found his way to a flight of steps. A chain hung across the entrance. "OUT OF BOUNDS. CREW ONLY". Alex unhooked the chain, stood on the first step and then replaced it. He steadily climbed to the top deck. The wind was howling; he was absolutely frozen. He worked his way slowly along the ship towards the stern, pausing by a huge part of the superstructure which, when he stepped behind it, immediately cut out most of the wind. A few feet in front of him he saw what looked like a massive box. He went to look. Not locked. He lifted the lid: life jackets. He took one out and looked at it. He laid it on the steel deck in front of the superstructure. Then he fetched three more and stacked them one on top of the other and sat down. *A chair; not bad!* The superstructure stopped all the wind and the life jackets stopped the cold from the deck. By midnight you'd be walking through six inches of vomit downstairs, particularly since it was New Year. He'd rather freeze to death up here!

Eventually, the ship hauled anchor and made its way out to sea. Making himself as comfortable as possible on his improvised seating, his mind drifted back to the last time he'd been out of bounds on the top deck of a ship ...

He'd been just 15 at the time. It was Easter 1953, and he'd been on a school trip to Koblenz in the French military occupied zone of Germany. The second day there and he'd spent all his money on an Agfa box camera. Not a particularly bright thing to do since he was now penniless, but an Agfa had been top of his wish list from the moment he'd signed up for the trip. He'd got caught in a storm and the rain had soaked through his brand new sports jacket. When it dried out the canvas in the shoulders had puckered up and he couldn't wear it anymore. Everyone had laughed. Everyone except the Indian, Shimanlal Shah, and his mate George from Singapore. Although part of the school trip, they were actually students at university in London.

Shimmy took Alex to his room, opened the wardrobe and said: "Choose!" Alex had never seen so many jackets. Between them they chose a beautifully tailored double-breasted, dark blue blazer. Then came a shirt, tie and light grey slacks.

Shimmy, George and Alex became inseparable from then on. Shimmy said his father was one of the largest arms manufacturers in India. "Don't worry about money," he'd said, "we've got plenty." And how he'd spent it! Nightclubs every night where Alex was introduced to girls whose uniform appeared to be bare breasts and bottoms to match.

On the first evening after a dinner, with perhaps a little too much wine, Shimmy had spoken to one of the girls. Money changed hands and Shimmy led her back to the table. 'Alex,' he said, 'Time for a little education. Renate here is going to show you what to do with your willie.'

Alex went bright red but Renate smiled at him, took him by the hand and led him away, where she did indeed show him what could be done with a willie. Several happy willie-instruction-nights followed during the next twelve days. His initiation to manhood.

Dr Barnard, their German teacher and group leader, threatened to have him expelled when they returned home but Alex didn't care. He'd learned more here in twelve days than he had in five years at grammar school. He was drunk, he was happy and he had a sore dick. Life was great!

On the way back to England they'd changed trains in Cologne and it was here that he met Kristin. Kristin came from Bielefeld and was on a school trip to Neath in Glamorgan, Wales. Shimmy and George had paired off with two other girls. The six had grabbed an empty compartment, lowered the blinds and got down to the serious business of knowing each other better. By Brussels they were all bosom pals. Onto the boat in Ostend and Alex and Kristin had disappeared on the top deck where they spent the whole trip in a life boat while Alex gave her instructions based on Renate's teachings of "Ten Things to do with a Willie."

Alex smiled to himself at the memories and sighed.

No Kristin on this trip!

He made himself as comfortable as possible and at long last fell into a fitful sleep. Finally, when he could no longer doze, he realized he'd slept on and off for the best part of five hours. Midnight. New Year had come and gone, and he'd been blissfully unaware of it.

It was still dark when they docked. By then, Alex had been downstairs, armband and whistle removed. He'd been right about the vomit; everywhere stank. Toilets and sinks were blocked. He pitied the cleaning crew.

Out onto the dockside where Travel Marshals tried unsuccessfully to make them line up in threes. Looking along the platform Alex could see two Redcaps at the far end of the train. Hooking up his whistle chain and slipping on his armband again, Alex left the crowd and headed towards the MPs. No-one stopped him.

He reached the MPs, introduced himself, and they began to chat. It turned out they'd brought a prisoner down from Oldenburg who was being shipped back to the UK. They were going back to camp and actually had a reserved compartment. They pointed. A sign read "RESERVED" on the window. Could he join them, Alex asked. "Sure, why not!" was the reply.

They all climbed aboard. Blissful warmth. Wonderful!

They sat there and chatted while the train filled up. Eventually it moved out and they chugged their way across Holland, lost in the depths of a blizzard, and then over the border into an eerily white and silent Germany. The train finally wheezed to a halt in what appeared to be the middle of nowhere. The Army stayed put. All RAF personnel de-trained and piled into a fleet of buses. Next stop RAF Wildenrath and an overnight bed in the transit block – Alex wangled his own single room. Oh, the power of that little silver whistle!

Early next morning, following a remarkably varied and filling breakfast, everyone was shepherded into a huge, empty hangar. No instructions were given. Airmen just stood around in informal groups; no attempt was made to sort them out into the usual three lines.

Alex wandered aimlessly through the crowd – there must have been at least two hundred of them. He counted seven more whistle chains; eight in total. They'd all drifted to the far wall as if seeking safety in numbers; outcasts perhaps. Four station police and four Provost.

They were called to order by a Flight Lieutenant assisted by a Warrant Officer and two Corporals. The officer stood, the rest sat behind a table covered in papers. Number, rank and name would be read out, and the person would present his ID to the Warrant Officer at the desk and in return he'd receive his documents for onward travel from Wildenrath. As the Flight Lieutenant started reading out the names, the door next to Alex and the other seven opened and two Snowdrops walked in. Alex stared. He'd never seen an on-duty Snowdrop dressed like this before. They were identical; cloned, as if seeking anonymity, yet at the same time acceptance: boots, no white gaiters, no white belt or webbing, the inevitable whistle chain, black and red armband (both on the left arm), and white hat. Both had on well-worn sleeveless leather MT jackets – unbuttoned. They leaned against the wall and lit up. Alex wandered over. 'Hi. Where are you from?'

'Geilenkirchen. We're here to pick up the new postings. Provost. You Provost'?

Alex nodded and pointed, 'And those three over there. Where's Geilenkirchen?

'Not too far from here, thank God. About an hour, and the roads are bloody terrible. Not far from the Dutch border.'

At that moment two of the Provost were called to the desk. Documents changed hands; both to Gatow, Berlin.

'Right,' said the taller of the two, 'you must be coming to us then, along with him over there, unless there's anybody else hiding in the crowd'.

'Corporal Grapes, Provost, RAF Geilenkirchen.'

"Him-over-there" walked to the desk and picked up his papers.

Then Alex was called, also RAF Geilenkirchen. He fetched his papers and returned to the group.

'OK,' said the tall one. 'I'm Nick, this is Jock, and who are you?' He pointed at the other new guy.

'Corporal Grapes. Call me Bunchie, everyone else does'.

'Alex.'

'Right, let's pick up your kit from over there and bugger off. Just in time for lunch.'

Geilenkirchen

10- Accident: Welcome to Geilenkirchen!
11- Convoys
12- Vater Rhein
13- The Short Straw: Replacing the Famous Five
14- Bye-bye Katie - Hello, Beate
15- SOXMIS-BRIXMIS – A little Military History
16- The Russian Military Mission or
Two can play at your Game!

Chapter 10

Accident: Welcome to Geilenkirchen!

RAF Geilenkirchen was a military airfield built by the British, which became operational in May 1953. Home to Strike/Attack fighters, it lay hard up against the German-Dutch border in North-Rhine Westphalia and was known by the locals as "Flugplatz Teveren" after the nearest village, which regularly had its peace and quiet disturbed by the low-flying fighter aircraft. In 1957-58 it was home to Nos. 2, 3, 59, 96, 234 and 256 Squadrons, and housed just under 3,000 airmen.

* _*

Apart from the operational squadrons Geilenkirchen also housed No 12 Provost and Security Services Detachment up on the main drive, 500 metres or so from the main gate. Alex saw three Landrovers and two Kombis parked in front of the building.

'OK. Billet first, then nosh,' said the ever practical Nick.

They dragged their kit into the billet and Alex's heart sank. Duxford all over again, only worse! Eight beds on each side separated by lockers and wardrobes and two stoves in the middle. It was like an oven in there.

'Shit,' said Alex.

'Och, it's not too bad, man,' said Jock, grinning. 'We're left alone in here. Nobody bothers us, no inspections; it's not bad at all.'

Alex dumped his kit on an empty bed in the middle of the room and Bunchie took the one opposite.

'Grub's up,' said Jock. 'Let's go to the mess, food's pretty good here. I used to be at Marham and that place was shit. After lunch, just sort your kit out and settle in. No rush. We can go to the Detachment and do the arrival bit in the morning. The Old Man's away with the WO-man at Two TAF. Flight's away too and there's nothing to do anyway.'

'What's Two TAF?' asked Bunchie.

'Headquarters Second Tactical Air Force. It's over at Mönchen-Gladbach,' replied Jock.

'Stay away,' said Nick, 'it's all bullshit.'

Alex's heart sank to his boots. The billet was a dump. The camp was out in the middle of nowhere. Nobody seemed to give a shit and there was nothing to do. *Wonderful! Duxford Mark Two!* Well, at least the food was good.

Next morning Alex and Bunchie met the WO-man – Warrant Officer Joe Adams and the Flight, Flight Sergeant Templar, known behind his back as The Old Crusader. He had a large, lustrous and beautifully combed moustache, while the WO-man's forte was to continually click his top row of false teeth with his tongue – down, forward and back up again in one fluid movement. He'd obviously practised a lot. When not required to speak – and alone in his office – these teeth sat in a glass of water on his desk. He explained that nothing was moving at the moment because of the weather and the holidays, but normally there were runs to RAF Wahn, Bitburg and patrols in Cologne. Convoys would also be a regular feature in the coming months. A lot of heavy equipment was being moved out of Berlin. If the convoy didn't come through Geilenkirchen we picked it up at the East German border and took it, via a stop-over at RAF

Eindhoven in Holland, down to the docks at Antwerp in Belgium. Small convoys; that is, one or two tank transporters, usually had a motorcycle escort, and three or more required a Landrover plus a motorcyclist. Alex was a motorcyclist. He felt his heart begin to quicken. This was more like it! East German border, Holland, Belgium. This sounded like fun. They were both given arrival cards which had to be signed in strict sequence of number. Number 1 was the bedding store; Number 2 was the other side of the airfield, and so on. Some deranged person's idea of fun, and, oh yes, you had to walk.

Welcome to Geilenkirchen!

Alex and Bunchie wandered into the duty NCO's room. Jock sat behind a desk, feet up, reading a book. 'Fancy a cup of coffee at the NAAFI?'

Alex looked at this watch. 'It's half past ten.'

'I know. Time for coffee.' He stood up and took a set of keys from the key cabinet. 'Coming?'

'What about the office,' asked Alex.

'Oh, Tina will answer the phone,' said Jock.

'Who's Tina?'

'The WO-man's daughter, she works here. Next office. Does the filing and stuff.' Jock opened the door. 'Listen for the phone, will you Tina? We're just off to the NAAFI. Oh, and this is Bunchie and this is Alex.'

Alex looked. Now, that was something! Nothing false there… Geilenkirchen was beginning to look up!

They sat in the Corporals' Club drinking coffee and chewing the fat. Jock looked at his watch, 'Twelve o'clock. Too late to do anything now, lunch in half an hour. Start arriving after two, they'll all be drifting over to lunch in a bit, may as well take it easy while we can.'

Three thirty and Alex was walking across to the Detachment, he'd done 9 of the 22 on his list, the rest could wait until morning; he was knackered. Just then the door of the Detachment flew open and a tall, skinny Sergeant ran out, large box in his left hand, keys in his right. Seeing Alex, he stopped.

'You a new arrival?'

'Yes'

'Driver?'

'No. Motorcyclist.'

'Never mind, get in,' he said, unlocking a Kombi. He turned, 'Ever done an accident?'

Alex looked blank.

'Ever covered an accident, a traffic accident?'

'No.'

'First posting overseas?'

'Yes.'

'OK. Get in.' Alex climbed in the Kombi. 'Right. We've got a traffic accident a couple of kilometres down the road. Car under a lorry. Two dead. That's all I know.' Alex felt his stomach tighten.

'Just do as I say. You'll be OK. This is the accident box. Contains everything we need. When we get there we measure up, cover the angles, take photographs, put it on paper. Forget Police School; this is real life. The German Police are already there. When there are Service people involved, or their families, we get called out.'

'Do you get many accidents?'

'Enough. You'll get used to it.'

Alex could see the accident. A lorry with sheets of metal hanging over the back was parked at the side of the road, and literally under it was a green Volkswagen Beetle jammed up against the back axle. The sheet metal had torn the top of the

Volkswagen completely off and was hanging over the back of the car.

Alex got out, feeling very nervous. It was then that he saw the tarpaulin. The two German Police on the scene came over and saluted; the Sergeant returned the salute. Alex felt incapable of moving; he couldn't take his eyes off the sheet. They moved to the grass, one German policeman at either end of the tarpaulin and together they pulled it back.

Two bodies; the man in uniform – a Sergeant – the female in civvies, and what was left of two heads placed side by side, next to the woman.

Alex looked. It registered; then he ran to the ditch and vomited – several times. When he turned round, all three were looking at him. Nobody was smiling and the bodies were covered up again.

'Feeling better, lad?'

'Yes, Sarge.'

'Alright. Now we go to work.'

They measured the width of the road, the length of the skid marks from the Volks, chalk marks here, chalk marks there. The Sergeant took photographs. An ambulance came and took the bodies away. And then it was all over.

On the way back the Sergeant said, 'You did OK back there.'

'I was sick.'

'So? We're all human. Now you've seen it; you'll see a lot more. Learn to detach yourself. They're not human. They're objects. You move them. You pick up the bits. You blank out. If you don't, you won't survive. It'll drive you round the bend. Blank it out.'

From then on Alex was a natural; he blanked it out.

And later, everyone called him a hardnosed bastard.

Arrivals finished, and with it a further week of doing absolutely nothing, Geilenkirchen was beginning to pall by the minute when—

The WO-man stuck his head round the door of the duty NCO's office.

'Alex, got a minute?'

Alex followed the WO-man back to his office. 'Sit down, Alex. How're you finding Geilenkirchen?'

'Boring.'

'Hmm. Might be able to change that. Fancy a convoy run?'

Convoy? …'Yes!' *Anything to get out of here!*

'OK. Next week Monday we're picking up four tank transporters and taking them to the docks in Antwerp. We go via Eindhoven, stop overnight and then on to Antwerp and drop them off. You either come straight back here or, depending on the time when you drop them off, you stay overnight in Antwerp or go back to Eindhoven and overnight there, then back here next day. Up to you, really. You make the call depending on time and weather. Roads are open, but everywhere is snowed up. It's bitterly cold, so make sure you're properly dressed. Jock and Nick will be in the Landrover, but you will be on a bike. Don't freeze to death, OK?'

'OK!'

… Antwerp, here we come!

Chapter 11

Convoys

Monday morning and Jock, Nick and Alex met up with the convoy at Heinsberg, the end of the motorway. From there it was due north on normal roads to the Dutch border, then, via Roermond, on towards Eindhoven. Light snow was falling but the roads were clear. It was explained to Alex how he would ride in front of the convoy, down the centre of the road holding the lolly stick in the left hand and indicating to oncoming traffic that they should move over as far as possible into the gutter, giving the tank transporters in the convoy sufficient room to pass. At crossroads Alex had to stop all traffic coming from right or left, giving priority to the convoy; the same applied at traffic lights. Stop the traffic, never mind the red light: the convoy has priority. Once the convoy has passed, Alex would leap on his bike and chase after it, slowly working his way to the front again . . .

-

The above dozen lines or so are all that remain of 30-odd pages of type; victims of our Bulgarian thief!

I more or less lived on the road for the first 3 months of 1958 – a dreadful winter; snow, snow and more snow!

I loved the convoys, and I hated the convoys.

I loved them for the freedom they gave me; I sometimes hated them for the physical duress they put me under.

Although it became a love-hate relationship, when I was offered the opportunity of running my very first convoy, all I could think of was "freedom". Just what I wanted . . .

I was out there, on my own. No-one to get in my hair and tell me what to do or how to do it. I was given a job and provided it was done properly I had the run of the place.

A personal dream come true.

I loved the bike rides. I loved visiting all these new places. I loved the freedom I had after having safely delivered my loads to the Antwerp docks.

I remember with fondness the night I spent in Antwerp, Belgium, where I slept in the Movement Officer's private office – no bed, no blankets and no toilet – which meant that when nature woke me in the middle of the night due to an intake of too much wine, the only course of action was to open the window – I was three stories up – hang on to the window frame and let fly into the street below . . .

Oh Happy Days!

Or the visit to "The Black Cat" in Eindhoven, Holland, supposedly the Number One out-of-bounds place in the city. Jock, who was the Landrover driver, was away for the evening having a fling with – if my memory serves me right – the daughter of a town councillor. I, meanwhile, accompanied by my trusty white hat, spent the most enlightening evening with a beautiful and truly striking blonde who spent the entire evening drinking beer after beer into which she poured two spoons of sugar, then whisked it all up and drank it down. At the end of the evening she was in what I can only call an extremely "amorous mood". A walk to her house, a welcome pause, followed by a five kilometre hike back to camp, since Jock, having had his own wicked way, had completely forgotten to come and pick me up!

And I also remember how, after one particularly taxing and trying return ride from Antwerp back to Geilenkirchen in the midst of that cold winter, I arrived almost frozen stiff – barely hanging on – and scarcely having the energy to push the horn, trying to draw the attention of somebody – anybody – inside the Detachment to come help me off the bike. In the end I switched on the klaxon. Bunchie heard the noise, came running out and dragged me off the bike.

I swore there and then NEVER AGAIN! I'M NEVER AGAIN GETTING ON THAT BLOODY BIKE . . . only to be eager for my next excursion as soon as I was thawed out and after a good night's sleep.

Convoys was longer, much longer, but under the circumstances, it will have to end here . . .

But, as I said: OH, HAPPY, HAPPY DAYS!

Chapter 12

Vater Rhein

Vater Rhein was notorious.

It stood in the Deutz district of Cologne, adjacent to the river that dissected the city: the Rhein. Hence the name *Vater Rhein* – Father Rhine.

Vater Rhein gloried in its notoriety.

Twenty eight houses in all; fourteen on either side of the road. Each house was divided into four rooms and each room was occupied by one girl. One hundred and twelve girls in total on one shift. They worked double shifts. Two hundred and twenty four girls. A giant sex factory, a bordello, a brothel, a knocking shop – call it what you will.

Sex was for sale for eight hours a day, every day. Strictly regimented, it opened at 8 p.m. each evening and closed at 4 a.m. next morning. The girls changed shifts at midnight. They needed to; it was the epitome of the *wham-bang-special.*

On any given Friday and Saturday night, they'd be queuing down the street three deep, as though on parade, eager to get their collective ends away; "they" being the Brits, the Canadians and the Belgians. The military. A German wouldn't be seen dead in the place. Nor were there any signs of the Americans. It wasn't that they were more fussy; they had their own equivalent to *Vater Rhein* down the road in Kassel.

With prices set to attract the target market –the military– business was always brisk. In and out in five or six minutes. Conveyor belt sex. You could even keep your trousers on! The customers seemed happy. They entered through a front door, paid their money to a girl behind a desk who was usually one of the girls who would begin her work on the next shift, or one who had just completed one. Above each door were two small lights, one red, one green. When the green one glowed it was your turn. Generally the customers took pot-luck with the girls, although some of the regulars – and there were many – preferred to use the same girl. Two Deutsch Marks extra, regardless of the specialty requested.

Vater Rhein stood in the middle of nowhere. Behind it the river. To either side and immediately in front for about three hundred metres was desolation. Beyond that was the main road. In between nothing but rubble awaiting redevelopment. Somehow the bombing raids had missed this stretch of twenty eight houses in the same way that Cologne cathedral was left standing while all around it the city was flattened.

One bitterly cold Monday morning in the middle of March, the WO-man called Alex into his office - radiator full blast, electric fire on two bars; it was like an oven. Outside the snow stood the best part of seven or eight inches deep. He pointed to a chair in front of his desk. Alex sat.

'Alex, we've had what I would call an interesting little job dumped on us. I thought it might be up your street. Do you know *Vater Rhein?*'

Alex shook his head, 'Heard of it, but never been there.'

'Right. Well, it seems that some of the lads who frequent this establishment have gone and got themselves a dose of clap. The MO here has reported four cases in the last two weeks. It seems the same at Butz, Wahn and Düren. He's also made enquiries at a couple of army bases. Seems their cases have peaked over the past three weeks. The German police have been on to the Boss. Four girls registered positive at last Friday's inspection. Every week they're supposed to be tested. Don't know what went wrong, but the problem is being dumped on our doorstep. Based on our limited knowledge of throughput, this figure could easily be over the hundred mark by now. As of today *Vater Rhein* has been placed out-of-bounds to all military personnel. We're putting in a patrol each weekend: Friday night, Saturday night and Sunday night. Back here Monday. Interested?'

'Hmm. Yes. Could be fun.'

'Alex, you have a strange idea of fun. You could get your teeth dumped down your throat if you don't handle it right.'

Alex just grinned.

'I take it that means you're up for it?'

Alex nodded.

'Who'd you like to take with you?'

'Well, none of the married guys in quarters for a start. I don't think their wives would be too happy knowing hubby's spending the weekend in a brothel. I think Paddy might be best. I know he's married, but his wife's in Ireland, plus he's built like a barn-door. If he puts on the right face he intimidates people.'

'So, Paddy it is then. You'll be staying at Wahn and the German police will be there to assist if needed.'

Alex and Paddy arrived at Wahn mid-afternoon Friday and secured themselves a room each in the transit block. At 19:30 they parked in the middle of the street opposite *Vater Rhein.* No German police, no punters; just one or two girls straggling in for work, just like any factory girl. Without exception they all gave the Landrover a hard stare. At 19:45 the first of the punters arrived by car. They were warned off and left. 20:00, several more appeared in the street. They were also warned off and left. 20:15, the German police arrived in a Kombi. They introduced themselves. They would sit at one end of the street. If they were needed, they'd come. By 21:30 the floodgates opened; they were streaming in by the dozen. Paddy switched the headlights and blue light on. The German police did the same. They worked the crowd, warning people off. Many went, but many stayed. Among those that stayed the attitude was "Fuck You! What can two of you do!" When Alex pointed to the German police Kombi, one squaddie gave a laugh, 'They've already lost twice. Do they think it will be third-time-lucky?'

Alex and Paddy stuck at it until 04:00. They were both knackered. They'd called the German police in twice when it looked like they might be flattened. Both agreed on one thing: with only two men working the crowds, it definitely was not going to work.

Saturday evening, 19:30, and they were back there again. No-one about, just some of the girls arriving for work. Then Paddy nudged Alex, 'Looks like we've got a delegation.'

They climbed out of the Landrover. Three gorgeous and scantily clad young ladies walked up to the Landrover. Working Girl dress! The one in the middle spoke to Alex. 'I am Beate, this is Ulla, and this is Ilse. We're here to offer you a proposition. You are bad for business. Last night we lost a lot of money. All the girls agree. We will all pay each of you one Mark a night that you are here. That is Friday, Saturday—' and she looked at Alex, eyebrows raised, 'Sunday?' Alex nodded. 'That is a lot of money. We have two hundred and forty girls. For each of you for the weekend that is 720 Marks. You come, you collect, you go, and we carry on as before.' She looked at

Alex again. 'Plus, you want a girl it is free, whenever you want.' Ulla stood back and struck a provocative pose. She looked Alex in the eye and slowly raised her short skirt. She wasn't wearing panties. 'You like?' she asked, 'anytime!' Then the girls turned and sauntered away toward the end house on the right. Ulla turned and blew them a kiss before they disappeared into the building.

Alex and Paddy climbed back into the Landrover.

'Jeezes, Alex! 720 Marks for doing sweet bugger all. We'll be rich. What do you think?'

'Are you serious, Paddy? We can't take that money.'

'A bit of nookie then. On the house.'

'No nookie, Paddy; you might get a dose. Remember? That's why we're here.'

Saturday night was a repeat of the night before. Some success, but overall they were on a loser. They called the German police in three times between 9 p.m. and midnight.

At midnight Beate appeared; alone. She headed directly for Alex. 'This is no good, we need to talk. Not now, but perhaps tomorrow. Can you come tomorrow, say twelve o'clock?'

'Of course we can come,' said Paddy, beating Alex to it.

Beate nodded and walked away.

05:00 a.m. saw them back in Wahn – out for the count.

At 12:00 noon they were back in front of *Vater Rhein.* Beate opened the door of the end house and beckoned. They followed the finger. This house was different to the others they'd seen, not larger, but laid out differently. As you entered the front door you stood in a very small box-like hallway. Stairs immediately in front of you led to an upper floor. Beate saw Alex looking. 'Work rooms,' she said and opened a door to her left. The wonderful smell of cooking wafted out. Alex sniffed the air.

'Lunch,' said Beate. 'Today we eat, drink and talk, and who knows … today we are off duty, no?'

'Today we are off duty, Yes!' jumped in Paddy. He rubbed his hands together and licked his lips. 'I'm hungry already.'

Alex broke in, feeling the conversation was drifting the wrong way. 'We're off duty until 7:30 tonight, Beate, then the white hats go back on. Sorry. It's the job.'

'Ah, the job. Believe me, I know all about the job. But,' and she turned and looked directly into Alex's eyes, 'until then you are free, yes?'

Alex nodded, 'Until then we are free.'

He looked around. The room was fitted with two white leather settees, each a two-seater and seemingly filled with burgundy coloured silk cushions. A dark, wooden dining table with glass top fitted against the wall opposite the entrance door, the length of the table stretching towards the centre of the room. Two dining chairs with white leather seats stood on either side of the table. To the right, in the far corner, was the doorway to a very tiny, but expensively fitted kitchen.

Ilse came in from the kitchen, holding a tall, slim flute of what looked like champagne. She held it up, 'Welcome, everyone,' and then took two delicate sips, 'lunch will be half an hour. A drink anyone?'

'Please,' said Paddy.

Beate nodded.

Ilse looked at Alex. 'Alex? May I call you Alex?'

'Of course. Is that champagne you're drinking?'

'Never drink anything else,' answered Ilse.

'Not for me, thanks. I hate the stuff. Do you have any dry white wine?'

Beate looked at Alex with incredulity. 'You don't like champagne? It is the best, you know.'

'Not for me, I prefer non-fizzy wine.'

'Your wish is my command, dear Sir,' mocked Ilse.

'But only until 7:30, eh, Alex?' chuckled Beate.

They all laughed. Whatever ice there had been was firmly broken. Lunch was a delight. A joint of beef with Brussels sprouts, horseradish and roast potatoes. There were four individual and perfectly made Yorkshire puddings. 'In honour of our English guests,' smiled Ilse.

'I'm Irish,' said Paddy, half rising from his chair next to Ilse.

'Sit down, Paddy, today you are English,' admonished Beate. Ilse stroked the back of his head. Beate and Alex exchanged glances. It looked like Paddy had been claimed.

Lunch finished, Ilse and Paddy cleared away. They returned from the kitchen holding hands. Ilse led him across the room to the door. She looked at Alex, 'If you would excuse us, please.' Paddy grinned and lifted his shoulders in a shrug. He'd gone bright red and looked like a little schoolboy, caught with his fingers in the sweet jar. After the door had closed behind them, Beate looked across at Alex.

'I'm not quite sure how to put this because you seem very different to the type of person I usually deal with, and I don't mean the men that come here to visit the girls. So, I'll just be direct and hope not to upset you.'

She reached across and took hold of Alex's hand. She squeezed it and held it tight, 'We, too, could …' She hesitated, 'Oh dear, this isn't coming out too well.' She lifted her head to indicate upstairs.

Alex looked at her for a few seconds and then said, 'Beate, tell me, where did you learn to speak such good English?'

Beate collapsed in laughter. Finally, she looked at him, tears running down her face. 'My, my, my ... You really are different. I try – and not very well, I admit – to entice you to bed, and you ask me where I learned my English.'

She collapsed in laughter again. When she finally composed herself she looked Alex seriously in the face. 'I could like you, you know? Perhaps too much, I think, and that could be bad for both of us.' She squeezed his hand and then stood up. 'More wine is needed, I think. And if I understand correctly, I have just been rejected.'

Alex just looked at her for a while and then said, 'You yourself gave the reason, Beate.'

Beate nodded, and as she poured the wine, said, 'I'm not a prostitute, you know, and I never have been. I run this place, along with others who will not take kindly to your interference. You will need to take care, even with our police force here.' She handed him his wine and then she leaned over and kissed him lightly on his cheek. 'I should hate you, but I don't. And I don't understand why not. You want to close me down, you don't want to sleep with me – I should be furious, but I'm not. I even feel I could care for you, and for me this is not normal.' She snuggled up to him, linked her arm through his and laid her head on his shoulder. 'Is this OK?' She looked up at him. 'Very OK,' he replied, and kissed her forehead.

At five o'clock Paddy appeared with Ilse in tow; they held hands. 'Look,' smiled Beate, 'I do believe they're in love.' Paddy blushed, deep crimson. His hair was all over the place, his shirt undone and he was minus shoes and socks. On the left side of his neck he had two very distinct deep red and blue marks. Alex pointed, 'Ilse get hungry, did she? I should keep them well hidden from the WO-man if I were you. Otherwise it'll be your first and last trip down here.'

Paddy and Ilse went to get showered – together.

'Do you think you'll be here next week, Alex?' Beate asked.

'Yes.'

'The week after?'

'I think so.'

'That is when it could become dangerous for you. One week, two, they will stand … But then it could become different. You are not the German police, Alex – they will not care. They will hurt you, or they will kill you. It is not worth it, Alex. Tell your people to give it up. You English are stupid, you don't even carry weapons. The Americans, Canadians, Belgians – their police all carry weapons. How can you protect yourself, huh? Tell me that!'

Alex smiled, 'Charm?'

She stared at him, mouth open, then she burst out laughing and threw her arms around him. It was only when his shirt felt wet that he realized she was no longer laughing.

He gently pushed her away.

Tears were rolling down her cheeks. 'What's the matter?' he asked softly.

'You stupid English Mister Policeman, do you not understand?'

'No. What's the matter?'

She hit him in the chest. 'You're unlike anybody I've ever met … and I think I'm falling in love with you. That's what's the matter!' She turned and ran out of the room, slamming the door behind her, and dashed upstairs.

Alex slumped in the couch, dumbfounded.

Beate remained upstairs until after Alex and Paddy had gone.

Paddy was mooning around like a lovesick teenager. He couldn't stop rambling on about Ilse. She wanted to come to

Geilenkirchen with him. She'd get a job and look after him. She'd have children with him. She didn't care about his wife. She loved him. Alex held up his hand. 'Paddy. Stop. How old are you?'

'Thirty five. Why?'

'I reckon you've got the midlife crisis right on time. You're married, she's a prostitute. For Christ's sake, get things in the right perspective!' For a minute Alex thought Paddy was going to hit him. He glared, then walked to the end of the street and worked his venom out on a group of squaddies who'd just appeared. He must have won. They left without too much backchat.

Compared to Friday and Saturday, Sunday night turned out to be a doddle; only about a third as many people to turn away. At 4am *Vater Rhein* closed its doors. Alex was exhausted, drained. Paddy wasn't speaking.

They awoke at noon on Monday and wandered over to the mess for something to eat. The first thing Paddy did was to apologise to Alex. 'Sorry, Alex, I got carried away. Shows what a bit of nookie'll do for you. But isn't she gorgeous,' he laughed, punching Alex on the arm, 'absolutely, fucking gorgeous!'

'Paddy, if you want to screw her, OK, but don't let her get in the way of the job, and don't let her into your life – unless of course you want to dump the missus.' He laughed, 'Do you?'

'No way, Alex. I've got a super missus, but you know how it is. You're away a long time, no home comfort, somebody shows you a bit of kindness or whatever, you know, and before you know it, you've got your dick out. It's only normal, isn't it?'

'Don't ask me, Paddy. Apparently I'm not normal.'

When they arrived back at the detachment all the daytime wallahs had left. Paddy looked at the duty roster, 'Hey, Alex, we've got two days off. I can use it. I'm knackered.'

'Must be all the shagging you did.'

Paddy laughed and held his hand up. 'Fair comment, I suppose.'

Nick wandered in, he was pulling duty NCO. 'Alex, the WO-man wants to see you tomorrow. No urgency. Whenever you can.' Alex nodded.

After lunch the next day, Alex walked across to the detachment. Paddy was still in the land of nod, snoring contentedly.

'So, Alex, pull up a chair and tell me all about it. How'd it go?' Alex sat down. 'I now know how King Canute felt. It's like trying to turn back the tide. It's impossible!' He went over the weekend in detail, omitting, of course, the part Beate and Ilse had played.

'So, in short,' the WO-man summed up, 'you reckon we're on a loser?'

'Can't see how we can win,' replied Alex. 'Two of us against hundreds of them. Not possible. Without the Kraut police we'd have been duffed up several times.'

'Are you OK for another go this weekend?'

'OK for back up there again this weekend?' laughed Alex. 'Why not. I suppose we managed to turn away about half, but with the tough boys, no chance. Still it's good fun.'

'Good fun? You're not normal, you know that?'

'So people keep telling me.'

Alex and Paddy were back at Wahn before noon the following Friday. Transit rooms claimed, they had an early lunch, then drove into Cologne to have coffee in the shadow of the Kölner Dom – Cologne Cathedral – and do a spot of sightseeing, that is if you can do sightseeing wearing a white hat on top of an RAF uniform and having half the German population stare at you. Still, the weather was beautiful, bright, warm and sunny. It was certainly better than sitting around at Wahn, twiddling your thumbs. Perhaps the lull before the storm.

They pulled up outside *Vater Rhein* at 19:30 on the dot and were surprised to see not one German police Kombi, but two, plus a black unmarked Opel with a blue light perched on top. *Kripo?* Standing beside it not the usual two uniformed police, but six, together with two people in plain clothes. Alex and Paddy wandered across.

The uniforms momentarily stood to attention while the one with the pips on his shoulders saluted. Alex would never get used to this; he still found it highly embarrassing after nearly four months in the country. He returned the salute.

Pips addressed Alex. He spoke flawless English. He introduced the two in plain clothes, who were indeed *Kripo*. The bigger of the two – silver grey crew cut and tortoise shell glasses – as Captain Otto Fleischmann. He also spoke excellent, though heavily accented, English. His companion was Klaus, his driver, who only spoke German, and that appeared to be the *Kölsch* dialect, which was Double Dutch to Alex. He couldn't make out a single word of what Klaus uttered. It may as well have been Mandarin Chinese. Captain Fleischmann took command. He gestured towards one of the police Kombis, 'Let us sit inside, it will be more comfortable to discuss things.' Alex and Paddy climbed in, only the Captain followed them and slid the door to behind him.

Captain Fleischmann began, 'I suggest we dispense with rank, it only makes things more difficult. This is essentially a military problem, we are here to assist if needed. Please call me Otto, and you are?' he pointed at Alex.

'I'm Alex, this is Paddy.'

They all shook hands again. The atmosphere thawed immediately.

'Right,' said Otto, 'we commence. These buildings that you know as *Vater Rhein* are occupied illegally. However, about two years ago, they appear to have been issued with a licence to operate their business. How this happened we do not as yet know. We believe money changed hands. This eventually we will find out. As you see all around us is desolation. But,' and here he raised his right hand and wagged his first finger, 'the area is scheduled for development. Unfortunately, though, not for at least one year. So – and this has been a discussion of some importance – I have spoken with my superiors to see if there is anything we can do to assist in the present problem. We believe that if the military ban on this place were lifted the problem would go away. We recognize that is not likely to happen, at least in the short term. Our opinion also is that if the military insist on keeping the ban on the premises war will break out, and you two gentlemen will most certainly be the losers. With this in mind we are providing extra resources.' He gestured to the rest of the German police standing outside. 'This can only be a short term solution, and I confess to not being happy with it. We have also decided to apply to the Courts and have the licence revoked, after all the people are here illegally, but they have been here for several years, so it is not exactly straight forward. They are involved in other illegal activities within the Cologne area, so on a personal level, I would like to see this place closed down. If you like, it would be a goal to us. I will now leave, but the uniformed men will stay. As well as providing back-up they may also act as a psychological deterrent.'

*

Friday night and Saturday night were a replica of the previous week – the off-duty troops arrived in similar numbers but the sight of three police vehicles sitting there, with their blue lights flashing, was indeed a deterrent to many; they simply turned around and left when told to do so by either Alex or Paddy. Some of those that stayed and started to argue thought better of it when they saw the German police move towards them. Then you had the hard core, maybe ten percent in total. They told everybody to fuck off and went in to get their jollies. Both Alex and Paddy realized what a tight-rope they were walking and knew when to stand back from physical confrontation. They might have been given special powers of arrest, but a piece of paper was no deterrent to a group of six or seven half drunk, testosterone-loaded, squaddies.

At 4am Sunday morning, the external lights at *Vater Rhein* were extinguished, the German police departed and Alex and Paddy climbed back inside the Landrover and heaved a collective sigh of relief. 'Fuck me gently, but I'm knackered,' intoned Paddy as he leaned back in his seat and closed his eyes. As if on cue there was a gentle knocking on the Landrover's door. Paddy looked out. 'Holy Mary, Mother and Joseph! If it isn't the darling Ilse!', and he was out of the Landrover in a shot, sweeping her off her feet in a giant bear hug, she planting little kisses all over his silly grinning face. Then came the big one. Alex looked away. It was embarrassing. Then followed a rather earnest, whispered conversation.

Paddy took Ilse by the hand and led her to the Landrover. He cleared his throat. 'It seems there's a question of Sunday lunch. What I mean is, would we like one, you know, like last week, here.' Alex looked at Paddy. He was actually standing there nodding his head up and down and grinning like a stupid puppy.

‘Am I welcome after tonight?’ asked Alex.

Ilse answered, ‘Beate sent me. She cannot be seen to come and talk to you, but she wants you to come. Please.’

Paddy was still nodding his head, but he was no longer grinning, he now had an earnest, imploring look on his face. It said “Pleeease”!

Alex nodded, ‘OK, twelve noon. Now kiss the girl goodnight, Paddy, and for Christ’s sake, let’s get to bed, I’m done in.’

Paddy obliged and they were in bed by five.

They arrived for lunch a full fifteen minutes ahead of time; it was Paddy itching to get there to see Ilse. Wifey, back home in Ireland, seemed to have been forgotten. As they entered the small living room, Beata rose from the settee. Both Alex and Paddy gawped, she looked gorgeous. Her shining dark hair was pulled severely back into a bun. She wore a very fine tiara encrusted with tiny stones that glistened when she moved her head. But it was the dress that made them stare. A shining deep blue, it fell to the floor. Pencil thin shoulder straps and a neckline that stopped just short of the navel. She appeared to be wearing nothing underneath it.

Alex continued to stare. ‘Beautiful,’ he said. ‘Absolutely beautiful. Are we going out?’

‘No,’ she smiled.

‘What’s the dress for?’

‘Not what, who?’

‘OK, who’s the dress for?’

‘You,’ she said, walking across and planting a gentle kiss on his cheek.

After lunch Paddy and Ilse disappeared upstairs. Alex and Beata sat on the couch. She poured him an *Asbach Uralt*. ‘For digestion,' she explained. Then she linked an arm through his and rested her head on his shoulder. 'I can't stop them, you know.'

'What do you mean?' he asked, puzzled.

'They want to hurt you, and there is nothing I can do. It's silly, isn't it, comical even. I have more feelings for this policeman that I hardly know than for the business that he is intent on destroying. I must be mad, but I can't help it, and to add insult to injury, he doesn't even want to sleep with me.'

Alex put his arm around her and kissed her hair.

'You're wrong, very wrong, but I have a job to do, and I must do it.'

'But who would know?'

'I would.'

'You're a strange man, Mr Alex Policeman, but then that's what I like about you. Tell me, when all this is over, do you think there could be a chance that maybe we could meet, somewhere where no-one knows us?' She looked up at him.

He squeezed her to him, 'There's always a chance,' he said.

'Please,' she whispered.

They were back outside by 19:30, Paddy complaining he was exhausted, that his dick ached, that his joints hurt and that he hadn't done as many gymnastics since he was in Kindergarten back in the Emerald Isle.

'God, isn't she just gorgeous,' he mooned.

Alex refrained from mentioning – yet again – that she did this for a living.

At 19:45, the two Kombi-loads of German police arrived, followed fifteen minutes late by Otto.

'Just thought I'd put in an appearance,' he commented as he shook hands with Alex and Paddy. Alex told him about the threats that were being issued. Otto looked at him and shook his head. 'If they're saying it, then they'll do it. Leave it with me, I'll see what I can do.'

The night passed peacefully, a lot less people and not a single threat. They crashed out at 5am. They arrived back in Geilenkirchen after everyone had left for the day to find they'd again been given two days off. Alex was requested to see the WO-man "at-your-convenience".

Bright and early the next morning Alex was across at the detachment and over a pot of tea – my, things were looking up! – briefed the WO-man on the happenings of the weekend. He omitted to mention the threats that Beata had brought up and he didn't breathe a word relating to Paddy's gymnastics. Paddy was still in bed, sleeping it off.

'So, Alex, what's the bottom line this week. Still think we're on a loser?'

'Long term, yes. We can't keep this up forever, and the moment we don't go they'll be back in droves. I think we should give it one more week and see what Captain Fleischmann comes up with – if anything – and then somebody in the Big Brass needs to make a decision; withdraw the ban or increase our presence.'

'We haven't got the manpower to put half a dozen of the lads in Cologne each week for three days and keep them there indefinitely, and like you say, the moment we pull them off, the hordes will be back.' He paused a moment for thought. 'Right, we'll give it one more weekend, and then you prepare a report, listing your findings, and we'll kick it upstairs. OK with you?'

'Sure! You're the boss.'

The WO-man looked across at him and grinned.

'Nice of you to acknowledge it, Alex, although I sometimes wonder . . . Off you go now. Unless anything happens, same time next week.'

The following Friday, Alex and Paddy once more pulled up in front of *Vater Rhein*, ready to commence the weekend. The two Kombis full of German police were already in attendance. Surprisingly to Alex, by 21:00 only some twenty odd people had turned up and they had no problem in turning them all away. Maybe the happenings of the previous two weekends were making a difference after all! Alex felt the German police presence was invaluable. They kept their blue lights flashing, as did the Landrover, and they maintained a highly visible presence rather than just sitting in their vehicles.

By 23:00 they'd turned away another 48 people – visitors were definitely down – and they hadn't had one really stroppy person.

At 23:20 Captain Fleischmann appeared. As he shook hands, his face was wreathed in smiles. 'By early tomorrow morning I will have a court order to close this place down. The Commissioner, the Mayor, the City council, they all sat down together yesterday with the people from the legal department. This afternoon a special court was in session and the City's case for closure was presented. Closure has been approved. Tomorrow morning I will have the papers to attach to these buildings to enforce the closure. The people will have two working days to remove personal effects; that is Monday and Tuesday. On Wednesday the bulldozers will move in and by Wednesday evening *Vater Rhein* will look like that.' He swept his arm in the direction of the surrounding desolation.

'Good,' said Alex. 'So, by Sunday morning, we can all go home.'

Paddy looked as if he was attending a funeral.

'Well, actually, Alex,' said Otto, looking a little uncomfortable, 'the Mayor and the Commissioner were wondering if we could do it a little different. If we just move in sometime during the day, deliver the notices and seal the area off, it will be like a damp squib, nobody will notice. If, however, we were to do this at, let's say, ten o'clock tomorrow evening, we will have people here, your people. Punters, as you call them, but not too many. We would bring a police photographer, take pictures, put the notices up, all in time for the Sunday morning papers. Good publicity for the city, good publicity for the police, and of course none of this would have been possible without the valuable assistance of the Royal Air Force Police.' He pointed at Paddy and Alex, all smiles. 'Well, what do you think?'

'I don't. It stinks,' replied Alex. 'If I ask for approval to stage this, my boss will say no. I guarantee it.'

'So?' Captain Fleischmann spread his hands wide, 'What do you suggest?'

'When will you get the court order?'

'By nine tomorrow morning I will have it.'

'Can you be at Wahn guardroom by, say, eleven, with the court order?'

'Of course. What do you have in mind?'

'I have an idea, but I need to think it through.'

'Fair enough, I will see you at eleven then.' And he gave a little salute, headed over to his car and was driven away, offering a little toot on the claxon as he went.

Paddy climbed in the Landrover and sat sulking. Alex looked at his watch, nearly midnight. He'd be glad when it was over. It all seemed a pointless exercise now; tomorrow the place would be closed down for good. He briefly thought about warning Beata but dismissed the idea immediately. It could be totally counter-productive and backfire. Somebody could get hurt. No, much better to keep the element of surprise; that way there should be no injuries.

With agonizing slowness the clock edged its way towards 4 a.m. Alex had been able to turn away every single group that showed up without argument. One exception was a group of eight Poles who claimed to be construction workers. With their crew cuts and bearing, Alex was sure they were visiting military but he had no intention of pushing it to find out. Tomorrow – no, today – was close-down. Finally the lights at *Vater Rhein* went out. This was the signal for Ilse to appear for a goodnight cuddle with Paddy. She wanted him to stay. His eyes were full of pleading when he looked at Alex, but Alex shook his head, and they wandered off together into some dark corner and did whatever it takes people fifteen minutes to do in a dark corner.

They wearily climbed into bed at 05:30. Three hours later Alex was up and in the shower. He didn't go next door and wake Paddy. If things went wrong, it was best he wasn't involved. At 10:00 Alex entered the guardroom and over a cup of coffee asked the LAC minding the shop to get his boss over. It seemed the Flight Sergeant in question was having a dirty weekend with a WAAF from the Sergeants' Mess in Königswinter, a picturesque, romantic tourist town on the banks of the Rhein, famous for its castle ruins atop the Drachenfels – Dragon's Rock – mountain.

Sergeant McMann, the second in command, put in an appearance inside ten minutes. When Alex told him what he wanted done, the Sergeant seemed struck dumb. He did, however, agree to call the NCO i/c of the MT Section together with Sergeant Dale, who was in charge of the dogs. Fifteen minutes later, and over yet another cup of coffee, Alex explained to the three main players exactly what he wanted to happen that evening. Looking at his watch he began, 'In about half an hour we will be having a visit from a Captain

Fleischmann from the *Kripo* here in Cologne. He will have in his possession court documents ordering the closure of *Vater Rhein* at 22:00 this evening. There will be a heavy German police presence, and because the place is very popular with service personnel, we have been asked to be present in case of any problems. None are anticipated, but the German police would rather we dealt with that side of things, while they handle the closure, deal with the girls and any other civilians that are there. Based on numbers of service men there at 22:00 on the last two Saturdays I anticipate we will need three or four buses.' He looked at Sergeant Coates, the MT Sergeant, 'Can you handle that?' The Sergeant nodded, 'Four buses and drivers. Can do.'

'OK,' said Alex, 'now dogs. I would like a show of two dogs. As I said, trouble is not anticipated, but the sight of four white hats and two dogs should intimidate people sufficiently to make them climb on the buses quietly. Once the buses are full I'll go to each bus and make them an offer – a trip to Wahn and be charged, or dump them all outside Cologne railway station. My guess is nobody will want to come back here. If I just offer the railway station, over half the people will probably want to go somewhere else and we'll spend the next hour arguing.'

At that moment, Captain Fleischmann and his driver pulled up outside the guardroom. Alex looked at his watch, 11:00 on the nose. You really could set your clock by them.

Introductions were made and a chair found for Captain Fleischmann. His driver could stand. Alex turned to Captain Fleischmann and set about telling the story again, only he began differently. 'I have explained to my colleagues here the plan that has been drawn up by the German police at the instigation of the police commissioner, the Mayor of Cologne and the City Council, and their wish that we participate in the closure of *Vater Rhein*, only insofar as it involves British Servicemen. In fact, we are there only as a gesture of goodwill and to highlight the level of cooperation between the civil police and the Royal Air Force police. My colleagues here have agreed to provide the four buses you requested and also to provide the two police dogs, purely for show of course.'

Captain Fleischmann didn't bat an eyelid.

He behaved exactly as he would if this had been his own plan and he was hearing it again for the umpteenth time.

'Thank you, dear colleagues,' he nodded toward the three Sergeants, then stood and withdrew several sheets of paper from his inside pocket. He held them up.

'Earlier this morning I took possession of these documents issued by the German Court demanding the closure of the *Vater Rhein* premises. We will act upon this court order at 10pm this evening. Now, the German police do not want any confrontation with British servicemen and it is for this reason that we have asked for your cooperation. It is very much appreciated. Thank you.' He sat down, speech over.

The three Sergeants preened themselves, happy to be of service.

'I'll just see the Captain out,' said Alex, rising. 'And then we can discuss the method of operation for this evening.'

They stood beside the *Kripo* car; the Captain held out his hand, 'Alex, that was masterful. I almost believed it myself. You are wasted as a policeman. I felt like standing up and applauding. They are all senior in rank, you're a Corporal, and yet they follow you. Unbelievable!

Alex looked him in the eye, 'Hitler was a Corporal, and the whole country followed him, remember?' Otto winced. 'Ouch. Touché. My sincere apologies, Alex. That was unworthy.' Alex nodded, 'By the way, Otto, how many men are you putting in tonight?'

'Four Kombis. Four men in each. I had thought of using a small bus, but thought that more vehicles, lights flashing, would create a stronger impression. What do you think?'

'Oh, I agree, Otto. The more the merrier. Should make it easier for us.'

'By the way, Alex, you're invited to the show on Wednesday. Will you be there?'

'I should really be back in Geilenkirchen on Monday, might be a bit difficult – unless I receive a direct request, of course. I couldn't refuse that, now, could I?'

Otto nodded, 'I shall see to it. I also understand that a letter of commendation will be sent to your commanding officer relating to your work here. It will be on behalf of the City Council and the Police Force. It should halt any problems before they begin. What do you think?'

'Gratefully received, Otto, thank you.'

He nodded and climbed in the car. 'See you tonight, Alex, and don't be late for the show.'

Buses, drivers and dogs were organised to arrive as near to 22:00 as possible. The dogs and handlers would travel on one of the buses rather than with Alex and Paddy; they would arrive at 19:30 as usual. Alex felt that buses and dogs arriving together would create a greater impression than if the dogs were to simply wander around aimlessly for an hour and a half. Fortunately, everyone agreed. Alex and Paddy arrived at *Vater Rhein* at 19:45, two Kombis and four German police were already there. Vater Rhein was already all aglow. There were two parallel roads leading to the buildings, each roughly 300m long where they joined the main road at one end and the Vater

Rhein road at the other; quite like a letter U with a flat, rather than rounded bottom. The twenty eight houses stood on the base of the U – fourteen either side of the road. Immediately behind the houses an embankment led to the river.

By 20:45 they'd turned away only one group of six Belgians.

Alex was beginning to think that tonight might be a damp squib. He went with Paddy over to the German police. 'We've got roughly one hour to when the fireworks start. Perhaps if we turn all the blue lights off and just sit in the vehicles, we might get a better crowd by 22:00.'

All lights were turned off and they retreated to their respective vehicles. Ten minutes later, several groups had arrived. They eyed the silent police vehicles with suspicion, then one or two went into the brothel. No attempt was made to stop them. Ten minutes before ten, a nice little crowd was milling around outside in the roadway. At two minutes to ten flashing blue lights appeared at the top of each of the parallel road. Two vehicles with lights coming down the right hand road leading two buses, and one vehicle proceeding down the left, again leading two buses.

Alex, in the Landrover, turned on his headlights and blue lights.

The two stationary police Kombis did the same.

The German police vehicles pulled up in front of Vater Rhein, while the two buses in each road drove forward as far as they could and then stopped, totally blocking each exit from *Vater Rhein.* The only way out was to scramble across the rubble in the direction of the main road – nobody tried it. One handler with dog dismounted from each leading bus and stood by that bus.

They did not attempt to join the crowd.

Captain Fleischmann, his driver and a police photographer exited from a *Kripo* car. He waved to Alex to join them. Together they made towards the end house, Beata's accommodation. Well before they got there the door opened and Beata, followed by Ilse, stepped into the street and waited.

Otto stopped directly in front of Beata and bowed slightly.

'Madam, I have here a court order authorising the closure of these premises with immediate effect.' He handed over one set of documents. 'I also have a second court order, authorising the demolition of these premises. That will take place in four days' time. Next Wednesday.' He handed over a second set of documents.

'Everyone must now vacate these premises. You have thirty minutes. A police presence will remain here until the demolition is complete. You have two working days, Monday and Tuesday, to remove all personal effects from the premises, should they not be removed, they will be seized.'

The photographer was busy flashing away at everything, dogs, buses, police wagons, Captain Fleischman and Alex. He turned to take one of Beata and Ilse.

'Stop!'

He looked at Alex, unsure what to do.

'Please do not take photographs of these ladies.'

The photographer looked at Captain Fleischmann, who took a moment to consider. Finally he nodded at the photographer, 'Elsewhere, please.'

The photographer went into one of the buildings, happily flashing away.

Beata looked at Alex, her eyes were glistening. 'Could I speak with you a moment, please. Alone?' She turned and headed back into her accommodation. Alex followed her into the living room. She stood facing him, fighting hard to hold back the tears. 'Well, Mister Policeman, you did it. I never thought you would succeed.' Alex waited. 'I should hate you for what you've done, but I can't, and you know why.' She took her bag from the table, opened it and handed Alex a finely engraved card. 'When all this mess is over, I want you to call me. I want you to visit me.'

Alex went to speak but Beata put her hand gently over his mouth. 'Not now; it is the wrong time. Sometime, when this is all blown away, and we can simply be Alex and Beata.' She leaned forward and kissed him softly on the lips. 'Now you must please leave me, I have only twenty minutes left to get changed, before the good Captain comes to throw me out.' She sighed. 'Quite a night, Alex… One I shall never forget. A story to tell our grandchildren. When they are grown up, of course.' When she caught the look on his face, she burst out laughing. 'You should see your face! I did not mean our—' She stopped suddenly, 'But why not? What a wonderful thought!' She kissed him on the cheek, 'Out, Alex! Let the lady get changed.' And with that, she moved with him towards the door. 'Please, Alex, when this is over, call me.'

Outside in the street, Paddy and the German police were ushering people on to the buses. When everyone was aboard, Alex counted them – only forty seven, about a third of the number that would have been here a couple of weeks ago. He addressed the reluctant passengers. 'Your choice! A drop off at the central railway station with no further action or a trip to Wahn to be charged.' Nobody asked for Wahn.

Alex stood talking to Captain Fleischmann while the latter's men tacked a copy of the Court Order to every front door. No need to show his face again, it was now German police jurisdiction. He noticed Paddy had disappeared; no doubt making his own future arrangements.

They were back in Wahn before midnight. Alex didn't ask, and Paddy didn't tell.

Sunday afternoon, Alex phoned the Duty NCO at Geilenkirchen with details to be passed on for the WO-man's consumption; he'd be back with Paddy Wednesday evening.

Wednesday morning broke grey, wet and windy. It had been throwing it down all night and everywhere was sodden. Alex and Paddy arrived back at *Vater Rhein* just before nine; the bulldozers were hard at work. Four houses had already gone. German efficiency. Captain Fleischmann paddled over to the Landrover, umbrella held high.

'Welcome, Alex. Welcome Paddy; don't get out. Not exactly what we'd hoped for, but nevertheless work is proceeding.' He waved vaguely in the direction of the houses. He reached inside his coat pocket and withdrew an envelope which he passed through the open window to Alex.

'From my boss to yours, it's very complimentary – I've read it.' He chuckled. 'I'm off now. Everything is under control. By tonight you'll only see more of that,' and he pointed towards the main road and the desolation. 'If you're in town again and fancy a beer, a coffee or just a chat; call me.'

He offered his hand to both Alex and Paddy; then with a wave he headed for his car. Job over. Done and dusted.

-

As I've already said: Life is sometimes stranger than Fiction!

Fast forward almost fifty years to 2005.

Emm discovered she had a half-brother, Dieter, whom she never knew existed. To cut a very long story short - we found him, and his family, and we had several visits to his home town of Leverkusen, roughly midway between Düsseldorf and

Cologne. During the course of one conversation Dieter began to talk about his early life . . . in Cologne!

We couldn't believe our ears.

It turned out that Vater Rhein had been rebuilt in 1960 within the redevelopment plan, and issued with a legal licence to carry on business as a brothel. In his twenties, Dieter had worked for the people who owned the brothel ... as an enforcer!

Chapter 13

The short straw: Replacing the Famous Five

Alex wandered into the detachment. It was a beautiful spring morning, bright blue sky, glorious sunshine, one of those days when it was good to be alive. Last night he'd returned from taking yet another convoy via Eindhoven to Antwerp, 5 transporters, and all on his own. At the rate equipment was heading back to the UK there'd soon be nothing left in Berlin. He went into the duty NCO's room – nobody there. He sat down behind the desk and picked up a magazine.

'Alex, got a mo?' The WO-man stuck his head around the door.

'Sure.' Alex idly wondered what he'd do if he'd said no. Not worth trying; the old boy treated him well. The odd night's baby-sitting – unfortunately not Tina – a few drinks and a bite to eat in his married quarters now and then. The WO-man was OK. He liked to shout a bit, but his bark really was worse than his bite – certainly with those teeth that seemed to spend more time in a glass of water than in his mouth.

'Sit down, Alex. And, oh, shut the door if you will. No need to let the world know.'

What? thought Alex, as he grabbed the chair in front of the Wo-man's desk. *Sounds ominous*. The WO-man looked at him.

'You happy here, Alex?'

Jeezes! Now what! Alex thought. 'Yep! I like it here.'

'Why?'

What the hell is this…? 'Well, many reasons, really. First, I suppose, is because I've got a lot of freedom.'

'You mean the convoys?'

'Yes. It lets me do exactly what I want to do. Travel around. No real restrictions. Different countries, different people. It's great.'

'It's going to stop'.

'What? Why?'

'Don't know, but we've only got one more convoy scheduled for the next two months. Also, we're going to be cutting back on weekends in Cologne. Deemed not necessary any more. Probably down to you, that one. You and your mates in the *Kripo* getting *Vater Rhein* bulldozed. Done yourself out of a job there, lad'.

'Shit!'

'Quite.'

'So what's left?' asked Alex. 'There's nothing much round here. No convoys. That's Holland and Belgium out. No Cologne, what does that leave us? Not a lot!'

'Nope. It's going to clip your wings, Alex. Oh, there'll still be enough work. Traffic. The odd convoy. The odd patrol. But that's not you, is it, Alex? That's not your style. We've got four here going back to the UK or civvy street in the next three months. My guess is not everyone will be replaced. Times are changing, son!'

'OK. I see that, but there must be something else.'

'There is.' The WO-man opened a drawer in his desk and took out a blue file. 'This.' He laid it on his desk but did not open it.

'Know where Sundern is?'

'No.'

'Gütersloh?'

'No.'

'OK, we can look at the map in a minute. Basics first. Sundern is HQ for No 1 Provost & Security Services Detachment. Big area to cover. East German border, down to the American zone and way up north. Ex SS barracks, not too big. Provost billeted separately, either single or no more than two to a room.'

'Nice!'

'Yep, thought you'd like that. I've spoken to the Warrant Officer in charge there, Warrant Officer Smith, an old mate of mine, he gave me all the gen. They're busy. Too busy. There's a big airfield on the other side of Gütersloh, several thousand bods there and enough trouble in town every night to keep even you happy. One patrol out every night and two at weekends. Also, they put out patrols to Bielefeld, Münster and half a dozen other places. Problem is they're stretched. Just lost five men. Seems the AOC has himself a place in a town called Rheda, not too far from Sundern. He went away for a week and the Detachment was supposed to keep an eye on it. Seems they did that with a vengeance. First patrol went by and spent the next four hours in the kitchen, drinking coffee and chatting up the housekeeper, who apparently is a looker. Back to camp, next shift goes out there and does the same. To cut a long story short, over the next six days, five of our brethren had themselves a ball. They drank all the AOC's booze, slept in his bed and shagged his housekeeper plus, by all accounts, assorted friends. Problem was the AOC came back early without warning, and walked in on what he described as "one gigantic fuck-in". He called the Detachment CO who got himself one gigantic bollocking and poor old Smudger had to go out there with four of the lads and a couple of Kombis to arrest everybody. This was followed by the quickest Court

Martial in Air Force history and the Famous Five, as they're now called, were reduced to the ranks and kicked out of the police into GD. Hence, Sundern is five bods short.'

'And you're asking me if I want to go?'

'Well, somebody's got to. I thought since things are going to get a little quiet around here you might like to see what you can find up there.'

'Can I think about it?'

'For today. And mum's the word, OK?'

'What if I decide against it?'

'That's up to the Old Man. My guess is it's between you, Bunchie and Ralph. Jock, Dennis and Nick will be out of here soon. That leaves you three.'

'Hmm. . . I think Bunchie's in for the long haul. Good guy, maybe a bit quiet. Ralph's a pretty mean boxer, could be good news for the Detachment. That leaves me, so I think I'd better jump before I'm pushed.'

'That's the way I figured it, son.'

'OK, when?'

'How fast can you pack a bag?'

'You're joking!'

'You've got two weeks from today. Oh, by the way, talking of Ralph. I heard a story that it was you who split his lip some time back. True?'

Alex nodded. 'Yeah, *Rosenmontag.* He was pissed and causing a spot of bother down town. Several people asked him nicely to pack it in but he didn't. I asked him twice – then I told him. He put his fists up, so I clocked him before he clocked me. End of story.'

'Any problems afterwards?'

'No. Bunchie and I stuck him in a taxi, and Bunchie came back to camp with him. He was bleeding all over the place.

First off, Ralph was apparently going to kill me, but the lads stuck him in a shower and he cooled down. When I got back he'd sobered up. When he first walked toward me I thought he was going to deck me, but he stuck his hand out and apologised. Could hardly speak. His lip was huge. We've been great pals ever since. Wouldn't like to meet him in the ring, though; he'd kill me. It was a one off.'

Alex looked the Wo-man in the eye, and almost as an afterthought, asked, 'Boss, can you swing a patrol to Cologne this weekend?'

'Why?'

'I want to say goodbye to Katie and her grandma.'

'Are you . . . err . . . you know?'

'No, I'm not. But they've been good to me. Food every time I call in, and I stayed there over Easter. Had a super time. Walks in the park and long talks with Katie'

The WO-man raised his eyebrows.

'No, no. She's trying to get over Dennis, the prick!'

'Ah…'

'Anyway, can you swing a trip?'

'On your own?'

'Preferably.'

'Motorbike then.'

'Thanks.'

'Bring the docs in for signature Friday morning. Then you can vanish. Be back here Monday morning. OK? In the meantime, I'll have a word with the Old Man and tell him you volunteered.' He grinned at Alex.

Alex grinned back. 'I've a feeling I've been conned.'

First thing Alex did when he left the Detachment was visit Ali in the MT section. Ali was not only the real power here but he was also a driving instructor, examiner and the person who put the official signature on RAF driving licences. A power way beyond his two stripes.

'Ali, I need a favour. I'm being posted and I need a driving licence.'

Ali looked at him and laughed. 'Don't want much, do you? Can you actually drive?'

Alex told him that when he was night duty NCO he would lock the Detachment up at about three in the morning and take a Landrover out onto the runway for half an hour and this way he'd taught himself to drive.

'Jeez, Alex! How long have you been doing this?' Ali exclaimed in horror.

'Every time I pull nights.'

'Does anyone know about it?'

'No.'

'Ever driven in town?'

'No. Never driven anywhere except the airfield when it's dark. Ali, I need this badly.'

'OK. Look, this afternoon, three o'clock meet me here. We'll go down town and you can drive around for an hour. If you don't actually kill anyone, I'll fix you a licence.'

'Thanks, Ali, you're a gem.'

'Not so quick, Alex, this is gonna cost you. I want something in return.'

'What?'

'Next week we've got the Top Brass coming. I need defaulters for some cleaning and painting jobs.'

'I'll talk to the guardroom and get them to send over whoever's on jankers for the next week. OK?'

'Done deal, Alex.'

*

Alex didn't kill anyone, and by 18:00 was in possession of a brand new driving licence for vehicles up to seven tons. Three lads on jankers were already hard at work.

Done deal, as Ali had said.

Chapter 14

Bye-bye Katie - Hello Beate!

Alex waved goodbye to Katie and her grandma, climbed on the motorbike and made his way to Cologne's central railway station. He'd always loved it there; it smelled of cigars and strong coffee - much different to England. He looked at his watch as he made his way to the bank of telephones next to the ticket kiosks. Still only 8:30; he could be in luck. He took the card from his breast pocket and dialled. It rang six times before finally a sleepy voice answered, 'Hallo.'

Alex chuckled into the phone, 'I'd recognize that beautiful voice anywhere. Sounds like you're still asleep.'

'Alex? Alex, where are you?'

'Cologne'

There was a pause.

'Duty?'

'No.'

'How long?'

'Today and tomorrow.'

'I'm staying where I am. Press the button when you arrive, I'll release the door. Think you can find me?'

'I'd find you anywhere, Bee.'

She was chuckling as she hung up the phone.

-

This is another one of the chapters that suffered a "major loss" when Emm's bag disappeared in Sofia. It deserves more attention than I have given it here, but I simply don't have the heart to re-write it all again.

Katie and her Grandma ran a small, working class, restaurant in Köln-Kalk – a district of Cologne – that was a favourite meeting place for all members of the Provost Detachment at RAF Geilenkirchen.

*If we were working anywhere within 25 to 30 kms of Cologne we would always find an excuse to visit Katie and Grandma to devour their wonderful platters of "*panierte Koteletts mit Kartoffelsalat*" – breaded pork chops with potato salad – washed down with a Pils and followed by a pot of their delicious home-ground coffee.*

We never encountered any antagonism here from customers. Grandma made it clear to everyone that we were always welcome; a considerable "olive branch", since both her husband and Katie's parents had been killed in the allied bombing of Cologne during the Second World War.

After leaving Geilenkirchen I still managed to steal the occasional trip down to Cologne to see them.

Grandma died in 1960, the same year that Katie met and married a Belgian who had a business in what was then known as the Belgian Congo. After the wedding Katie accompanied her new husband back to Africa.

It was with a great deal of sadness that I later learned that both Katie and her husband had been killed in one of the frequent uprisings there.

Katie and Grandma invited me to spend the whole of Easter 1958 with them. I have never forgotten the walks in the park nor our conversations that literally lasted for hours.

Katie was a lovely, lovely lady and I still think about her and talk about her with Emm to this day.

Another "stranger than fiction" story: While Alex was enjoying his visits to Katie and Grandma in the winter of January to March 1958, little did he know that Emm, at the time just a toddler, was staying with her own Grandma in Köln-Kalk, literally round the corner from the restaurant. Afternoon playtime was on the swings and roundabouts in the park where Alex and Katie took their walks!

Chapter 15

Soxmis - Brixmis: A little military history

SOXMIS was the Soviet Military Mission to West Germany while BRIXMIS, its operational "liaison" equivalent, represented the *British Commander-in-Chief's Mission to the Soviet Forces in East Germany*.

On 16 September 1946, the British and Soviet Commanders-in-Chief signed what became known as the *Robertson-Malinin Agreement* under which each side had the right to deploy military liaison teams within each other's sectors of Berlin, and indeed Germany. In March 1947, the Soviets signed a separate agreement with the United States and one month later they signed a third agreement with the French.

The British had by far the largest contingent of accredited military members, thirty one in total. The US had some fourteen accredited military personnel. Simply put, the rules of the game stated that a military mission had the right to travel anywhere within the opposition's designated zone with the exception of certain restricted areas; usually military bases and airfields, training sites and Displaced Persons camps. In reality, these restricted zones were exactly the places that the various military missions sought to enter. Carrying weapons was strictly forbidden.

Not far from RAF Gütersloh airfield was a DP Camp from which it was possible to observe through binoculars the comings and goings of both aircraft and personnel. A SOXMIS team made regular visits to this camp and on two occasions

Alex and colleagues chased them away. On one occasion, Alex managed to overtake the SOXMIS vehicle and forced it to stop directly in front of RAF Gütersloh's main entrance. The car contained three Soviet observers, in uniform, carrying side arms. They refused to leave their vehicle. Alex called the duty officer who, when he arrived did not know how to deal with the situation and knew of no standing orders at Gütersloh for dealing with a Soviet military mission. He suggested letting them go – complete with unauthorized weapons.

Alex's suggestion, which was not acted upon, was to "box the buggers in and let them starve. Three or four days of living in their combined shit will have them begging to be let out." Not an unreasonable suggestion, he had thought. Ignoring Alex's suggestion, who was after all at the sharp end of things, contrast this to treatment meted out by both Soviet and East German troops to BRIXMIS personnel, of which there were hundreds of such incidents over the years.

One evening in September, at approximately 18:00, two motorcyclists deliberately forced a BRIXMIS car off the road near the town of Finsterwalde. As the driver tried to regain the road, the vehicle was deliberately rammed by a nine ton truck that literally ran up the near side of the car, over the bonnet and front right side of the passenger area, before itself turning over onto its side. One of the BRIXMIS personnel lay trapped inside the vehicle for one hour with head and rib injuries. His right leg was also fractured in four places. East German soldiers, who were present at the scene, were forbidden by their officers to help. German civilians eventually freed the man and he was transported to an East German hospital to suffer what can only be described as nightmare treatment.

In September two years earlier, an RAF team made up of a Squadron Leader, Flight Sergeant and a Corporal were attacked by a group of twelve Soviets, later found to be a *Spetsnaz* group acting under specific instructions. The car was ransacked and the three were finally tossed into the back of a Russian truck with their hands tied behind their backs. It took twelve hours of high level negotiations to get the three released. One of them had suffered a broken collarbone. The Russians never did apologize and we quietly let the matter drop.

Cars were repeatedly rammed by Soviet or East German military vehicles. One BRIXMIS car was deliberately rammed by a tank transporter. Over the years BRIXMIS vehicles were repeatedly –yes, repeatedly– fired upon, and one RAF Corporal almost died from bullet wounds as a result. BRIXMIS crews were beaten up with everything ranging from rocks, bricks, tyre levers, shovels, pickaxe handles to the butt of an AK47. It needed a very special type of person to belong to such a group. Brutal intimidation was the norm. Fortunately, Brits are extremely resilient by nature and the more adverse the situation, the greater their resolve. Why is it that so many of the High Command still think that war, even the cold war, requires a level playing field?

To paraphrase Colonel Blimp: 'Oh, war begins at twelve, does it? Does the other side know? They do? OK, we kick off at six!'

Contrary to popular military myth, not all service personnel were issued with what became known as the SOXMIS card. During the period 1958-1960 neither Alex nor his colleagues were ever issued with SOXMIS cards, nor, it appears, did the guardroom or Duty Officer at Gütersloh receive any instructions on how to deal with such incidents.

It was also known that Soviet Military Mission members would attempt to intimidate people who were resident in the DP camps. Almost without exception their former homes lay in

Soviet occupied territory and if the Soviets discovered the former addresses of these people, then relatives who were still living at home could and would be intimidated, thus forcing the Displaced Person to supply information to the Soviet Mission.

Both British and French military missions suffered fatalities in incidents. Both Governments shamefully preferred to brush these incidents under the carpet. After all we mustn't upset the Soviets, must we?

The Americans suffered one fatality in 1985.

Little appears to be publicly documented about SOXMIS. The Soviets always held their cards very close to their chest – unless, of course, it suited them to do otherwise.

All military missions were closed down in 1990.

Chapter 16

The Russian Military Mission, or: Two can play at your game!

The phone in the Duty NCO's room rang at exactly 10:30 that Friday morning. Alex was behind the desk reading a three weeks' old News of The World that had been left lying around; nothing but sex, murder, intrigue and more sex. Infidelity seemed to be the main game in town back in the UK. Alex had been left to man the phones; everybody else had wandered over for a NAAFI break. 'P&SS Detachment Geilenkirchen.'

'Good morning. Would by any chance your Corporal Alex be available to speak?'

Alex recognized that voice, but from where? Definitely German, but… And then the penny dropped.

'Otto?'

A throaty chuckle came down the phone. 'Gotcha, as the *Amis* would say.'

'So, Otto, and how's life treating you in the great metropolis? Got enough work to keep you out of mischief?'

'Huh! You know how it is, Alex. Work we have plenty, too much, in fact. My wife complains she never sees me. You see more of your driver, than you do of me, she says.'

'I have a solution, Otto. Divorce your wife and marry your driver. No more complaints.'

'My driver is a man, Alex.'

'I know, Otto Just joking. What did you want me for anyway? *Vater Rhein?*'

'No, Alex, that now blends into the area very well. It's just a mass of rubble. But, you mention the Rhine, so I speak specifically of the Rhine, as in the river. You understand?'

'Understand what, Otto? I don't follow you.'

'Have you been in Cologne recently, Alex. I need to know.'

Alex's heart seemed to stop momentarily. *Cologne, Rhine... Oh, shit!* 'Why Otto, you have a problem?'

'Well, it depends. Can you speak freely?'

'Yes, everyone's cleared off for a NAAFI break, I'm manning the phones. We can speak.'

'Good. Yesterday morning a report came to my desk for action. It seems that two nights ago a SOXMIS vehicle was pulled out of the river by a police breakdown crew. Inside had been three Russians, very wet, but amazingly not hurt. They refused to talk to us, or more correctly, to our Russian interpreter. They claimed, as they are allowed to do, diplomatic immunity. Now, as I understand it, this happened just before three in the morning. The Russians were not in any off-limit zone, but, I ask myself what are three Russians doing in a SOXMIS car, in this area at three o'clock in the morning. So, Alex, do you know what I did?'

'No, Otto, do tell. I'm intrigued.'

'I went to look at the site, and do you know what I think, Alex?'

'Otto!'

'OK, OK. I look at the road. I look at the tight bend to the left. I look at the road and the kerb before the bend. And you know what? I think they were being chased. I think that whoever was chasing them caught up with them and then forced them off the road. They made it impossible for the SOXMIS vehicle to turn into the bend and therefore the driver braked, but it was too late. He went over the kerb, hoping to stop on the pavement – there are marks – and in the grass, but he could not stop. He was going too fast and went down the embankment and into the river. I kept asking myself, why would he not stop? Why? He was not in a forbidden zone. OK, it was the middle of the night, which was strange, but… And then it hit me. He did not stop because there was something in the vehicle they did not want anybody to see. So, I think, perhaps whoever chased them already see what is in the vehicle and that is why they chased them. So, Alex, do you know what I do?'

'Otto, I have the distinct feeling you're playing with me. Tell.'

'OK. I tell. I fetch our police diver and he looks along bottom of the river. Guess what he found, Alex? Go on, I want you to guess. Please. Just be kind to me, for once.' Now he was laughing down the phone. 'Come on, Alex, please!'

'OK, Otto. I would guess that if your theory is right, and someone chased them because of what they saw in the vehicle, then your diver would find weapons, several weapons.'

A whoop came from the other end of the phone. 'You'd make a great policeman, Alex. Your powers of deduction are wonderful.'

'I am a policeman, Otto.'

'Yes, I know. But I mean—' He stopped suddenly.

'A real one, Otto?' said Alex into the silence.

'I apologize, my friend. But I knew. I knew! You see, there was one witness, not a very good one, he was more drunk than sober, coming home from a club, and he saw a Landrover, he thinks, leaving that road very fast. He thinks, only thinks, that above the back number plate there was something painted – he thinks – black and red. So, then I think, who drives Landrovers with black and red flashes? And guess what? I think of you. I think, Cologne, Landrover patrol, Geilenkirchen, black and red, RAF police… Alex. So, I telephone for a little chat. How am I doing?'

'You're gloating, Otto.'

'What is gloating? I do not know that word.'

'It means you are showing an excessive amount of satisfaction. You're enjoying this. You're rubbing salt into the wound. OK?'

'I plead guilty,' and he roared with laughter. 'But my friend, what do you think to my theory?'

'I think it's a very good theory, Otto, a very plausible theory. It could have been just as you say. So, what now?'

'Well, so far the theory is just that – a theory – and it is mine. The Commissioner does not want trouble with the Russians. Nobody wants trouble with the Russians. So, since they will not speak to us, and since we have now found weapons were in the car and were then thrown away by the Russians, what do I do?'

'How many people know about this?'

'Everybody. They're Russians, so everybody knows. Why?'

'The Press?'

'No. So far nothing.'

'OK, I suggest you call everybody together and tell them that this matter is being dealt with diplomatically and it is now out of your hands. Also, tell them that this is to be kept quiet – no press, no friends, nobody, or else… If the Russians were going to do something, they would have done it. They had weapons and by now they probably think that you know they had weapons. So, it's stalemate. Take the file, and with the Commissioner's permission, bury it; only bury it where you can find it should you ever need it again in the future. OK?'

'You always come up with a very good solution, Alex, just like at *Vater Rhein.* Did they give you a medal?'

'No, Otto, nobody gave me a medal. The Old Man called me in, read the English translation of the Commissioner's letter, shook my hand, told me "Well done" and said it would be filed with my record. End of story.'

'The Amis would have given you a medal.'

'The Yanks give you a medal if you survive basic training.'

They both laughed.

'Alex, you trust me Alex?'

'No.'

More laughter down the phone.

'OK, that's fair. May I ask, have you been to Cologne on patrol lately?'

Alex was thinking fast. Now was the time to jump, close your eyes, cross your fingers and hope. 'I guess I have to trust you, eh, Otto?'

'I think, Alex, yes.'

'OK, ask. Tactfully, though!'

'Were you on patrol two nights ago in Cologne?'

'Yes.' It had actually been Alex's first trip as a fully-fledged police driver; brand new licence from Ali; trip courtesy of the WO-man – for experience!

'Is my theory of what happened correct?'

'One hundred percent. You'd make a good policeman, Otto.'

More hearty laughter down the phone.

'By the way, Otto, I'm leaving here sometime in the next couple of weeks, going to a place called Sundern, near Gütersloh. Know it?'

'I should do, my father was born there. In Gütersloh that is. Why are you leaving?'

'I jumped before I was pushed. Long story, but I'd have drawn the short straw from three possibles. So, I think that was probably my last trip to Cologne. I was also in Cologne last weekend, saying goodbye to friends.'

'I know.'

'What? How?'

'How doesn't matter, but I have excellent sources of information.' He paused, 'She's beautiful, isn't she?'

'Yes.'

'Be careful, my friend. Very, very careful.'

'I will, Otto, and thanks for the chat. Maybe we'll meet up in Gütersloh sometime.'

'I guarantee it, my friend. Until then, Alex, take care.'

Sundern

17- Welcome to Sundern!

18- Naked in the WAAF Block

19- Dear John,

20- Upside Down in a Ditch with Lynn

21- Christmas Dance

22- Dinner at the Top Three Club and introducing Debs

23- Adolf Hitler's 70th Birthday

Chapter 17

Welcome to Sundern!

To Alex, Sundern was a dream posting. First, it was small, at the most maybe 700 people. From the main entrance you could see to the far end of the camp; just three blocks either side of the main camp road. First block on the left of the road, shaped like an H, was the P&SS Detachment. The imaginary central bar between the lines was PBX and the end leg of the block was occupied by a mix of army and RAF techies. The second block on the left was the Sergeants' Mess. Attached to this was the main mess hall with a small parade ground in front and at the end a separate dining room for NCOs. After this, more accommodation, again mixed, army and RAF, while at the far end of this block, and at the very end of the camp, stood the RAF Police Provost accommodation. Two separate entrances: one for two bedrooms and a bathroom upstairs, and one for the downstairs accommodation. Through the main door and into a central square-shaped hallway from which led four separate rooms. First left: Big Bill and Andy. Second left: MacDonald. Far right: Brian and Jim. Front right: Alex; a double room with a view, and all to himself. Even a washbasin. Paradise!

The rest of the mob lived in married quarters or hirings in town. Well, it was certainly different. A huge step in the comfort direction as far as Alex was concerned.

First morning there, Alex showed his face in the duty NCO's room. Only person there, sitting behind one of the two desks and puffing away at a cigarette while reading the newspaper, was Paddy. Another one! The entire Provost Service seemed to be full of Jocks, Taffs and Paddies.

'Is it always this quiet?' asked Alex.

Paddy looked at him.

'It's only just nine o'clock, in the morning, by the way! Not much happens here at nine o'clock in the morning. Nine o'clock at night now, that's a different thing altogether. Let me see now. We have two out on convoy, be back this afternoon. Two out in town – a little breakfast time shunt. Two out with a *Kripo* guy at the local hospital, taking statements from some prossie who's given one of the pongoes a dose of clap and—' He stopped in mid-sentence, his eyes fixed at some point behind Alex's back. 'Right. So you've arrived then.'

Alex turned. Standing in the doorway, cigarette in mouth and surrounded by a cloud of blue smoke, stood an RAF Warrant Officer in Number One dress uniform who, Alex thought, would make a very good Friar Tuck should he ever wish to change careers. Twinkling blue eyes, the right one screwed up and squinting against a rising spiral of cigarette smoke, chubby red cheeks and the perfect Friar Tuck haircut: bald pate and a reddish, ginger-grey fringe all the way round. A reddish, nicotine-stained moustache and complementing this, one of the most ample girths Alex had ever seen in uniform. He looked Alex up and down. 'Right, lad. Let's go to my office.' And with that he turned and waddled down the corridor, puffing out clouds of smoke with every step. Alex followed - well back and to the right. 'Close the door, lad, and stand easy.' No "pull-up-a-chair", Alex noted.

'My name is Smith. Warrant Officer Smith, and contrary to what you may hear elsewhere, I run this detachment. Is that clear?'

Alex nodded.

'I said, is that clear?'

'Yes, Sir.'

'Right, then. I've been reading your file here.' He tapped a buff coloured folder lying in front of him. 'OK as far as it goes, I suppose. You seem capable enough. It's what it doesn't say that interests me, though.'

He took another puff from the cigarette, which seemed a permanent fixture between his lips, blew out smoke down his nose, and at that moment a length of ash fell down the front of his bemedalled tunic. He left it there.

'I've been speaking to your former Warrant Officer, or to put it more correctly, he called me.'

Alex did not move.

'Now then, lad. Seems you're not too keen on discipline, don't like parades – in fact your uniform seems to visit the dry cleaners at the very mention of one – you like to be left alone to do things your way, you hate having your hair cut, but even more so, you hate calling anyone "Sir". How am I doing so far?'

Alex just stood there. *Shit!*

'Well?'

'Sir.'

'What, Sir? Am I right?'

'Yes, Sir.'

'Now, that wasn't too hard, was it?'

Silence.

'Was it?'

'No, Sir.'

'On the plus-side, your ex-Warrant Officer speaks very highly of your work ethic, your reliability. *Totally trustworthy*, is what he called you. Suggested you might try putting your brain into gear before engaging your tongue, though. Know what I mean?'

'Yes, Sir.'

'I've just had my balls personally toasted by the AOC following the shenanigans of our *Famous Five*. We can't afford any more cock-ups like that. Do you understand me?'

'Yes, Sir.'

'Right, that's it for now. Any questions?'

'Yes, Sir. Where are the rest of the new postings?'

'New postings? You're it, son, for the time being. Two more next month, all being well. That it?'

'Yes, Sir.'

'Right. Your first job here will be to go and get your hair cut, then report back to the duty NCO's room. This week you'll sit, watch and fill in. Next week, full shifts. OK?'

'Yes, Sir.'

'By the way. Are you driver or motor cyclist?'

'Both, Sir.'

'Handy. OK. Dismissed, and keep your nose clean, son!'

Chapter 18

Naked in the WAAF Block

It was 19:30, Alex was off-duty and had decided to have a quiet drink with a book in the Corporals' Club, that is, until he walked through the door. Mac and Steve were ensconced at their usual table near the window in the far corner of the room – *Stammkunden!* – and even with all that crowd Mac spotted Alex the moment the door opened.

'Alex!' he shouted across the room. Everyone looked. Under the circumstances what could he do but be polite, wander across and say hello. Fatal. A chair was pulled out and as soon as he sat down a pint of sludge appeared in front of him, as if by magic. So much for a quiet evening! To be quiet with Mac around was impossible. He was always the noisy, boisterous – usually at least half drunk – life and soul of the party with a seemingly endless supply of dirty jokes, and his impersonation of the Station Commander went down a storm. Mac knocked Alex's arm and pointed towards the bar, 'You're wanted.' The bar tender was waving a telephone receiver in the air. *Shit.* Phone calls when you are off duty are never good news. He took the receiver; it was Little Nick from the guardroom. 'Alex, we've got a problem. There's a guy running around starkers in the WAAF block. Can you sort it out?'

'Nick, I'm off duty. And anyway this is a station police job. Get one of your lot to deal with it.'

'Can't find anybody, Alex. Nobody answers the phone in the block. You know how it is.'

Sensible people, thought Alex. Don't answer the phone, it's always trouble. Pretend you're not there. Let some other silly sod deal with it. This time Alex appeared to be the silly sod.

'OK, Nick. Call our duty driver and get him to do it.'

'Sorry, Alex, the patrol went into town about half an hour ago, there's only Charlie in your office. He's on his own.'

'Right. Call him. Tell him to lock up shop and bring the spare wagon down here to me. I'll drop him off at the Detachment on the way to the WAAF block.'

Alex waved to Mac, mouthing "Duty Calls" and went outside.

Charlie arrived within five minutes, grumbling as usual. Alex tuned him out. He couldn't stand Charlie; he was one long moan. Nothing was ever right. Got a beautiful wife, though. To a man, the Detachment wanted to screw her.

They switched seats at the Detachment and Alex drove down to the WAAF block. Outside everything appeared normal. As he walked through the front door, the noise hit him. The Corporals' Club all over again, but an octave higher. It seemed that every WAAF in the block was either shrieking or screaming. Those from the first floor had decided to come down to the ground floor and join in the fun.

The "fun" appeared to be a naked male – naked that is, except for moustache and pubic hair – prancing up and down at the far end of the corridor, performing a rather unprofessional, albeit quite comical, impression of *Swan Lake*. He saw Alex. The dancing stopped and he backed up into the corner, cupping his hands over his willie. *No erection*, thought Alex, *probably not sexual then*. The girls also stopped their antics. Alex walked slowly along the corridor toward the aspiring Nureyev.

'Right, ladies. I'd like everyone in their rooms and all doors closed. I need to deal with this quietly.'

'NOW!' he barked, when no-one moved. One by one the doors closed. Nureyev didn't move, but his eyes seemed to be everywhere; up, down, side to side. *Very nervous.* At least he wasn't frothing at the mouth. Alex started picking up the clothes that were strewn along the corridor – two stripes on the blouse: a Corporal. Alex didn't know him other than to have seen him in both the NCOs' dining room and the Corporals' Club. He found a wallet and 1250 in one the blouse pockets. The 1250 gave the owner's name as Derrick Beswick. Alex looked at Nureyev and then back at the ID card. Same person in the photo, minus the moustache. He put the things back in the blouse pocket and walked slowly towards the now spasmodically shaking figure in the corner. He held out a vest. 'I'd like you to start getting dressed, Derrick. You'll catch your death out here without your clothes.'

Derrick just looked at him. Nothing seemed to register. Alex dropped the clothes on the ground in a heap, except for the shirt, which he held out. 'Put your shirt on, Derrick. Here, let me help you.' And he slowly lifted Derrick's left arm away from his body and into the shirt sleeve. Then the right arm. Slowly he dressed Derrick, then took him by the arm and led him outside to the Kombi. Derrick turned his head towards Alex. 'Are you going to lock me up?'

Alex hesitated. 'Well, I'll have to take you to the guardroom. Too many people know about what's happened. You'll be alright.'

'Can I have a room to myself?'

No problem, Alex thought, *all cells are singles*. 'Is that what you'd like?'

'Yes, please.'

'Would you like something to eat?'

'Yes, please, I'm hungry.'

'Right, we'll get to the guardroom and Nick will brew a nice pot of tea and somebody will nip to the cookhouse to get you something to eat.'

'Bacon and eggs, toast and brown sauce. Can I have that?'

'You can have whatever you like, Derrick, provided the cookhouse has got it. Mind you, I don't think they do caviar at this time of night.'

Derrick laughed. 'Thank you,' he said.

'All part of the service, Derrick.'

'No, I mean, for not shouting at me.'

Alex kept quiet. He led Derrick to a cell, while Nick brewed a pot of tea. He then did the paperwork, informed the orderly officer, and called the cookhouse to order bacon, eggs, toast, *and don't forget the brown sauce!* He looked at his watch. Just before 21:00. He didn't fancy going back to the club. An early night beckoned.

Next morning Derrick appeared before his CO. Unblemished record, never once been in trouble during his fourteen years of service. The CO gave him a dig.

That evening Alex was Duty NCO. The crew were down at the railway station, in reality probably having *Koteletts mit Kartoffelsalat* across at *Steiners*.

Then the phone rang.

Alex automatically looked at his watch – 20:15.

'Alex, Yorkie here. Guardroom. You know that nutter you brought in last night? Well it seems he's at it again. WAAF block just called. Chummy is running up and down the corridor bollock-naked. Can you sort it?'

'Sure, Yorkie, see you in half an hour or so. Better get the kettle on.'

Alex locked the Detachment and drove over to the WAAF block. The scene was identical to the night before. There was

Derrick in all his glory doing pirouettes before a crowd of laughing, clapping girls. Tonight they were all in the corridor, not just leaning out from their doorways. Alex pushed his way through the crowd and turned to face them.

'OK, ladies, same drill as last night. All back to rooms, please. And close the doors. I need quiet.'

No-one demurred. When the last door had closed, Alex turned to Derrick, who had again retreated into a corner and was covering himself with his hands. Tonight the eyes were normal, Alex noted. 'What's up, Derrick? Fancy some more bacon and eggs? Not forgetting the brown sauce, of course.' Derrick actually smiled at Alex who went and collected the scattered clothing. 'Need any help, Derrick, or can you manage?'

Derrick was hopping about on one leg, trying to get into his underpants. 'Are you going to lock me up again?'

Alex shrugged. 'What do you think?'

Derrick nodded. 'Can I have the same cell, please?'

This guy is really not right, Alex thought. 'Sure, was it comfortable? Warm enough?'

Derrick nodded again, as he struggled into his trousers.

'Fancy a mug of tea, and bacon and eggs, Derrick?'

'Yes, please, Corporal.'

Alex thought of telling him to drop the Corporal bit and call him Alex, but somehow it didn't seem quite appropriate. He led him to the Landrover and helped him in.

'Why, Derrick? Why do you do it? You got a problem?'

Derrick stared at Alex. He didn't answer, but he gave a nod. Just one. Alex followed the previous night's routine, paperwork, ordered food and called the Duty Officer himself. After fifteen minutes the Duty Officer still hadn't appeared. Alex called again, 'Now, please.'

He arrived in a huff. Alex explained about Derrick; how he'd done the same thing the previous night; that he'd got a problem and that he thought the MO should be called. The Duty Officer listened and then said, 'I'd like to see him.' Yorkie unlocked the cell and went in with him. 'Alone, please.' Yorkie shrugged and walked out.

Alex remembered Duxford. Maybe Derrick would become violent and strangle the little bastard. *Wishful thinking . . .*

Five minutes later – and wish unfulfilled – the Duty Officer advised Alex and Yorkie that, 'I have spoken to Corporal Beswick, he seems very calm now, realizes fully what he's done but would like to return to his own room in the block. After he's eaten, I shall release him to appear before the CO in the morning.'

'But the guy's sick. He needs a medic.' Alex got no further.

'Are you trying to tell me my job, Corporal? What I can and cannot do?'

'No, but that guy is sick. Twice in two days. It's not normal.'

'Corporal, I'm releasing him to his own bed. Tomorrow he can explain his actions to his CO.'

Alex shrugged, picked up the Landrover keys from the desk and walked out. *Asshole!*

Lunchtime next day, Alex was off duty in the NCOs' dining room, eating a delicious Nasi Goreng, topped with fried egg – the Dutch cooks were on again; always a pleasure when they prepared Indonesian food – when Little Nick popped his head around the door and caught Alex's eye.

'Can I come in for a sec?'

Alex pointed to an empty seat in front of him. 'Sit, young man, and confess all.' Nick sat. He stared at Alex's plate, fried rice mixed with congealed egg yolk and various other indiscernible bits. ‘That,’ he said pointing, ‘looks disgusting. Yuk!’

‘You’re simply a peasant, Nick. Now, before you get thrown out of here, what do you want?’

‘You know that guy you knocked off last night and the night before, the one who was starkers in the WAAF block, well, he didn’t turn up for CO’s report this morning. Some of your blokes are down town looking for him.’

Alex stopped eating. He suddenly had a bad feeling; queasy, and it wasn’t the food. ‘What have you done about it?’

‘Me? Nothing.’

‘You say our blokes are down town; what’s been done on camp?’

‘Nothing. We tried his room, but the door is locked.’

‘And?’

‘And what? Nothing.’

‘Nick, this camp needs to be searched before everybody starts trotting off down town. First, if he’s not turned up for the CO, he’s either sick, hiding, done a bunk or dead. Now, while I’m still here, go and search his block. All open rooms, store rooms, washrooms and toilets. You’ll probably find the poor sod’s hung himself in the shit house. Go.’ Nick scuttled off. Alex carried on eating.

Five minutes later, Nick came bursting into the Mess, panting and pale-faced. ‘I’ve found him! He’s dead! He’s in the toilet. Alex! Come quick!’

Everyone within earshot stopped eating and looked up, knives and forks held in mid-air.

‘Nick, calm down. First of all, if he’s dead, he’s not going anywhere. Let’s walk over there nice and quietly.’

Nick nodded, still panting. Nerves.

They entered the washroom and Alex looked to the left, the entire wall was divided up into eight separate toilets and there, in toilet number six, he could see, quite clearly, what looked like several neckties joined together and wrapped around a wooden support above the top of the closed door. Beneath the bottom of the door he could just see the fronts of two shoes. Alex walked into toilet number five, climbed on the seat and looked over. That was Derrick alright – quite dead, and a bit of a mess. The problem now was to get him out of there. Alex climbed down from the toilet and turned to Nick. 'Got a knife?'

'Yes.' He pulled out a jack knife.

'Sharp?'

Nick nodded; a flicker of fear in his eyes.

'OK, we need help.'

Alex walked out into the corridor. Just before the exit door was a figure he knew well. 'Lance Corporal Summerbee!'The figure turned. Alex beckoned, 'Come here. Now!'

Summerbee walked back up the corridor with a look of *What-have-I-done-now?* written across his face. Alex led Summerbee into the washroom and pointed to number six. 'There's a guy behind that door who's hung himself and I need you to help me push—' He didn't get any further. There was a dull thud. Summerbee had fainted. Out to the world! Alex looked across at Nick, 'Some tough guy, huh!' Alex stood and thought for a minute. 'I think there are three ways to try this. One is we both try to force the door open if we can, and then one of us supports him while the other cuts him down. Two, one of us climbs the partition and cuts him down. Or three, we get someone from Maintenance to cut through the partition and remove it. That's the easy way. OK, which do you fancy?' Nick was now very, very pale. He shook his head. 'Don't fancy any of them.'

Meanwhile Summerbee had come round and staggered over to the washbasin. He stuck his head under the cold tap.

'Right then; let's get this sorted. First we'll try and force back the door. I'm slimmer than you so let's see if I can squeeze in. I'll try and pull his body away from the door while you squeeze in and then we'll support him while we cut him down.'

They both pushed against the door. Slowly it moved back. Alex jammed his leg and shoulder in the opening to stop it closing. 'Summerbee, come and give Nick a hand on the door.'

'But Corp—'

'FUCKING WELL DO IT, Summerbee!'

Summerbee joined ranks with Alex and Nick. There was a thump as Derrick's body moved and his shoes knocked against the toilet's wooden partition. Alex squeezed in. 'Right, I'm in. Now, on the count of three I'll pull his body back and you two push the door. Nick, you squeeze in with me. Give Summerbee your knife; he's taller than both of us. Summerbee, you cut through the ties while we support him. OK?'

'Right.'

'Three, two, one, PUSH.'

They pushed while Alex pulled Derrick back by his legs. Nick squeezed in; just.

Alex laughed. 'Not much room in here with the three of us to do anything, is there?' Nick looked at Alex. 'How the hell can you joke about it? This guy's dead.'

Alex had still got an arm around Derrick's legs.

'Let me tell you something, Nick. Many moons ago, a wise old Sergeant told me to be detached unless I wanted bad dreams. I'd just puked several times into a ditch. My first accident. Two dead bodies plus two detached heads. So now I practice detachment. I suggest you do the same, Nick. This is not Derrick. It's just something we have to get down from this beam. An object. It can't hurt you. OK, Nick?'

Nick nodded, but he still looked decidedly un-OK. Alex looked across at Nick. 'I'm going to wrap my arms around Derrick's chest, you hold below the hips and when I tell you, Summerbee, you saw like fuck and cut him down!'

'Right,' mumbled Summerbee.

Alex wrapped his arms as far as he could round Derrick's chest. Nick bent down to support his legs and promptly stood up again. 'Christ, Alex, what's that smell?'

'At a guess, I'd say, he's filled his pants, wouldn't you? Grab him, Nick, and let's get this done.' Nick grabbed him.

'OK, Summerbee, cut those fucking ties!'

The body dropped, nearly putting Nick head first down the toilet. He struggled out from under and they managed to sit Derrick on the seat. Alex held him there. Not a pretty sight. Poor Derrick hadn't broken his neck when he stepped off the toilet; he had died from strangulation. Slowly, by the look of it. He'd obviously tried to prise the neckties away from his throat – an impossible task – and in his agony he'd clawed through both sides of his neck.

They left Derrick sitting on the toilet, head and right shoulder leaning against the wall. They then squeezed out and into the washroom. Summerbee had gone. The jack-knife was on the floor.

'Fetch the Meat Wagon, Nick. I'll stay here.'

-

On a sidenote

In the investigation into Corporal Derrick Beswick's suicide Alex was assigned to go through his personal belongings. It was the only time he ever felt dirty. Reading through Derrick's diary and the kept copies of letters he'd written to his wife and her replies, it was easy to build up a picture of Derrick's distress. He'd been married only one year. For months he'd begged his wife to keep her promise and join him in Germany. She refused to leave her mother – and it went on from there. Derrick begged and pleaded, then he'd tried to seek help and draw attention to his plight by performing his two nightly acts in the WAAF block. When nobody in authority asked him why, he killed himself in despair.

Chapter 19

Dear John,

From somewhere at the back of his mind he heard the incessant hammering. It didn't stop. Slowly he surfaced. The hammering again. 'Alex, open this fucking door. It's Sid! Alex!' More hammering. Alex forced his eyes open and looked at the bedside clock. In the dark he could just make out the position of the hands; 10:00. Ten? He slowly came to and his brain began to function. Ten! He'd been in bed exactly one hour.

The door again. 'Alex, wake up!'

The door handle rattled. He always locked the door when he slept, otherwise he'd never get any rest.

'Stow it Sid, I'm awake. Let me get something on!'

He struggled into his pants and trousers, couldn't find his socks, so padded barefoot to the window and drew the curtains. The sun streamed in. God, that was bright! He closed his eyes again. Sid hammered on the door again.

'Alex, wake up! We've got a problem. You're needed.'

'Can't find my socks, Sid, hang on.'

'Open the fucking door, Alex.'

Alex padded to the door and turned the key. Sid walked in. Sid being Sergeant Greenhough from CIS. He looked at the bed. 'What? Sleeping alone today, are we Alex?'

'Fuck off, Sid. I'm not in the mood. Last night while you were pissing it up somewhere, I was down town three times. Two accidents, one of 'em a piss artist and one battle royal in the *Krone*. Four of our lot from Gütersloh versus four pongoes.'

'So I heard. Who won?'

'I did.'

'Oh, very droll, Alex. Very droll!'

Alex found his socks and sat on the bed to put them on. The shoes followed. Then he walked to the wash basin and turned on the water.

'You've not got time for all this crap, Alex, the boss sent me. There's a guy in one of the blocks running round knife-happy. He's barricaded the entrance and won't come out. We've emptied the block. Everybody's there, Old Man, WO-man, Flight. Everybody.'

Alex turned to look at him, the tap still running. 'So, we've got the best part of what, twenty or so of our lot out there, he's barricaded himself in, the block's empty and you want ME? Why?'

'Alex, how the fuck should I know? The Old Man says "Fetch Alex", I fetch. That's it!'

'Sid, I'm having a wash. Chummy's obviously not going anywhere. If he wants to cut his wrists, it's not my problem. Let somebody else deal with it.' Alex stuck his head under the cold water tap and blew bubbles.

'It's a mate of yours.'

Alex stopped.

'Davy Knight. Corporal Davy Knight.'

Alex grabbed a towel and started drying his face and hair vigorously. He looked across at Sid who was now sitting on the bed. 'First, Davy Knight is not my mate. And second, Davy is probably the most gentle and timid person I've ever met.'

'The same. Only this time Davy has scared the shit out of half the block.'

'Anybody hurt?'

Sid shook his head.

'No. We've been lucky.'

Alex pulled his blouse on and picked up his white hat. 'OK, Sid. Let's go and kick the shit out of Davy. Should be able to manage that with twenty or so of us.'

They drove to the block and parked on the opposite side of the road. Alex started counting. 'Jeezus, Sid, what a fucking circus! We've got three Landrovers, two Kombis and three Volkses. And all with their pretty blue lights flashing. What's the theme? Intimidation?'

'Nice to see you're on form today, Alex. Go to it, Rover.' He punched Alex on the arm.

Alex climbed out of the car and made in the direction of the Old Man who seemed to be having an earnest conversation with Flight. Arms were waving – somebody wasn't happy. Alex stopped before the Boss and Flight, still buttoning up his jacket. 'Morning, Sir, seems we've got a bit of a problem.'

'Morning, Alex,' said the boss, nodding – and ignoring the fact that Alex didn't salute. 'Sorry to wake you. Heard you had a bit of a rough night last night, but thought this might be one for you, particularly, as I understand he's a friend of yours.'

Alex smiled. 'He's not my friend, Sir. We met up at square bashing. Somebody was taking the mickey and I sort of stopped it. Davy kind of hung around after that. He's a nice lad, but a bit shy. Then two weeks after I arrived here, Davy turned up. Sometimes we have a beer together. That's it.' He turned and surveyed the scene, then turned back to the CO. 'Somebody expecting a war? May I make a suggestion, Sir?'

'Please, Alex, go ahead. That's why you're here.'

'Kill the lights; everything back to the Detachment except two Kombis and six of the guys.' He pointed at Big Bill. 'I want him here. Also get a Meat Wagon. You never know.' The CO nodded.

Alex beckoned Bill over. 'I'm going in, Bill. I want you at the top of the stairs, here in the doorway. You. Just you. Nobody else. I want the others in a ring at the bottom of the stairs, facing inward. If he makes a break, we'll have to bring him down. Knife or no knife.' He turned to the CO.

'I don't suppose anybody thought to bring a truncheon, did they?'

The CO looked extremely uncomfortable. 'You know the official point of view, Alex.'

'With all due respect – to you Sir – it is not the official point of view that is going in there. It's me. And somebody could get hurt. I don't think he'll go for me. Probably the only person on camp he'll trust now is me. But, if it goes wrong, Bill will have to bring him down, and a gentle tap across the wrist in the circumstances might work wonders.'

The Old Man turned to Flight. 'Flight, nip up to the Detachment and bring two truncheons. One for Alex and one for Corporal Cannon.'

Alex shook his head, 'Uh-uh. Only one Flight. For Bill. If I show one, with Davy it could be counter-productive.' The CO nodded again.

Flight leapt into a Landrover and roared off to the Detachment. At least he didn't turn on the siren. Alex walked up the outer steps with Bill. 'Stay in the doorway, Bill—' He stopped and looked at the mess in the corridor. 'Is this the barricade they're talking about?'

Bill shrugged. 'He's dragged out two clothes lockers and laid them across the corridor.'

'OK Bill, you stay here, this side of the lockers. If he tries to run, he's got to climb over all this shit. If he's carrying the knife, whack him. If he's not, then bring him down. You're a big boy.'

Bill nodded. He looked nervous.

Alex climbed over one of the cupboards and walked slowly along the corridor.

'Davy? Davy, it's Alex. I'm coming in, OK? Just me. You OK, Davy? I'm coming in.' Not a sound.

Alex reached Davy's room, the last on the right. The door was open. Davy sat on the bed, a large wooden-handled knife in his right hand. Tears were streaming down his face. Alex leaned against the door frame and stuck his hands in his trouser pockets.

'Bad time, eh, Davy?'

Davy looked across at Alex, he tried a weak smile. 'Bad time, very bad time,' he whispered.

Alex noticed an envelope on the bed together with two pages from a letter; a third page was on the floor. *Oh, no! . . .*

'Trouble at home, Davy?'

Davy nodded. 'She's left me. Dumped me! Eight years...' He sobbed quietly.

'Mind if I come in, Davy?'

Davy shook his head. Alex walked over and sat on the bed next to Davy. He let Davy cry. They just sat there quietly for a while.

'OK if we talk, Davy?'

Davy blew his nose and wiped his eyes. He nodded, 'I'm sorry, Alex, for all this. It just sort of blew up. We've been together for eight years. We met when we were both fourteen. We were going to get married next year. Been saving for four years.' He gestured towards the letter. 'Then this arrived. She's gone off with somebody from Trinidad. TRINIDAD! Can you fucking imagine?'

Alex couldn't. Also, he'd never heard Davy swear before. He pointed at the knife. 'What's with the knife, Davy?'

Davy shrugged. 'I don't know. It just sort of happened. I wanted everyone to just leave me alone, you know, to just be alone.'

'I know, Davy. Think I could have the knife?' Alex held out his hand. Davy nodded and handed it across. Emergency over.

Alex stood up and walked into the corridor. He slid the knife along the floor toward Big Bill. 'Give that to the Boss and tell everyone to sod off. I'll handle this. Meat Wagon there?' Bill nodded. 'Tell them to stay. You stay as well.'

He went back into the room and sat on the bed again, next to Davy.

'You going to lock me up now?'

'Nope,' Alex replied.

Davy looked at him. 'But all the trouble I've caused. The knife and that. You know, the people I frightened. I don't know what happened, I just flipped!'

'It's OK, Davy. Really, it is. Nobody was hurt. I know you couldn't help it. Tell me, how do you feel about the Air Force? Do you like it? Do you want to stay in?'

'I like it. I'm good at my job. Dawn, my girlfriend – well, ex-girlfriend, I guess – thought it would be a good life together. I don't really know what to do. What do you think?'

'I think we should tread softly. I've got an ambulance outside.'

Davy's head shot up.

'It's OK, Davy. I've also got a Landrover. I just thought that maybe instead of going to the guardroom it might be a good idea to go and talk to the MO. You know, sort of feel things out. Maybe he could get you sent to Wegberg where you could talk to somebody. Believe me Davy, it's better than going the guardroom route.'

'I know why you're doing this.'

'You do?'

'It's Derrick, isn't it? He killed himself, and you think I might do the same. I won't, you know.'

Alex patted Davy on the knee. 'It's partly Derrick, I agree. He'd never been in trouble in his life. He had a problem and didn't know what to do. When he did something out of character, something outrageous, nobody really wanted to know. If somebody had paid attention, I think he'd still be alive. I want somebody to pay attention to you.'

Davy laughed. 'And they say all coppers are bastards. You're not, you're different.'

It was Alex's turn to laugh, 'Try telling that to the nine I slung in the nick last night.'

'Nine?' Davy's eyes opened wide.

'Busy night, Dave. Shall we wander across to see the MO? We'll walk. Blow the cobwebs away.'

He stepped into the corridor. 'Bill, can you take the Landrover, or whatever's out there, back to the Detachment? And tell the Meat Wagon to disappear – Davy and I are walking across for a chat with the MO.'

* _ *

On a sidenote:

Following Davy's chat with the MO he was sent to Wegberg for counselling. He remained there for eight weeks and was then posted back to the UK. Nothing negative ever appeared in Davy's personal file relating to the knife incident. Alex filled out the paperwork, but didn't submit it for processing.

Strangely, no-one ever asked for it – a technical oversight, perhaps. Davy stayed in the service, married – not Dawn – and had two daughters. He retired in 1978 with the rank of Flight Sergeant.

Chapter 20

Upside down in a ditch with Lynn

Wednesday 5th November 1958.

Alex pulled the window open and stuck his head out. The rain was still coming down in torrents and it was misty. He could smell wood smoke in the air. It reminded him that tonight was Guy Fawkes Night back in the UK. Bonfires, fireworks, that wood smoke, jacket potatoes in the embers – super! He'd loved Bonfire Night when he was younger.

'Alex! You deaf or something?'

He pulled his head back into the duty NCO's room; much too hot as usual. It didn't matter which way you turned the knob on the radiator, the heating stayed the same and everyone melted.

Paddy was waving the phone at him, 'Girlfriend wants you.'

'What girlfriend?'

Paddy shrugged and rolled his eyes.

Alex took the phone. 'Yep.'

'Alex, it's Lynn.'

'Hi Lynn. What can I do you for?' She laughed.

Alex and Lynn were what you might call an "on-off item". Sometimes they went out together; to the cinema on camp, or perhaps a drink downtown. A bit of nookie if they felt like it. Nothing too serious. Good fun was Lynn. Her younger sister, Pat, was head over heels in love with Alex. Or so she told anyone who'd listen. She was only just 16 and worked in the Malcolm Club. Alex stayed clear. Nothing to do with age. Her father was the most fearsome Flight Sergeant on camp, and if he caught Alex sniffing around, he'd have his balls for breakfast. Policeman or no policeman! No sense in courting trouble, especially since big sister was so accommodating!

'Alex, I've got a bit of a problem. There's a dance on over in Hövelhof tonight. Everybody's already gone on the bus that was laid on. I had to work late and missed it. Any chance of a lift over there?'

Alex looked at his watch, 20:15. 'Look, Taffy's over at the NAAFI at the moment in the duty vehicle. He'll be back soon. If I pick you up outside the WAAF block in half an hour, how will that suit?'

'Alex, you're an angel. Thanks.'

'I'll refrain from saying it'll cost you!'

'Any time, Alex, you know that,' she giggled and broke the connection.

'I heard that, you dirty devil,' said Paddy. 'I don't know how you do it. You're getting more than me, and I'm married!'

'That's why, Paddy, that's why!' grinned Alex. Life at Sundern was good. Particularly if you wore a White Hat.

'I'll tell you a story about Hövelhof,' said Paddy, looking across at Alex. 'It was New Year's Eve before you arrived here. Anyway, there was a big dance on over at Hövelhof and half the lads from camp went. It's not too far from Sennelager, so again, half the pongo tank crews were there, and for some reason there was also a group of squaddies from the paras. God knows what they were doing there, maybe learning how to jump out of a tank.' He sniggered at his own joke. 'Everybody was expecting trouble, so we had two patrols out with old Flight Sergeant Morris in charge. You never met him; a right prick. He got posted to Marham back in March. Serves the bugger right. Hope the food chokes him.'

'Paddy,' Alex interrupted, 'the dance; Hövelhof… Remember?'

'Sorry boyo. Get carried away when I think of that asshole; find one everywhere. So, the Flight and two of the boys, Norm and Bolo, wandered into the dance hall. Just before midnight it was. The place was jam-packed full and everybody was half pissed, or more. Away in one of the corners a group had formed a circle around some guy who was doing what appeared to be his version of the Highland Fling while balancing one of those grey steins of beer on his head. Of course the inevitable happens: the stein falls off his head and, hey presto, one litre of beer goes all over him. This guy is dripping wet, but laughing away with his mates. They're having a great night. Anyway, everybody claps and cheers and thinks it's great fun. That is of course except our very own Flight-Sergeant-fucking-Morris. He goes up to this guy, who's causing nobody any trouble, and sticks his nose in his face. "Now then, laddie, we'll have less of that", says Flight. 'This guy looks at him for a minute and then says, "Fuck off! And don't call me laddie!" Morris says to him, "I beg your pardon?", and this guy says, "Fucking deaf as well, are we, crap hat?", and promptly knocks Flight's white cap off his head. Flight bends down, picks up his hat and puts it back on again, turns to Bolo and says "Corporal, arrest this man!" Can you imagine? Bolo! Never arrested anybody in his fucking life! Flies a desk in Traffic! So, Bolo steps up, goes to put his hand on this guy's arm and the guy promptly decks him. Flight steps forward and he gets decked as well. At that moment – and here you've just *got* to believe in God – the main door opens and in walk a bunch of MPs, eight up. Flight picks himself off the floor, and guess what? He blows his whistle. Can you imagine? He blows his fucking whistle! I've never blown my whistle in my entire fucking life and I've got twelve in! Don't even know if it works!' And with that he pulls his whistle out and blows. It emits a high pitched squeak. Paddy peers at it. 'Full of fucking dust or something. Anyway. Flight's whistle was the call to arms. The MPs run forward to grab this bloke who, instead of running, goes straight into the middle of these Redcaps and starts swinging. He drops two on his own and then his mates join in. A right old farce. Anyway, it took the best part of twenty minutes to get it under control and that was only after two Kombi-loads of *Kraut* police turned up.'

He chuckles at the memory, and continues, 'So, they stick the cuffs on these guys – there's five of them and they're Paras – and as they lead them out this first guy, I'll never forget his name, McKinley, Pete McKinley, sees Flight's hat on the floor and promptly jumps on it. Both feet. He looks Flight straight in the face and says "Fucking-Crap-Hat!" The Redcaps dragged him and his mates out and threw them in the Champs. Never did hear what happened to them, but when I go to the Club now and then for a beer I lift my glass and give a toast to dear old Pete McKinley, wherever he may be. Whoever can fuck old Flight Morris up is a mate of mine!'

At that moment Taffy walked through the door, rain dripping from his cap and running down his raincoat. He tossed the vehicle keys to Alex. 'Pissing down out there, hope we don't get called out tonight.'

'Too late, boyo. You're playing taxi for Alex's girlfriend tonight!'

Taffy looked at Alex. 'Which one?'

'Lynn.'

'She's OK. No problem. When?'

'Now. We're going over to Hövelhof. There's a dance on. The bus has already gone, so we can justify a patrol on the docs.'

'OK, but I don't like the way this Volks handles. The steering feels a bit..., you know, wobbly. Is there another vehicle we can take?'

Paddy looked in the key cabinet.

'Sorry, lads, there's four still out. One Kombi, two Landrovers and a Volks. You're stuck with the thing out there, won't do more than 90 flat out. It's clapped out.'

Alex and Taffy left to pick up Lynn.

'Sit behind Taff, Lynn. That way I've got more room for my legs.' Taffy got out into the rain, dropped his seat forward and let Lynn into the back. Alex reversed the car and then headed out of camp, turning left towards Verl.

Alex turned to Taff. 'These wipers hardly take the rain. Look how slow they are. And the steering is ever so sloppy. Look at this.' He turned the steering from left to right and the car kept going straight on. 'I've got my foot to the floor and we're not even doing 80. This Volks is ready for the knacker's yard!'

They passed through Karmitz and into the long right-hander a couple of kilometres before Hövelhof. Alex turned the steering wheel to the right. The car went straight on.

'Steering's gone!' he shouted, and touched the brake. Mistake. BIG mistake! The back end swung first to the right and then to the left. Alex turned into the skid. Nothing happened, the car continued to turn across the width of the road. Alex glanced at the speedometer. 70. They hit a sapling on the far side of the road and uprooted it. It immediately broke their speed before they headed through the barbed wire fence and straight into the concrete manmade water channel, three metres wide and one and a half metres deep. Somehow they were upside down.

'Everybody OK?' shouted Alex, uncomfortably squashed against the inside of the car roof. A whimpering sound came from the back of the car.

'Lynn?'

'I've hurt my back.'

'OK. Keep still. Taff?' Taffy grunted.

Alex tried his door. It opened, and somehow he managed to crawl out and then promptly fell into some twenty centimetres of water at the bottom of the ditch. He made his way round to Taffy's side of the car and tried that door; it also opened. He dragged Taffy out into the water.

'Lynn, can you move?'

'Yes, I think so.'

'If I hold this seat forward, can you try and crawl out?' Lynn gingerly crawled out and rolled sideways into the water. Alex and Taffy pulled themselves out of the ditch and up on to the grass. Then they hauled Lynn out. She screamed. There was obviously something seriously wrong with her back. She couldn't stand, and collapsed. Alex took his rubberised raincoat off and laid it on the grass. They dragged Lynn onto it. Taffy covered her with his own raincoat. They became aware that a car had stopped and the driver was running towards them. He'd seen the whole thing, he said, and would drive on into Hövelhof to fetch the police. 'We *are* the police,' Alex told him. He looked around. Maybe two hundred metres away stood two houses. Their lights were on. A phone line ran from a wooden pole to both houses. 'No need to call the German police,' Alex told the man. 'We'll deal with it.'

'Taffy, go to that house and call George in the guardroom. Tell him what's happened. Tell him to get hold of Mac from the MT section and Stevie, the medic. Find them. They're probably both in the NCOs' club. Half pissed as usual. Get them to the guardroom. Give George the telephone number of that house and tell him to call it when Mac's in the guardroom. I want to speak to him.' Taffy left.

Alex looked down at Lynn. 'How's your back?'

'When I'm lying down, it's OK. Standing's the problem. My legs won't take the strain.' Alex looked at her feet. She'd lost her shoes. He bent down and wiggled her toes – first right foot, then left. 'Feel that?'

'Yes,' she giggled. 'I feel stupid, lying here like this in the pouring rain.'

'No comment.'

She stuck two fingers up at him.

Taffy returned. 'OK. The guardroom's going to find Mac. They'll ring back. The old lady at the house is making coffee. She'll call when it's ready. She wants to know if anybody wants to eat.' They looked at each other and then shook their heads. 'Not really, Taff,' said Alex. 'Why don't you go and sit in the house, out of this sodding rain. There's no point in all three of us being soaked.'

'Alex, in case you haven't noticed, I'm already soaked. Lynn's got my mac.' Then they turned. The old lady at the house was waving and making strange sounds. Alex walked towards the house, the old lady pointed at the telephone, receiver off the hook. Alex picked it up.

'Who's there?'

'Alex? George, I've got Mac and Stevie here. They were both where you thought they'd be.'

'Give me Mac.' The strong Scottish accent – slightly slurred, Alex thought – came down the line. 'What the fuck have you been and gone and done this time, Alex?'

'Mac, I want a straight answer. Are you pissed, sober or somewhere in the middle?'

'Well, err, we've had two or three in the club, but it's early days yet, the pissed bit comes later.'

'Mac, can you drive?'

'Course I can fucking drive!'

'Mac, shut up and listen. Are you in a fit state to drive or not?'

The voice seemed to sober up immediately. 'I'm OK, Alex. Seriously. What's the problem?'

'I've put the Volks in this manmade ditch just before Hövelhof. Lynn's hurt her back and can't walk. I need Stevie and somebody else to bring the ambulance out; no blue light, no siren. Nobody's dying. Nice and easy. OK? I also want you to bring a crane out here to lift the thing out of the ditch. And we'll also need a flatbed to take it back to camp. Before you lift it, I want you to look at the steering; it's upside down, so it should be easy. I want to know what's wrong with it BEFORE we go back to camp. OK? Any problem with that?'

'None, Alex. But when you fuck up, you really fuck up, don't you? You got docs to cover that run, Alex?'

'Not a problem, Mac. And by the way, bring your wellies. You're going to be working in water half way up your legs.'

'I'll be at least an hour, Alex. You want the ambulance first?'

'Yes. Send Stevie to pick up Lynn and Taff. I'll ride back with you. Remember, nice and quiet. No lights and no siren, OK?'

'Aye, Alex, one hour.'

Thirty five minutes later Stevie arrived with the ambulance. They manoeuvred Lynn onto a stretcher. She hurt; that much was obvious. Thirty minutes after the ambulance had left Mac arrived with the crane and flatbed. He was driving in wellies. He jumped down from the cab and made straight towards the upturned Volks. Alex tried not to laugh as Mac eased himself down into the ditch in front of the Volks. Without question Mac had to be one of the fattest men in uniform. Well, Alex thought, eight to ten pints of sludge a night in the club. Seven nights a week. For how long? Must be twenty years, maybe more, since Mac was well into his forties.

With a great deal of puffing and panting Mac struggled back up out of the ditch. 'Bolt's missing. Not sheared. Missing. You're very lucky not to be dead, Alex.'

'Thanks, Mac. That's me off the hook. That Volks should have been in for servicing about two weeks ago. Flight stopped it, said we needed the vehicle on the road. To my knowledge two people have complained about wobbly steering, and then Taff mentioned it to me again tonight.'

'So that's Flight in the shit then.'

Alex looked at Mac. 'Mac, what am I?'

Mac pondered. '… A prick?'

'Mac!'

'Aye, aye! I read it! You're a cop. Flight's a cop. Nobody's in the shit. Right?' Alex nodded. 'My report goes in tonight. I needed to know exactly what the problem was BEFORE officialdom got involved. My report will be mentioning this and quoting you, OK?' Mac agreed. 'Will say the bolt was missing. It will also say the Volks was overdue on a service.'

'Are you out to sink the Flight?'

'No. That report is going on the WO-man's desk, not the boss's.'

'I don't get it.'

'Mac, the WO-man is not going to sink Flight, but both will know the cause of the accident was a missing bolt. Both will know that I know this and both will know who stopped the Volks's service, and again, both will know that I know.'

'I don't get it.'

'Somebody, Mac, with more on their arm than me, is going to owe me.'

'You crafty bugger!'

'It's called survival, Mac. And while we're on the subject, why do you think nobody slings you in the nick when you're pissed as a newt and causing a ruckus in the club? Why do you think our boys pick you up, give you a lift back to your room and drop you on the bed?'

Mac looked at Alex and shrugged – then the penny seemed to drop. 'You?!'

'Correct, Mac. And why do you think I called you tonight and nobody else? Mac shrugged again.

'Because you owe me, Mac, and tonight helps even up the score.' Mac grinned.

'I get it! You scratch my back and I'll scratch yours.'

'Something like that. Tell me, Mac, how long have you been in?'

'Twenty eight years. Joined up in '30. Loved practically every minute of it.'

'I hate to point this out to you, Mac, but after twenty eight years you should be at least a Flight Sergeant, or maybe WO-man.'

Mac looked up at Alex. 'I was a Sergeant once, long time ago now, but I got busted.'

'Booze?'

Mac looked down and shuffled his feet in the sodden grass. He nodded. 'Got pissed and wrecked the Sergeant's Mess. Back in Blighty it was, just after the end of the war.'

'Ever been married, Mac?'

'No, thanks! I've got a good job, nobody bothers me 'cause I know what I'm doing. I get food, I've got my own room to bunk in and good mates to have a jar or two with in the evening.'

'And somebody to make sure you don't get busted down to LAC.' Mac grinned.

'Aye, and that too. Me, I'm staying in till they sling me out.'

_

On a sidenote:

Mac

Mac stayed in the Royal Air Force till the end of his days. In March 1963 he reported sick with pains in his side. Following in-depth examinations he was admitted to hospital where he died five weeks later, aged 51. His liver had finally given up the unequal struggle. He was still a corporal.

Lynn

Following her accident in the Volkswagen with Alex and Taff, Lynn was kept in hospital for the next seven weeks. She'd ruptured a disk in her spine and apart from manipulation she spent most of her time lying flat on a board.

Following her release she started going out with L/Cpl Summerbee, who Alex considered to be the biggest pain in the arse on camp. Lynn, however, said it was love. When Summerbee's term of engagement was up he left the army and Lynn went with him. They lived for some time in Harrogate. Over the next six years, and not withstanding two terms of imprisonment, Summerbee managed to father two children. Daughters.

When Summerbee was nicked yet again and sent down for a third term Lynn divorced him. In 1974 Summerbee was transferred to Parkhurst on the Isle of Wight where he ran into somebody tougher than himself. They broke his back.

Summerbee, now aged 74, is back living in Harrogate. He is alone, dependent on Social Services, and confined to a wheelchair.

Chapter 21

Christmas Dance

Alex parked the Landrover opposite the guardroom, in front of the fire station exit, grabbed the bag from the passenger seat and ran across the road. The heavens had opened ten minutes ago, and now it was coming down in buckets. Not a night to be out. Gütersloh had been quiet, exactly the opposite of a typical Saturday evening. Still, it would be Christmas in two weeks, and everyone that would normally be in town was on camp. Plus the visitors. The annual Christmas dance! The camp was bursting at the seams. Cars were parked on pavements along every single road. The car parks were full. They'd parked the rest along both sides of the slip road leading to the camp. Even the Officers' Mess drive was full, and for once nobody complained. Everybody was getting kaylied in the ORs' dining room, commandeered for the occasion every year, since it was the only place on camp which could accommodate the goodness-knows-how-many heaving, sweating and drunken souls that seemed to find it fun. The band and noise could be heard in the guardroom, a good three hundred metres away. So far, so good. No calls for help to go and sort somebody out who'd crossed the line. Mind you, on such occasions, the line was rather elastic, plus every off-duty policeman – provost or guardroom – from Sundern and Gütersloh was there, complete with wife, girlfriend or current bed-warmer.

*

Alex had parked himself in the guardroom, together with Little Nick and the German barrier operator. The Detachment was locked, the duty NCO probably pissed by now, and all calls had been re-routed to thc guardroom. Alex, feeling in a generous mood, had called *Steiners* in town and asked him to prepare three lots of *Koteletts mit Kartoffelsalat*, with the gherkin but minus the fried egg – nobody really fancied congealed, cold fried egg; hence the trip into town. Nick had the tea all ready. They sat around the guardroom table, Alex looked at his watch. 23:15. Perfect! That's when the phone rang. Nick answered, 'Guardroom.' He listened, then passed the phone across the table to Alex, 'For you. Sid.'

'Yes, Sid.' Sergeant Sid Greenhough was tonight's duty CIS wallah.

'You're wanted.'

'Well, and a good evening to you too, Sidney.'

'Sorry, Alex. Boss wants you. Bit of a kerfuffle here. Army officer, pissed, making a nuisance of himself with some of the ladies.'

'Sid, did I hear you say army officer? You are of course setting me up, and YOU are of course half pissed. Not biting, Sidney.' He dropped the phone back on the receiver. It promptly rang again. Nick pointed, 'Bet that's a pissed-off Sid for you.'

Alex picked up the phone, 'Guardroom.'

'Alex, this is not a joke!' Sid again. 'The boss wants you here. Now! OK?'

'Sid, quick question. How many police are at this dance?'

'Dunno.'

'Flight?'

'Yes.'

'WO-man?'

'Yes.'

'And the Boss?'

'Yes.'

'And you. Plus maybe another, what, thirty or so? You are setting me up, aren't you?'

'Alex, God's honest truth! Your presence is requested. I'm just the messenger. Again! Not my idea, honest. The Boss asks, "Where's Alex?" and I'd like to answer "How the fuck should I know, I'm not his keeper," should I be so popular, but… well, you know.'

Alex sighed. 'On the way, Sid. On the way.'

The noise inside the Mess was deafening. Sid was waiting for Alex just inside the door, half empty pint glass in one hand, cigarette in the other and a very definite glazed look in the eyes. Half pissed as usual. He led Alex to the edge of the dance floor and nodded in the general direction of the other side, 'Him!'

"Him" appeared to be having an upset with three girls; or rather three girls appeared to be shouting at him - all at the same time.

'How do you know he's an army officer?'

'Boss told me.'

Alex sighed, let out a silent "shit" and slowly made his way around the edge of the dance floor until he reached the object of the commotion. 'Hello, Geoffrey.'

Geoffrey turned to face Alex, holding on, rather grimly, to a chair with his left hand. He blinked once, twice, screwed up his eyes and then said: 'Sorry, old man, but my name's not Geoffrey.'

'Really?' replied Alex, 'you look very much like Geoffrey to me. If you're not Geoffrey, who are you?'

Geoffrey took his time, looking Alex up and down, the penny slowly dropping. 'I'm Lieutenant Campbell, Corporal.'

'Not Geoffrey Campbell?'

Campbell took a deep breath and tried to get his eyes to focus on Alex. 'No. Alistair Campbell.'

'Lieutenant Alistair Campbell. You have an address to go with the name?'

'Haig Barracks.'

'Ah, Bielefeld.'

'You know it?' Campbell replied, apparently surprised.

'Know it well. Military Police Detachment at Haig. You have ID?'

'Why?' asked Campbell, swaying gently from side to side.

'Because, Lieutenant Campbell, you're Army and this is an RAF camp. And for all I know you might be Lenin in disguise.'

Campbell thought about this for a moment and then suddenly burst out laughing, nearly falling over in the process. 'But Lenin's dead,' he said, 'everybody knows that.'

Alex reached over, and grabbing a chair from the next table, manoeuvred Campbell onto it. 'If I were you, I'd sit down before you fall down. Now, ID!'

Campbell reached into his inside jacket pocket, removed his wallet and extracted his ID, which he handed to Alex. Alex glanced at it. 'Who's your CO?'

'Lieutenant Colonel James McDonald… Why?' he asked as an afterthought.

Alex ignored the question. Instead he said, 'Time for you and me to go a little walk. Outside. Breath of fresh air. Come on.'

Campbell looked up at him. 'You can't arrest me, I'm an officer.'

'Correction,' replied Alex, 'You're a drunken officer and I'm a policeman, plus I'm not arresting you, but you are leaving this Mess now, with me. And, as Cagney used to say, you can do it the easy way or the hard way.'

Campbell looked up at him. 'You wouldn't dare!'

Alex suddenly realised the music had stopped and they were the centre of attention for seven or eight hundred pairs of eyes. Alex bent down and whispered into Campbell's ear, 'Don't make a prick of yourself, Geoffrey, everyone's watching. Remember, easy way or hard way. I suggest a little dignity, OK?'

He stood up and took Campbell by the arm. 'Let's go.'

Campbell rose unsteadily to his feet and allowed Alex to escort him slowly across the dance floor. Halfway across the trombone player blew a raspberry on his instrument and the crowd laughed. Campbell stopped and tried to do a little bow, nearly dragging Alex over in the process. Alex stood him up straight and then said, 'That wasn't for you, Geoffrey, that was for me. After the event the copper's always the bad guy.'

The fresh air was too much for Campbell. Once in the car park he immediately vomited onto the bonnet of someone's highly polished burgundy coloured Borgward Isabella. Alex stood and watched. 'Feeling better, Geoffrey?' And again …

A nice surprise for somebody, when the dance finally turned out!

Nick made a mug of black instant. Alex led Campbell and mug to one of the cells. He pointed, 'In there. Shoes off. Coat off. Belt off. Tie off. Lie down and have a kip. You vomit, you clear it up. OK?'

Campbell was now as white as a sheet and shaking. He held the mug with both hands and took a sip. Then he looked across at Alex. Very softly he said, 'You can't arrest me, I'm an officer.'

Alex pointed to the bed, 'All off; now. This is the easy bit. OK? Don't cock it up.' Alex took his tie, belt, shoes, coat, and emptied his pockets. He sat him on the bed, propped him against the wall and covered him with a blanket. Then he left the cell, closed the door and turned the key in the lock. He heard a faint *please,* and what sounded like a sob.

'Who's on PBX?' he asked Nick.

'Fay.'

Alex picked up the phone and dialled zero. Ten minutes later he was talking to the Duty Officer at Haig and explained that, No, he couldn't help, only Lieutenant Colonel McDonald could. Did Alex realise what the time was? Indeed he did; it had just turned midnight. "Lieutenant Colonel McDonald only. It concerned Lieutenant Alistair Campbell and no, he couldn't explain further, Lieutenant Colonel McDonald only".

It was forty five minutes later when Lieutenant Colonel McDonald finally called. Alex explained the situation in great detail. Silence on the other side of the line; the Colonel was obviously digesting the news. Finally, a chuckle came down the line. 'You're making him sweat, aren't you? You've got the little bugger in a cell, and you're making him sweat.'

'Well, Colonel, this way it's still unofficial. I call in the Duty Officer, it becomes official. I'm happy to follow your advice.'

'Hmm. How long can you keep him there, shall we say, without problems?'

'07:30 latest. 08:00 there'll be a change of Duty Officer.'

Another chuckle. 'Someone will be along about 05:00, Corporal. Goodnight.'

The phone went dead.

Chapter 22

Dinner at the Top Three Club and introducing Debs

They discovered the US Air Base at Kassel quite by accident. They drove past a gap in the trees, and there it was, the main entrance. The fact that they shouldn't have been anywhere near it was considered to be totally irrelevant. It had somehow started out as one of those non-designated area patrols and developed into a trip down to the US sector. Alex was duty driver and waiting for Taffy to bring the Volks back from the NAAFI shop where he'd gone to pick up various odds and ends forgotten on a shopping trip with the wife earlier in the day. Flight nipped into the office to sign the MT docs authorising the patrol and was told that Taff had both car and docs down at the NAAFI; he decided not to wait. 'Do it in the morning,' he said on his way out – hence a patrol in a non-designated area.

Taffy finally arrived back at the detachment with both shopping and Pete, who was off-duty, in civvies and bored out of his mind with nothing to do.

'Where are you going tonight?' he asked Alex who looked across at Taffy and shrugged. 'Fancy anywhere in particular?'

He got a shrug in return. 'No idea.' Alex walked to the map of their area pinned to the wall. 'You can choose from Münster, Bielefeld and Paderborn.' He looked across at Taffy; another shrug. 'Right, let's do Bielefeld.'

'I don't fancy Bielefeld. Anyway, that's Redcap territory.'

'Jeezus! You're being difficult tonight.' He turned back to the map and traced the road with his finger.

'Anybody fancy a trip to the Yankee Zone?'

'Where?' This from Pete.

'You're off-duty.'

'I'll change into uniform, I've never been down there. Whereabouts?'

Alex continued to trace the road. 'How about Kassel?'

'How far is it?' Pete again.

Alex added up the figures. 'Roughly 110 kilometres.'

'We can't go down there, it's too far. Anyway, how do we explain being in the Yankee Zone if we have a problem? We'll get shot.'

'Taffy, you've got no sense of adventure . . . Pete?'

'I'm game.'

'OK, Kassel it is.'

Pete went and changed into uniform and white hat, and approximately two hours later they drove past the main entrance of the USAF base. Alex pulled to the side of the road and stopped. He looked at his watch. 'It's going on for nine. Anybody hungry?'

Taffy wound his window down as he looked up and down the road. 'Can't see much here; we'll have to drive into town.'

Alex pointed to his left. 'Here.'

'We can't eat there – it's an American Air Base!'

'Taffy, I'll drive up to the barrier, tell them we're hungry, and I bet they'll feed us.' He turned the car and drove down the wide driveway, stopping at the red and white barrier. An American Air Policeman, resplendent in white hat and polished black leather belt, cross strap and pistol holster, came out of the guard hut and stared at the black and red sign above the number plate: *RAF Police*. He peered through the windscreen and saw three white hats. He smiled, then he swung a salute. Alex rolled the window down and nodded. 'RAF Police. We've been on a job down here, saw your camp and wondered if you could possibly feed us before we head back up north.'

'You got ID?'

'Sure.' Alex handed over his Warrant Card. The American slowly read every word.

'Stay put, guys. I'll make a call.' He went back into the guard hut.

'Told you.'

'We're not in yet, Alex.'

'We're in.'

The Air Policeman reappeared, followed by a second who actually ran across the main drive and climbed into a jeep. The first one pressed a button and the barrier rose – modern technology; no little German in an old green Wehrmacht blanket here! He handed Alex his Warrant Card and pointed to the Jeep.

'Follow that vehicle, please, Sir. He'll take you to the Top Three Club. You are expected.' A smile, another salute and he vanished into the guard hut. Incredible!

They followed the Jeep through the camp and finally stopped in front of a sign which read *"Top Three Club, Senior NCOs only"*.

'I get it,' said Taff, 'it's the equivalent of our Sergeants' Mess. But what are we doing here, what's wrong with the cookhouse?'

Alex looked at his watch. 'It's going on for nine, Taff. Maybe it's closed. Anyway, we're wanted.' He pointed at the figure in a Steward's white mess jacket who had arrived and who was now holding the glass entrance door open. They climbed the steps towards the Steward.

'Good evening, Gentlemen, welcome to the Top Three Club. You are the guests of Master Sergeant McAndrew.' They looked at each other with blank expressions. Pete and Taff shrugged. 'Pray tell,' said Alex to the Steward, 'exactly who is Master Sergeant McAndrew?'

'Oh, you don't know him?' questioned the Steward, 'Well, Master Sergeant McAndrew is tonight's Duty NCO in charge of the Air Police.

Aha, thought Alex, the phone call. 'Is he here?'

'No, Sir, he's on duty.' *I wish he'd stop calling me Sir,* thought Alex, *typical Yank. They call everybody Sir.*

They followed the steward through the main entrance hall and turned right. To the left, Alex noticed, was a very large carpeted room with brown leather chairs and low tables plus a sprinkling of what looked like Chesterfield sofas. Some Sergeants' Mess!

To the right was the bar, equally sumptuous. Polished wooden top, padded brown leather front. A single continuous bench ran along the walls, also upholstered in brown leather and in front of which stood a series of glass-topped tables each with three chairs, with arms. The Steward led them to a table in the far corner that had been set for three; knife, fork, spoon, linen napkin, water glasses that positively sparkled and looked like crystal, while in the centre stood a sweating bottle of *Staatlich Fachingen*, Adolf Hitler's favourite mineral water. Nice touch! As they sat a second Steward appeared, handed them each a menu, turned and left. They looked at each other, not sure that it would be right even to speak. 'I know one thing for sure,' Pete finally said, 'we're definitely in the wrong bloody Air Force.'

They studied the menu, unable to believe the seemingly endless list of goodies. The Steward reappeared. They ordered roast duck, roast chicken, thick filet steak – medium rare – red wine, beer, beer and 'No, thank you, no soup to start.'

'I'm stuffed,' said Pete, finally pushing his empty plate away – and, 'No thank you. No dessert!'

There was a noisy party going on across the room, six men, four women. One of the men kept looking across at them and when the Steward had finally cleared the table, he came over. A little unsteadily, thought Alex. He held out his hand, 'Hi, I'm Derek.' They shook hands and introduced themselves.

'You guys really Brits?'

Wow!

They nodded in unison.

'Police?' he pointed at the three white hats lying side by side on the bench. They nodded again.

'We're all aircrew.' He made a rather sweeping gesture toward the table he'd just left.

'The ladies as well?' asked Alex, tongue in cheek.

'What?' The eyes had definitely lost their focus. He was now holding on to the back of Taffy's chair, quite firmly, by the look of it. 'What?' again. 'No, they're our wives.'

'Lucky wives.'

'Huh?'

'Four wives, six husbands.'

The penny – or dime – finally dropped.

'Hey, fella! Alex, is it? You're funny. I like you,' he quipped while Alex was thinking to himself, *Why is it that I always have this uncontrollable urge to take the piss out of Yanks?* 'Come on over and meet the gang.'

They walked – he wavered – across the room to meet "the gang". Introductions were made, spaces appeared and Alex found himself pulled by the hand to sit next to a very attractive dark haired, thirty-something who looked incredibly like

Audrey Hepburn. He raised her hand to his lips and gently brushed the fingers.

'Oh, my! A gentleman!'

'On occasions. But I'm sorry, I really didn't catch your name.'

'Debbie.'

'But you're German. What's Debbie short for?'

She shook her head. 'It isn't. My husband calls me Debbie, he doesn't like my real name, so he told me "From now on you're Debbie, OK?" So, I'm Debbie … asshole.'

'I heard that,' Derek grinned. She shrugged.

'What's your real name?'

'Dora.'

She looked at him. 'Not good, huh?'

'Nothing wrong with it at all. What would you like me to call you?'

She hesitated and looked across at her husband.

'Better call me Debbie or he'll be pissed off. That's one word I've really learned to understand in the English language.' She nodded across at Derek. 'He's either pissed, like practically every night, or pissed off. That's usually every time he's not pissed. Good word that, says it all.' She turned back to face Alex. 'Hope I don't upset you but, well, it's just the way it is. At least for now.'

'Tell me more.' She glanced across at Derek who lifted his glass to her and pursed his lips in a kiss. She lifted her glass in return, but didn't smile. 'That's all he's fit for; show. He's either flying or drunk, or both, for all I know. He doesn't stick to the abstinence rule. Sometimes I wonder how some of the planes actually get off the ground, the amount of booze these people put away. Anyway,' she squeezed Alex's hand, 'you don't want to hear about my problems.'

She glanced up at the clock on the wall – it advertised Bell's whisky. 'In fifteen minutes it will be *last drinks, please*, and then he'll ask you all to come back to the house to party there. Fifteen to thirty minutes after that he'll pass out and Joe over there – he's a real Red Indian, you know. Sioux or Cherokee or something, I can never remember, but he's real – will help me drop him in bed. The Sovs could drop an atom bomb, he'd never wake up.'

She started to giggle. 'I've just realised what I said. Nobody would wake up if they dropped the bomb. Must have had too much cherryade.' She nodded towards her glass, 'Campari-soda; love it!' She picked up the glass and drained it in one. 'Time for just one more before we leave, otherwise I'll finish up as bad as this lot. Want one?' She nodded across to Alex's glass. 'What's that?'

'Tonic.'

'Just tonic?'

'Yes.'

'I thought it was vodka.'

'No. I still have to drive tonight, two hours or so. It helps if you can see where you're going.'

'But you will come back to the house? Please?'

'OK, but only for half an hour or so, until Derek passes over.'

She giggled, 'if only! Stay till he's in bed, then we can talk. I'll make you boys coffee and sandwiches if you like.'

'We'd like.'

The prophecy came true. By 23:15 they were all back at the house and at 23:32 Derek started to snore. On cue, Joe – it transpired he was Sioux – and Debbie manhandled him upstairs to bed. That seemed to be the hint for everyone to take their leave. Everyone, except Joe. 'I think I'll stay for a while and have another drink.' He was eyeing Alex.

'Joe, out!' Debbie pointed to the door. Then she pointed at Alex, followed by Pete and Taff. 'He's a policeman, he's a policeman and he's a policeman. What do you think they're going to do? Gang-bang me? Wishful thinking.' She saw Joe's face.

'Joke, Joe. Joke! Now, go on home and leave me to the protection of the Royal Air Force Police. I'll tell Derek how concerned you were for me tomorrow; he'll love you for it. But for now, out!' Joe left, but it was clear he wasn't happy. Taffy started to yawn; then he spread his hands apologetically. 'Sorry fellas, I'm whacked. Think I'll go and kip in the car. Got the keys Alex?' Alex tossed them over and Taffy left.

Pete was in the arm chair, legs out, supporting his head on his left hand. Eyelids were drooping. Alex sat on the couch, Debbie sat next to him. Then she immediately stood up. 'Since I'm home, I'm going to have one more Campari. Have one with me?'

'Thanks.'

'I think your friend's out.' Pete was gently snoring.

Debbie sat back on the couch next to Alex again and told him how she'd met Derek, how they'd courted and why she'd married him even though she didn't love him. 'America,' she said, 'that's what I want. Derek has three more months to do here and then it's State-side. One year there, get my papers and then bye-bye Derek!' She saw Alex staring at her. 'Next month I'll be 32. When the war ended I was 18. You can't begin to imagine what it was like then. I'm just glad it was the *Amis* and not the Russians; they are animals! You saw the other three girls tonight; we're all after the same thing: America. America, and then my freedom. I'll be 34 and I'm going to make something of myself over there. Here it's impossible – too late. What do you think of me now then?' She glanced almost defiantly at him.

Alex smiled, 'I think exactly the same as I did when I first met you, all of three hours ago. You're beautiful. You look just like Audrey Hepburn in *Roman Holiday*, and I don't judge.'

Her eyes filled with tears. 'How old are you, Alex?'

'Next month I'll be 21.'

'What date?'

'Twelfth'.

Her eyes opened wide and she clenched her fists. 'I don't believe it! That's my birthday! Alex … Alex, Alex! We must spend it together! Please?'

Alex pointed upwards, 'And Derek?'

'Derek won't be here. We had a fight about it. The flight's in Finland, or somewhere. I'll be on my own. At night I'll have a party with the girls, but …' she hesitated, 'could you be here for breakfast, say by nine? We could be together until about two. Please?'

'I don't know, it's too early to say, but if I can I will.'

She leaned across and hugged him. 'Thanks, Alex. Another drink?'

'No thanks.'

She went and fetched another Campari from the fridge and then returned to the couch, put the drink on the low table, kicked off her shoes, sat on the couch and swivelled to face Alex, lifting and crossing her legs in an attempt to achieve the lotus position. She failed – her skirt was too tight. She stood up, lifted her skirt slightly and tried again. Success. Alex looked at her. She was smiling.

'Nothing like getting comfortable,' he remarked drily. 'There is one problem, though.'

'Oh, what's that?'

'Well, if I don't consciously force myself to look at your face, I can't help but look directly at,' … he glanced down, 'your rather skimpy, frilly, black panties.'

'That bother you?'

'No.' She had that dreamy look in her eyes. *Too much Campari?* Alex didn't think so.

'But?'

'No buts.'

She climbed off the couch and pointed a finger at him. 'Stay here,' she ordered as she headed for the bathroom. Alex had no intention of going anywhere. He glanced across at Pete who continued to snore gently. He was catching flies, out for the count. He heard the toilet flush, then water running from a tap. It seemed to run for a long time. Finally the door opened and she returned to the couch where she stopped, hitched up her skirt again, sat down, swiveled towards Alex, then lifted and crossed her legs. She didn't speak, she just looked at him.

Alex's hands were sweating and his mouth had suddenly turned dry. He cleared his throat. Then he glanced down. 'Jeesus!' he exclaimed.

'Jesus doesn't come into it,' she answered.

He continued to stare. Unadorned. She was as naked and pink as the day she was born. He had butterflies in his stomach and he felt himself beginning to rise to the occasion. He finally dragged his gaze away and looked across at her. She was still smiling; a beautiful, gentle, lazy smile. She leaned forward and lifted a hand toward him. He took it. She squeezed. 'Alex, can we make love?'

Alex nodded towards Pete.

'Is that a yes?'

He smiled. 'That's a yes.'

'Come with me.'

She took him by the hand and led him to the kitchen. She closed the door and turned the key in the lock. Then she looked up at him. Her hand swept the room; washing machine, cooker, kitchen table, four chairs, sink.

Her arms went round his neck. 'Improvise,' she said.

And then she kissed him.

Alex visited twice in the next three weeks. Improvisation seemed to be the new game in town. Then for his birthday he swapped shifts with Brian who'd do days while Alex took his nightshift. Alex decided to visit The Wire after he'd been to Kassel. He didn't know why, he just felt like it. He told Pete. Pete wanted to come, he'd never been to the East German border.

'It's just barbed wire and watch towers, Pete, that's all.'

'I'd like to see it. I come from Eastbourne, but I never go to the sea. I'm in Germany, but I've never been to the border.'

Alex called Debbie. 'Bring him. He can make breakfast.'

They arrived in Kassel just before eight in the morning. Pete made breakfast while Debbie and Alex "improvised". It was noon when they finally sat down to eat.

Mid-afternoon saw them on Route 7 heading out of Kassel, then turning off the main road at Oetmannshausen, on to a minor road to Eschwege where they took an even narrower road to Wanfried. They stopped. Alex pointed, 'The border.'

They climbed out of the car and walked slowly alongside the wire for a couple of hundred metres; not a soul to be seen anywhere. Alex gave his camera to Pete, 'I'll go to the wire, take a picture.' He did. Then he said very slowly to Alex, who had his back to the wire with right arm above his head and right hand holding on to a strand of barbed wire, 'Whatever you do, don't make any sudden moves. There's a guy in a watchtower about two hundred metres to your left pointing a rifle at you.'

Alex didn't move. 'Take another photo,' he said, 'so the guard can see what we're doing. Use flash.' Pete did. Alex then walked away from the wire and took the camera from Pete. He slowly turned and looked at the guard, and he waved. The guard lowered his rifle but didn't wave back.

As they headed back to the car it began to rain – steadily.

*

Alex opened the Detachment window and leaned out. Everywhere smelled fresh. The rain had stopped, the clouds had gone and the sky was bright with millions of twinkling stars. He reflected on the day. A great day - a great 21st birthday. He gazed up at the stars and idly wondered what he'd be doing in another twenty one years, and then another twenty one years after that. 63!

He couldn't imagine it.

It was simply too much . . .

Carpe Diem!

Chapter 23

Adolf Hitler's 70th Birthday

Monday 20th April 1959, would have been the 70th birthday of Adolf Hitler, the Austrian-born house painter and WWI army Corporal-turned-Führer of the short lived Thousand Year Third Reich, had he not shot himself at age 57 on the last day of April 1945 in his bunker beneath the Chancellery in Berlin.

Throughout the British Zone in Germany it was difficult to find anyone who had actually fought against us. Everyone, but everyone, had fought the Russians on the Eastern front. Strange really, how it took so long to get from the beaches of France to Berlin, when the entire German army was away fighting in the East. Just as strange was the fact that it was simply impossible to find a former member of the National Socialist Party – a NAZI. Nobody, it seemed, had been a NAZI.

Well, perhaps not quite nobody.

* *

The evening before, all members of the Provost Detachment had been called together by the CO. The German Police had passed on a message saying they'd heard that tomorrow a large contingent of former *Waffen SS* intended to hold a party in the village of Kransdorf to celebrate the late Führer's birthday. The same thing had happened the previous year, they said, but it had been much smaller, maybe fifty people or so, and in reality it had just been a group of former comrades in arms getting together for a party. There had been no problems and no arrests. There was nothing more to it than that, but they thought the Detachment should know.

'Why?' asked Charlie.

'I asked the same question,' replied the CO. 'They said, *information only*.'

'Has anyone else been advised?' asked Charlie.

'No, only us.'

'What are we supposed to do?' persisted Charlie.

The CO shrugged. 'I suppose, like all little Boy Scouts, we'd better be prepared.'

'Prepared for what, Sir?' Jock this time.

'Well, trouble, I suppose.'

'Do you want us to put out extra patrols in the area?' Jock again.

'No, I don't think so. I think a visible presence could be counter-productive. Best be prepared. OK then, Warrant Officer, everyone dismissed.'

And that was that; meeting over.

'And just what the fuck was that all about?' Charlie asked Alex as they walked back to the Duty NCO's office.

'Not got the vaguest, old son, but best be prepared.' He nudged Charlie in the ribs and laughed. Come on, let's go and eat.'

Alex lay on his bed reading when the field telephone standing on his bedside locker rang. Alex looked at his watch. Exactly 14:00.

'Yep.'

'Alex, it's Gerry, main guardroom.'

'No, I haven't got a spare pot of Brylcreem.'

'Bollocks.'

Alex laughed. 'Right, having got that out of the way, what can I do for you?'

'Not sure, really. But I've just received a garbled message from the *Kraut* police via our *Dolmetscher* that there's been a bit of a ruckus over in Kransdorf between a couple of guys from Gütersloh and that Waffen SS mob.'

'Anybody hurt?'

'No idea.'

'What am I supposed to do?'

'Dunno, but I thought you ought to know.'

'Wonderful. Gerry, get your *Dolmetscher* back onto the Kraut police and find out exactly what's happening or what has happened, OK? Do they need us? Call me back.' He dropped the handset back in its cradle.

Ten minutes later the phone burped again.

'Yep.'

'Alex, we've got a problem. A real problem! Apparently these two guys went over to Kransdorf for a few beers, one of 'em's apparently screwing something over there and, of course, that Jerry mob's having a party. *Adolf Hitler awake*, and all that shit. Anyway, nobody takes any notice of our guys, it's all "have another beer, Fritz" and "Fancy a *Bratwurst*, George?" until one of our guys notices that some Krauts have put up the old Jerry flag, you know, the Swastika, on top of the *Rat-house*. It seems these two Gütersloh guys are well pissed and they decide to get on the roof and pull the bloody thing down. What happens? They're seen and half a dozen of these Jerries hightail it up there and beat the shit out of our guys. They drag 'em down into the little square there and give 'em a good kicking. One managed to get away and ran like fuck across the fields. His mate's on the deck and nobody knows what state he's in.'

‘What are we supposed to do? Why don’t the Kraut police go and get him out?’

‘Dunno, and you’ve not heard the best bit. The guy that got away hitched a lift back to Gütersloh and now anything with wheels is rolling.’

‘What?!’

‘Yeah. The guardroom got the main gates shut, but word is two trucks broke through the fence at the back of the airfield. The *Krauts* would like a presence. I guess that means you.’

‘Be at the guardroom in a mo!’

Alex threw on his uniform and put his sheepskin lined coat over the top. Totally unofficial, but it was better than anything the RAF dished out. It could be a long do. He ran outside and started up the duty wagon – today the Kombi. His usual vehicle, the Landrover, was up the creek and the engine was spread out all over the MT section floor. “Four days minimum”, they’d told him. “Good”, he’d replied, “keep the bloody thing as long as you like. It’s useless. An embarrassment! Blue lights and siren on, and struggling to overtake granddad in his battered old Volks toddling along at 50!” He much preferred the Kombi; faster, and at least the heater always worked. Used to freeze your bollocks off in the Landrover.

He pulled up at the main gate and went into the guardroom. Gerry and the GD, Little Nick, were there.

‘OK, Gerry, I think we’ve got a bit of a problem. Pete’s supposed to be with me, but he sloped off somewhere. No idea where he is. Taff and the two Jocks are in married quarters and it’s too far to go and fetch them, even if they’re there. Bill’s got a new married quarter in Münster. It’d take me three quarters of an hour to get there. No Provost in Gütersloh, and it’s the wrong way anyway. That leaves you.’

'*Me?!* I'm not going! Could get yourself killed out there! There's supposed to be about two hundred of the buggers.'

'Gerry…there's me and there's you. Anyway, you're always on about how good the Provost have it and how you'd like to transfer. Consider yourself on loan for the duration. Nick here can mind the shop, can't you Nick? Lock the door and answer the phone. Get the Duty Officer over here, update and tell him to call the Boss. Then it's up to him. Gerry, let's go.'

'You're not serious.'

'Gerry, what's that on your arm? A propeller? What are these on my arm? When you get three of these, you can tell me what to do. Until then you do as I say. In the front of the Kombi. Now.'

Gerry climbed in, up front, a decidedly lighter shade of pale. Barrier up, blue light and siren on, Alex spun the wheels as they pulled away to the top of the street, turned left and headed for Kransdorf, some 20km away.

'Do you know this village, Gerry?'

'No. You?'

'No. Heard about seven hundred people live there, so it's not that big. I've passed the signs to it, but never been. Beats me why the Krauts chose this place for their party. Do you know?'

'No. Not really.'

'Listen, Gerry, when we get there you follow my lead. If I say you do something, you do it, OK? You do it immediately. No poncing about. We don't know what we're going to find. Fuck it up and we could get hurt, so watch me, OK?'

Gerry nodded. 'Big Bill says he doesn't know how somebody hasn't topped you yet.'

'What you mean?'

'Well, he says you walk into the middle of a punch up, drag the buggers out and sling them in the wagon, and never get a scratch. He went in with you a couple of weeks ago, you walked out with nothing, and he came out with a split lip and a broken finger, and he's twice as big as you. He said last week that you went into *Krone*, you know the out-of-bounds place, and dragged old Jagger out who was as pissed as a newt. Jagger had a glass; he broke it and was waving it about. Said he was going to cut off your fucking head. Bill said you pushed him against the side of a car, stuck your nose in his face and said "you might cut me, but see the big feller back there? He'll play football with your fucking head!" Old Jags dropped the glass and started to cry. Big Bill said you're not normal. One day someone will do you.'

'Well, Gerry, let's hope it's not today, because since you can't drive you'd really be in the shit, wouldn't you? Nearly there.'

They came to the turn off; the sign read Kransdorf 1km. A German police car was parked halfway across the road. They waved Alex straight through. On the edge of the village, roughly 500m from the main square, another police car stood, blue light flashing, also stretched halfway across the road. Behind it was a Kombi, parked on the grass verge. Six policemen were gathered in a group in the middle of the road, talking. Alex came to a halt and climbed out. He recognized the man walking towards him, Captain Helzer from Rheda. The Captain saluted. They all did this, the Krauts, regardless of their rank; they always saluted you. It was embarrassing. He returned the salute.

'Hello, Captain. How's life treating you?'

The Captain gestured towards the square where a huge crowd of people were milling around, many with bottles in their hands. Alex guessed there must be well over a hundred. Not funny.

'At the moment life is quiet but, well, you know, it could change.' He pointed, 'the Englishman is over there, on the floor. He moves now and then, so he's not dead.'

'What are you going to do?'

'For the moment nothing. I'm waiting for extra police to arrive.'

'Why?'

He looked surprised at the question, but waved towards the crowd, 'We are six; eight with you two. They are what? One hundred and fifty, two hundred maybe? I would say we're outnumbered.'

Alex looked at him. 'Are you looking to start a pitched battle?'

'No, of course not.'

'Then why do you need more men?'

'I need more men to establish control.'

'Captain, that man out there is an Airman. He could be dying, we don't know. We do know he obviously needs medical treatment. *You* may be into crowd control but *he*'s mine, and I'm going to get him out.'

'I cannot allow this.'

'Captain, I'm going in. Move your men out of the way,' Alex said. 'You, Gerry, get in the back of the Kombi! I'm going to drive up to the wall of the *Rat-house* with the sliding door facing the wall. We'll jump out and throw chummy in the back. You get in with him, close the door and lock it. OK?' Gerry nodded.

'OK. Let's go.' They climbed in the Kombi. Alex reversed until he was at the right angle to get past the parked police car, then switched on the blue light and accelerated. The policemen scrambled out of the way as the Kombi came at them. The crowd was watching. Suddenly, several men ran forward in an attempt to get in front of the Kombi. Alex switched on the siren and floored the accelerator. Third gear was screaming. He kept going towards the *Rat-house*, then swung the wheel hard over and stood on the brakes, screeching to a halt less than a metre in front of the motionless, battered Airman. They both leapt out, grabbed the Airman, dragged him to the open side door and heaved him in. Gerry jumped in after him, slammed the door closed and locked it while Alex scrambled back into the driver's seat, slammed his door shut and banged down on the lock. The crowd surrounded the Kombi, banging on the windows and sides. The noise was deafening. They tried rocking the vehicle from side to side. The crowd around them was maybe ten to fifteen deep; it was terrifying. Alex crunched the vehicle into first gear and accelerated. The Kombi only lurched from side to side like a drunken kangaroo. He took his foot off the accelerator and tried again. The vehicle bounced along as first one and then another drive wheel caught. Finally both wheels touched the ground at the same time – a puff of smoke from the tyres and he moved forward. People scrambled to get out of the way. One man slipped, tried to get up, but the Kombi hit him on the hip and threw him to one side. Alex kept going. *Fuck'em,* he thought, *it's us or them!* The crowd parted and finally they were through. Alex didn't slow down for either checkpoint.

Twenty five minutes later they were at the sickbay with the battered, still unconscious, Airman. Examination and X-rays showed four broken ribs, a broken left arm, a broken left leg, broken nose, five teeth missing and finally, twenty eight stitches were applied to lacerations in the head. Otherwise he was in pretty good nick.

Next day, Rheda police complained to the CO who had Alex on the carpet for a fifteen minute roasting, which resulted in an official reprimand being entered into his record. Alex later learned this was never put through.

Sylt

24- Introducing Kat
25- The Stolen Picture
26- Avenging Katrina

Chapter 24

Introducing Kat

Alex pulled into an empty parking space in front of the PBX and killed the engine. He laid his head back into the seat and closed his eyes for a moment; he was tired. He'd left home last night at 6:30pm, five hours down to Dover, including the run through Central London, and made it with half an hour to spare onto the midnight boat. Off the boat in Ostend at 06:10 and by 07:45 he was locked in the early morning traffic jams of central Brussels, only one wrong turn, where the signs switched from French to Dutch, then it was due east to Aachen-Lichtenbusch and over the border into Germany, grab a bite to eat, fill up and head north-east for Eschweiler, Frechen, Cologne, Leverkusen, his old stomping ground from what seemed like a lifetime ago when he was based at Geilenkirchen, yet in reality only just over 12 months. On, past Remscheid, Wuppertal, Hagen and just past Dortmund on to Route 2. Past Hamm, then the old Windmill cafe across on the westbound route of the motorway which was run by the Salvation Army, off at Gütersloh, along Verler Strasse and turn right onto the slip road and into Sundern – home, for what it was worth.

Alex loved it here.

He looked at his watch, 16:30. It had taken him 22 hours; 21 actually, since Germany was one hour ahead of the UK. Not bad at all. He glanced to his left and saw Pete hanging out of the Detachment window, waving frantically. He wound the car window down and waved, 'Hi Pete.'

'Don't even bother getting out of the car, you're off on detachment. Sylt.' He was laughing.

Alex slowly climbed out of the car. Mercedes or not, his back ached.

He turned to Pete. 'Welcome back, Alex,' he said, addressing Pete. 'Did you have a good leave? Everything OK? Nice to see you back here.' Pete stuck two fingers up at him and, still laughing, closed the detachment window.

Alex walked into the Duty NCO's room and planted himself down in the empty chair behind the second desk.

'Where's everyone?' he asked Pete.

'Where do you think they are at 4:30 on a Sunday afternoon? Nothing's doing. But, my friend, great things are in store for you. Do you know where Sylt is?' he asked with a grin, looking across at Alex.

'Up north somewhere.'

'It's an island off the coast of Denmark. NATO base I think. All nationalities there. Anyway, they've got big problems. Sounds like fights, riots and orgies every night. The police boss man, Flying Officer somebody-or-other has asked for help from Two TAF. They're taking eleven coppers from all over Germany and shipping them up there. One month detachment – and you,' he pointed at Alex, 'drew the winning ticket. It's not favouritism, it's just that everyone said "Oh, this'll suit Alex", plus of course the fact that no other silly sod was stupid enough to want to go. Why volunteer to get the shit kicked out of you every night on some distant island, when you can stay here and get the shit kicked out of you in *Krone* only on Saturday. See the logic?'

'Plus the fact that I wasn't here, of course.'

‘Well, I admit, that might have had something to do with it.’ He paused, ‘Oh, by the way, Sylt is apparently one big nudist colony. Just imagine all that nookie lying on the beach every day, starkers. Fantastic!’

‘If it’s that fantastic, Pete, why the hell didn’t everybody volunteer to go?’

Pete grinned. ‘Well, I think the idea that you might get both your head and your balls kicked in every night kind of outweighed the nookie side of things. I’ll tell you one thing, though – and don’t ask me how I know – apparently the WO-man didn’t want you to go. He suggested to the Old Man that blank pieces of paper go in a hat together with one for Sylt, whoever draws Sylt goes. First off, the Old Man thought this was a good idea, then later he called the WO-man in and they chewed it over again. The Old Man reckoned you were a natural for this, the WO-man agreed but still didn’t want to detail you for it. In the end, though, consider yourself detailed, and that’s the true version.’

Alex held his hand up. ‘Enough, Pete. I’m knackered. I’m going to have a big kip and don’t you dare ring that bloody telephone. See you later,’ and he was gone.

Next morning the CO explained the current situation on Sylt. Apparently, the behaviour of off-duty service personnel of all nationalities was causing concern among both the resident civilian population and the German police. Flying Officer Hansen, who was in charge of RAF Police on the island, admitted things were beyond his control. There were Belgian Air Police, German Naval Police and American Air Police on the island, and they would be working together. The Americans, though, tended to frequent their own places and in general didn’t mix with the European forces. It was therefore mainly the additional influx of Royal Air Force Police who would be expected to restore normality.

Alex left bright and early next morning. First, down the road to Bielefeld, then across to Hannover, due north to Hamburg. On to Neumünster, Schleswig and Flensburg. Just short of the Danish border turn left and head for Niebüll. At the railway depot drive onto a flatbed where straps attach the car wheels to the deck to keep it stable. Then, after the train has passed by Klauxbüll it heads out to sea; a single rail track along a man-made ramp: the *Hindenburg Dam.* At first the feeling of sitting in your car with nothing on either side but water can be a little disconcerting, but after roughly ten kilometres the train again hits dry land, the island of Sylt. On into Westerland, the island's main town and the rail terminus.

Tom and Gary were waiting for him as he drove down the ramp. He knew them both. Tom had left Sundern roughly one month after Alex's arrival and Alex had gone through Netheravon Police Training School with Gary.

Next morning Flying Officer Hansen held an informal meeting in an outer room next to his office for the new arrivals. Of the eleven who had been temporarily assigned to Sylt just six had arrived. It was hinted that the missing five might not be coming after all. Flying Officer Hansen called out the names of the six policemen and as he did each one walked up to the desk and was handed a black rubber truncheon, rather like payday back in West Kirby, but without the salutes and money. It turned out that the truncheons had been loaned by the German police and they wanted them back. During what Alex presumed was supposed to be a stirring call to arms, the Flying Officer used the phrase: "… and there may be occasions when it becomes necessary to use the truncheon first and ask questions later".

Alex tuned him out and studied him more closely. Roughly 45, thinning, mousy hair. He chewed his lower lip and played continuously with either a pencil or a ruler. Under the desk, his right foot was doing a tap dance. And he was still a Flying Officer. Alex summed him up: nerves shot to hell and completely out of his depth. *So much for leadership!*

After the meeting, a rota for the next week was handed out. Alex saw he was on duty that evening with a German Naval Policeman, a Belgian Air Policeman, George from Newcastle who was one of the new arrivals, and Tom and Gary. They would be six up in a Kombi. They would also be followed by a German civil police Kombi. Tonight was simply orientation for Alex, George, the Belgian and the German – all of them were new boys.

The first run into town was at 20:00. While Gary drove, Tom gave a running commentary on the delights –or otherwise– of the various establishments they passed. The place was deserted; he wondered what all the fuss was about. At 22:00 he found out. The streets were packed. They crawled down the main street, getting either one finger or two in rapid succession for their trouble. At 22:30 they met up with two German civil police who were on foot. The Belgian and the German Naval policeman left the Kombi. They would patrol on foot with the civil police. Everything remained quiet until 23:15 when, turning back onto the main road from a side street, they came upon a heaving mass of perhaps twenty people, at the centre of which two were attempting to slug it out. One of them was using a bottle. Gary turned on the siren and light and headed for the group. Tom leapt out and the crowd parted. As he got to the two combatants he simply swung his truncheon at the one with the bottle. Whack! It caught him somewhere below his neck and between the shoulder blades. He staggered and Tom hit him again. He fell to the ground. Alex and George dived out from the back of the Kombi and half dragged, half carried the now semi-conscious pugilist back to the wagon. They dropped him on the floor, between the two rear inward facing seats, slammed the rear door shut and Gary roared away from the scene. All very efficient. Action over in less than ten, fifteen seconds.

They drove back to camp but didn't stop at the guardroom. Gary continued on alongside the runway. He drove to the far end of the camp where a darkened building stood alone, isolated from everything else. He stopped and Tom climbed out, opened the door, stepped inside and switched on a light. They'd obviously been here before. Alex climbed out followed by George. 'What's this place?' he asked. 'You'll see,' was the reply.

Tom walked across to the back of the Kombi and shook the limp figure in the back, lying with his head towards the open side door.

'Out!' he ordered. Nothing. No reaction, except a groan. Tom prodded him with his truncheon, 'Out!' he repeated. The figure lifted himself slowly on hands and knees and shook his head as if to clear it.

'Out!' Tom banged his truncheon on the floor of the Kombi. 'Out, now!'

The figure started to crawl. The moment his head appeared outside the Kombi, Tom hit him. Not hard, but he tapped him across the back of the head with the truncheon. The man went out like a light.

Tom and Gary dragged him through the open door and into the empty building. Then they stripped him. Standing against the far wall was a bench, the type you might find in a gymnasium. Lying on the bench were what looked like four very dirty and blood-stained towels. Next to the bench was a bucket of water. Coming out of the wall was a tap with a hosepipe attached to it.

Alex could see that the naked man was now conscious. He was looking at Tom who had picked up the hosepipe, without expression. No fear; nothing. Tom turned on the water and directed the jet into the man's face. Then he ran it down his body aiming deliberately at the man's genitals. The man drew up his legs in a feeble attempt to protect himself. Gary, meanwhile, dropped two towels into the bucket of water. Tom turned off the water and took a towel. He told the man to stand up. Gary helped him to his feet, and then each armed with a wet towel they proceeded to whip him. The man screamed.

Alex stepped forward and stood between the man and Tom.

'Stop this crap now!'

'Get out of the way, Alex.'

Alex turned to George, 'George, help me get this guy dressed.'

Before George could move, Gary pulled Alex away from the man. Alex drew his truncheon and pointed it at Gary. 'You touch me again and I'm going to ram this thing down your throat until it comes out of your arse!'

Gary looked across at Tom as if seeking support. Tom shook his head. The pair walked outside and climbed in the front of the Kombi.

George and Alex helped the man get dressed. Turned out, he was an SAC from an Air Sea Rescue Flight. 'Do you want to do anything about this?' Alex asked him.

The man thought for a moment, then shook his head. 'No, I'll be OK. Just let's forget it.'

'Sure?'

He nodded, 'Yes, I'm sure. Thanks.'

They dropped the Airman off at his billet after which Alex told Gary to stop the Kombi. 'I'm finished with you two. I don't care what you tell the boss, but I'm not working with either of you again. Plus, if I hear of anyone else being beaten up, I'll shop you. You're a fucking disgrace. Get that roster changed and stay away from me.' And with that he climbed out of the Kombi and headed in the direction of his room in the transit block.

*

It was at lunch time next day that George sat himself down opposite Alex with a plate containing two pork chops and chips, and a second plate with two eggs and six slices of bread.

'Hungry, George?' George grinned. 'Always. Listen, Alex, about last night. It sort of took me by surprise. I've never seen anything like that before and I didn't know what to do. I'm glad you stopped it. That SAC may be a right arsehole – apparently he's always in trouble – but nobody should be treated like that.' Alex carried on eating.

'Alex, do you think we could work together?'

Alex looked at him, 'Don't know, George. I don't know yet how this place is rigged. If you can talk to whoever is drawing up the roster, I have no problem with it. Seems like it's all going to be night work anyway. That's when the fun and games start. Sure. Fix it if you can.'

Alex was lying on his bed reading when there was a loud rap on the door. 'Alex, it's Jock.'

Alex climbed off the bed, and checked his watch as he opened the door. 18:00. Jock stuck his hand out, 'Jock

McMahon, Alex. Thought I'd pop over to say hello. We're apparently working together tonight. Is it OK if I pick you up about eight, nothing happens before then.'

'Sure. Anybody else with us?'

'No, Gary is riding with George tonight – you know "Big George" – and a Belgian. Tom's off tonight.'

Alex nodded. 'Been here long, Jock?'

'Aye, just shy of two years.'

'What you think of it?'

'On the whole, pretty good. Now's the time to hit the beaches during the day. Grab a case of beer from Werner's and chat up the dollies in the dunes. Great fun. Winter's a bit grim though; we get a fair few storms. Night life's good though, can't complain.' He backed out of the door, 'See you in a couple of hours then.'

By 20:30 they'd toured the town; nothing. *Like Wales on a Sunday night*, Jock had said. Apparently he'd been stationed there before ending up on Sylt. An experience not to be repeated, he hoped.

They sat at an open air café and watched the world pass by over a couple of coffees. Jock looked at his watch, '9:15. I suppose we'd better make another pass. Things will start warming up in half an hour or so.'

Jock turned the Landrover around and they headed back for the centre. Alex reached inside his blouse pocket and pulled out a sheet of paper which he unfolded. The list of out-of-bound places the new boys had received at their first meeting. He looked across at Jock. 'Pigalle, what's that?'

'Stay away. That's official. The Yanks have taken it over. Bar downstairs, live music some nights, bedrooms upstairs. If you're not black, keep out. The air police check it out. Noisy, the odd punch up, but we're never involved.'

‘Cleopatra’s?’

‘That’s Werner’s place. Nice guy.’

‘And?’

‘And what? Nothing. It’s out-of-bounds.’ Jock shrugged. ‘We don’t bother Werner. He gives us a case of beer for the beach whenever we want it. He’s got his own boys in there to sort out any trouble. We leave Werner alone.’

‘Let’s drop by.’

‘What?’ He shot a look at Alex. ‘Why?’

‘Because it’s out-of-bounds, and I want to see it.’ Jock pulled to the side of the road and stopped. ‘Look, Werner’s OK. He brings girls up from Hamburg who’ve got an early case of bun-in-the-oven. He fixes them up and they go to work for him.’

‘Why’s he out-of-bounds?’

‘One or two punch-ups, noise after hours, a couple of cases of galloping knob-rot.’

‘How long’s it been out-of-bounds?’ Jock shrugged. ‘Seems like forever. Must be at least since I’ve been here. Don’t know exactly.’

‘Let’s go, I want to see this place.’

From the outside the building was completely unpretentious. A half-moon pink light above the black double doors, which flashed on and off, announcing to anyone who cared that this was indeed Cleopatra’s.

Alex climbed the three steps followed by Jock and found himself in a short corridor, perhaps six or seven metres long, then a set of glass doors behind which a hard nose crew-cut in black dinner jacket and trousers began making signs to someone out of view the moment he saw Alex and Jock. He opened the door and gave that typical German bow, *‘Guten Abend, meine Herren.’*

'Evening,' replied Alex, as he walked past into an extremely large, round foyer. Chandeliers, flock wallpaper, burgundy leather couches, thick carpets, girls. Alex counted. Thirteen. Unlucky for somebody, he thought, as he surveyed the scene. All conversation stopped – the music, however, continued. Six males, not German by the look of them. *Servicemen?* He looked again; officer material. *Could be fun*. Another dinner jacket came through a door in the far wall and headed for Alex, hand outstretched, plastic smile in place.

'Good evening, Sir,' he said as he offered his hand to Alex. 'I am Werner, the owner of Cleopatra's.'

Alex shook his hand, 'Do you think we could have a little chat somewhere?' The plastic slipped a little. He looked at Jock.

Alex turned just in time to see Jock making a "Don't ask me" sign as he raised his shoulders and spread his hands. Werner didn't speak to Jock. *Interesting,* thought Alex. 'Certainly, Sir. My office perhaps.' His English was excellent.

Werner closed the door behind them and indicated that they should sit in the two armchairs in front of his desk. Jock sat. Werner sat. Alex remained standing. He looked down at Werner who now realised he'd lost the initiative. 'I'm new in town,' said Alex, looking slowly round the room. *Lovely; money…* 'I just thought I'd call in to say hello.'

The plastic smile was back in place.

'Well, how nice. Always happy to make the acquaintance of members of the police. I'm sure we can continue to work well together. Anything you think I can do for you, simply ask. We always try to accommodate, don't we, Jock?' Jock seemed to sink into the chair.

Alex smiled at Werner, 'That's nice. A beer for the beach perhaps?' Werner smiled back and nodded.

'How about the odd lady now and then, Werner?' The plastic seemed a little unsure again. He took a chance. 'Well, I'm sure that could be arranged without too much trouble.'

'Free, Werner?'

'But of course.'

Alex leaned across the desk and looked down at Werner. 'I don't know what your arrangements were before tonight, but they just changed. Your bar, club, knocking shop, whatever you care to call it, is out-of-bounds and has been for a long time. I'm here to enforce that rule. As of tomorrow night, when you open, make sure that everybody who comes in here knows that, because when I come in here from now on I will arrest every serviceman I see, regardless of nationality and rank. Try and cause problems with your bouncer out there and I will come back with the German police. Understand?'

Werner just nodded. He, too, had slumped back in his chair.

'I'm not after you personally, Werner. I'm just here to enforce the rules. Understand?'

Werner nodded again. It seemed the stuffing had been knocked out of him. 'A piece of advice if I may, Werner. This place has been out-of-bounds for a long time. Why don't you go up to camp and put your case to the officer in charge of police to see if you can get the ban lifted.'

He looked at Alex – clearly surprised, 'I can do that?'

'Of course you can do it. Make sure all your papers are in order legally, check the girls regularly, you know the form. But, while the ban stands, I will enforce it. Every day if necessary.'

He looked at Jock in the chair. 'OK, Jock, next one. Good night, Werner.'

He turned on his heel, and with Jock following they left the building.

*

By 01:00 the process had been repeated three times. As they sat in the Landrover Jock turned in his seat and looked across at Alex. 'Tell me, arc you on some sort of personal crusade to close this town down? What's with you?'

Alex smiled. 'No personal crusade, but there are now six of us up here to do what you lot should have done in the first place. You take bribes, you thump prisoners and then, when it all starts to get out of hand your boss goes and whines to Two TAF. Result? We're here to clear up the mess. Get used to it Jock, because with me, this is how it's going to be. Who's next?' Alex looked down on the list.

'How about we visit one that isn't out-of-bounds; a nice classy place, just for a change?'

'Why, if it's not out-of-bounds?'

'Well, for a start, the owner's a real looker and she always makes us welcome. She doesn't mind us looking in now and then. Never been any trouble in the two years I've been here. She's got a couple of bird dogs there you really wouldn't want to argue with.'

'What's this place called?'

'Katrina's.'

'OK, let's go.'

She didn't need pointing out to Alex. He knew who she was the moment they walked through the door. She was standing by the bar, talking to some hard-looking guy with a crew cut. *One of the bird dogs*, thought Alex. She glanced over, saw the two white hats and smiled; a genuine smile. Not one of the plastic variety they'd been suffering all night. She walked directly towards Alex and held out her hand. 'Hello, I'm Katrina. You're most welcome.'

Jock was speaking but Alex wasn't listening. He held out his hand, 'I'm Alex.'

She held his eyes. Inside he started to tremble. 'I know who you are, your fame preceded you.'

'I don't understand.'

She smiled. 'Bush telegraph. You appear to have had a very busy evening. I should think that by now every club on the strip is awaiting your arrival with interest. I'm pleased that you decided to look in on us this evening. I hoped you would. I was curious.'

'You know what curiosity did?' She nodded, still smiling. She was radiant. 'Therefore, if you'll allow it, I should like to call you Kat – with a K, of course.' She laughed out loud. Beautiful sparkling eyes; deep blue. He was still trembling and suddenly he realised she was still holding his hand. 'Nobody has ever called me that before. I quite like it. If I am your Cat – with a C – will you make me purr?'

'I promise to do my best.'

The words were out before he had time to think. *Jeezus, where was this going?* His knees felt weak and he was sure she could feel him shaking. Her eyes changed; she seemed to be looking deep inside him. Finally, she whispered, 'I'd like that, Alex. Truly, I would,' and she squeezed his hand. 'Come, let me give you both some refreshment. I know you're on duty, but I would like you to have something.'

She led him over to an empty table in the far corner to the right of the bar. 'This is my table. No-one else sits here. Whenever you come, please sit here. Now, what would you like?'

It was then that Alex realised Jock was still standing in the middle of the room where they'd left him, looking rather lost. He laughed, 'I think we made Jock feel a little awkward.'

‘You felt it, didn’t you? I know you did, I felt you trembling inside. I’m still shaking too. I don’t know you, but I want to... Do you think I’m being very forward?’

‘No, I think you say what you feel and that’s good.’

‘And what do you feel?’

‘I feel electricity between us. I don’t know why but I’d like to find out. Not just for now; there’s something more, but I don’t know what it is.’

She nodded and squeezed his hand, ‘I know. I know exactly what you mean. What time do you finish?’ she asked.

‘When we leave here. Straight back to camp and check in.’

‘Can you come back’

‘Yes, I can.’

‘Will you, please?’

He looked at her; the trembling was getting worse. He couldn’t trust his voice.

He just nodded.

Chapter 25

The Stolen Picture

Alex took another forkful of scrambled egg and then looked at his watch, 02:15. It had been a quiet night, two drunks, no fights, in bed by 03:00. *Can't be bad.* He looked across at George who was trying, quite unsuccessfully, to force part of a double bacon and egg sandwich into his mouth. He watched as an egg yolk burst and slowly dribbled down George's chin. George made no move to stop it as one spot left the chin and landed on his tie. Alex grabbed a handful of paper serviettes and thrust them across the table. A muttered *thanks* found its way through the mouthful of food as George tried to wipe his chin with serviettes in his left hand and hold the sandwich together with his right. He failed. The bottom slice of bread broke in two and this, quickly followed by two halves of egg, landed on George's knee. The *thanks* rapidly became a series of *fucks*.

George was a slob. His main off-duty pastimes seemed to be smoking like a chimney, putting pints of sludge away by the gallon and seeing how many double bacon-and-egg-butties he could get past his teeth and into his stomach. George came from Newcastle. For some reason, though, no-one ever called him Geordie; always George.

George was a great guy to have around if there was trouble. Fearless. His working policy of *"I'd rather whack 'em than argue the toss"* definitely had something to do with it, together with the very visible fact that he was six foot seven and all of twenty two stone. People tended to scarper when they saw George ambling towards them.

At that moment Stan from the guardroom walked into the Mess. 'I thought I'd find the two of you in here,' he said as he plonked himself into the chair next to George and, reaching over, helped himself to a handful of cold chips from Alex's plate. Alex pushed the plate across, 'Help yourself.'

'Mm. Thanks.' He polished off the cold and soggy chips.

'Any tea?' Alex pointed to the large silver urn standing on the counter, 'Fresh. Cook has just made it. Full of bromide. Help you keep your dick in your pants.'

'Doesn't seem to work on you,' retorted Stan, as he took a mug and filled it with the dark brown liquid that came from the tap. It looked more like creosote with milk added. 'Never touch the stuff,' replied Alex, 'I want to live beyond twenty five.'

'Which brings me to the point of my visit,' responded Stan, as he sat down next to George again, spilling tea from his overfull mug onto the table top. 'Just had a phone call from Katrina's. Actually, it was from Katrina herself. Wanted to know if Alex was still on duty.' He leered across at Alex, 'Bit on the side, is it?'

Alex ignored him. 'And?'

'Appears she's had a painting stolen right off the wall in the bar. A copy of something famous, forget what, but expensive. Asked if you could go out there.'

'That it?'

'That's it.'

'By the way, Stan, who's watching the shop while you're in here stuffing your face?'

'Adolf.'

Alex and George looked at each other. George shrugged before biting into his second bacon-and-egg buttie.

'And who the hell is Adolf when he's home?' asked Alex.

'The old German guy that works on the barrier.'

'What? That little old fellow wearing that old green blanket uniform and the Africa Corps cap?'

Stan nodded, 'Good bloke, Adolf.'

'On whose shoulders rests the security of the great British Empire.' George tried to laugh at his own joke, but only succeeded in splattering bread and egg onto the table top. Alex looked across at him. 'If you can finish that lot without choking to death, I think we'd better go and take a look.'

'One minute,' came back the mumbled response.

It was 03:15 when they arrived at Katrina's. Still early. The place was full. It was one of the few places on the Strip where you knew that you would not be ripped off, be pestered by prostitutes or get duffed up. Katrina's really was a cut above – the slightest sign of trouble from anybody and one of Katrina's bodyguards, Karl or Heinz, would move in and quickly show them the door. They were masters of their craft. They did things quickly, quietly and efficiently, while the rest of the clientele would not be aware that anything untoward had happened.

Alex led the way towards Katrina's office, to the right of the bar. He knocked.

'*Herein!*'

They entered the office. Katrina herself was sitting behind an enormous dark wooden desk, a flute of champagne in one hand, and what looked like an empty picture frame in the other. She beamed a huge smile when she saw Alex and immediately rose from behind her desk, made towards him and planted a gentle kiss on his right cheek. George's mouth was practically hanging open.

Katrina pointed at George. 'Introduce me to your friend, Alex. I don't know him.' Alex did the honours. You could practically hear George purr. He wasn't used to being received like this.

'A drink for either of you? Wine, beer, tea, coffee?' Alex shook his head. George answered, 'No, thanks, Ma'am, we're on duty.' Alex had never known that stop him before. Neither politeness nor abstinence were George's forte. Katrina had him eating out of her hand. She pointed to the long cream-coloured couch that ran the entire length of one wall. 'Then I suggest we make ourselves comfortable, even though I find what we are about to discuss rather distasteful.'

Alex and George sank into the couch. Katrina showed them the empty picture frame. 'This is what Karl just found on the far side of the road, but perhaps I should start from the beginning. Tonight I arrived here a little after eleven. As I came to the entrance door I noticed a dark green Volkswagen parked in the side road opposite us. Two young men climbed out, ran across the road and entered right behind me. They took the table immediately to the right of this office door. One was blond and the other was dark. The blond one spoke excellent German, but he told me he was Dutch. Pilots; apparently here on exercise for a couple of weeks. They had a few drinks, some snacks, were no trouble, but each time I went near the table he wanted to speak to me, to what you Alex, call "chat me up". I take no notice, it goes with the job and I know that both Karl and Heinz are watching me wherever I go. So, no problem. They are still at their table when I come into my office to do some work at one o'clock. I go back outside again one hour later and they have gone – and so has the picture that was on the wall immediately above their table. The place was packed, room to stand only at the bar. I looked out into the street; the

Volkswagen had gone. I did not speak about this to either Karl or Heinz. If they had seen anything the picture would still be on the wall. I came back into my office to think. To do something or not do something. I decided to do something. These people are not children, they fly airplanes, they are adults and therefore they should know the difference between right and wrong. They cannot expect to steal my painting and get away with it. So I call the camp and ask if you are still on duty. They say they will find you, and,' she beamed a huge smile at Alex, 'now you are here. An unexpected bonus. Perhaps I should have someone steal a painting every day, then I would see you more.' George was sitting there staring at Katrina with adoration written all over his face. He really was smitten. Alex stood up. 'OK, we'll go back to camp and see if we can find the Volks and our two friends. What time will you be going home?'

'Probably five, maybe a little later. Will you come over?' George was positively drooling.

'I don't know yet. If we find these two characters it will mean paperwork. A bit unpredictable.'

'I will make breakfast for seven. If you can come it will be a pleasure. If not, after two?'

'I'll try. Can't promise, but after two definitely.'

As they walked across to the parked Landrover it was obvious that George was bursting to ask questions. He just wasn't too sure how to go about it. He looked across at Alex, 'Are you, you know, well, … are you two–' He paused, then tried again. 'Is that your lady friend, Alex?'

Alex looked at him and smiled, 'Something like that.'

'You lucky old sod. She's gorgeous! You've only been here two weeks. How do you do it?'

'I don't drink the tea, George'

Alex parked in front of the guardroom. The barrier was down and he could see Adolf at the desk reading a newspaper. Stan was nowhere to be seen. As they entered the guardroom Adolf snapped to attention. Alex waved him down.

'Sit down, Adolf. Where's Stan?'

'Sleeping in the back, Sir.'

'Leave him,' said Alex as George headed for the cells. 'Adolf, tell me. Have two Dutchmen in a dark green Volkswagen come through the gate in the last couple of hours?'

Adolf consulted a sheet of paper on his desk. 'Yes, Sir, they arrived here at precisely 02:21. A driver with one passenger. I checked their ID. Both Dutch.'

'You write all this shit down?' asked George in amazement.

Adolf looked pained. 'Yes, Sir.'

'And what do you do with it?'

'I give it to Stan or who is on duty for them to enter into proper book. I do not write English very well.'

'And where are these two Dutchmen staying?' asked Alex.

'In the transit part of the Officers' Mess.' Adolf looked surprised at the question.

'Thanks, Adolf.'

Alex led George back to the Landrover as Adolf threw up a salute.

'How the fuck did we ever win the war?' exploded George, once they were out of earshot. 'Stan, the lazy bastard, sleeps the night away, and some little old guy dressed in an army blanket checks people in and out and actually logs it. I bet Stan doesn't even bother to copy it. With idle sods like Stan around, no wonder they lost their grip on this place. If I ran this show

I'd stick my boot up the collective station police arse. Idle buggers.'

Alex stopped and held his hand up. 'Never mind Stan. Let's work out how we're going to do this.' George shrugged. 'Call the Duty Officer, his problem. We can't do much. We don't have the rank.'

'Let's find the car first, George, and then see,' said Alex.

They drove to the Officers' Mess. No Volkswagen to be seen. Alex then drove to the back of the Mess. 'Bingo!' he muttered. There stood the Volks. Alex felt the rear engine cowling – still warm. He tried the driver's door, it was unlocked. 'Didn't expect that,' he said as he stuck his head inside. He looked under the seats and in the glove compartment; nothing. He popped open the bonnet; the luggage space was empty. He stood and thought.

'George, go round the other side, slide the passenger seat forward and help me pull the rear seat out.'

George looked at him. 'We can't do this, Alex. Anybody finds out, we're in the shit.'

Alex raised an eyebrow. 'Yes or no?'

George shrugged, went to the other side of the Volks, slid the front seat forward, leaned in and took a grip on the rear seat.

'Right, George. Put your hand under the backrest and pull the seat forward and up. I'll do this side.' They pulled in unison and lifted the rear seat up and out. In the seat well lay a rolled up blue Air Force sweater. Alex lifted it out, laid it on the car roof and gently unfolded it. Inside lay the rolled up painting. 'Jackpot, George!'

'Now what do we do, Alex, this is illegal.'

'So is stealing, George.' He folded the painting back into the sweater and returned it to the seat well. Then they replaced the back seat and closed the door. Immediately in front of the parked Volks was a door leading into the back of the Officers' Mess. Alex tried it; locked. 'Front entrance, George.' They climbed back into the Landrover.

'Alex, it's Duty Officer time; there's nothing we can do.'

Alex didn't reply as they pulled up at the front entrance to the Mess. He took the torch from under the dashboard and made for the doors.

'Alex,' whispered George, 'we can't go in there, even on duty. We need an invite.' Alex ignored him and walked into the Mess. A startled orderly looked up from the book he was reading behind the front desk.

'I'm sorry, Corp,' he said, addressing Alex, 'but you can't come in here, and you have to remove your hat. Etiquette.'

Alex looked at him. 'I'm staying, and so is my hat. Now, I need to know something. Did you see a couple of Dutch Officers come in here at around 2:30 this morning? One blond hair, one dark?'

The LAC hesitated. Alex just waited. Finally, 'Yes, Corp.'

'Where are they bunking?'

'You can't go in there,' the Steward answered in a shaky voice, 'It's not allowed.'

'Where?'

The Steward looked at George for support. George ignored him. He pointed. 'Down that corridor, last door on the right.'

'Right,' said Alex to the Steward, 'I suggest you go and take a crap; fifteen minutes or so.'

The Steward turned and left, grabbing his book as he went.

'Alex, let's be serious, just for a minute. We have no authority in here. All we're going to get at the very least is one great big bollocking. If we're not lucky, a rocket. Jeezes, man, you're not really going to do this, are you?'

Alex grinned at him. 'You can always go and sit in the Landrover.'

George looked him in the eye and then grinned back. 'No way! I've only been working with you for a week or so, and already I've got a dozen stories to tell my future grandchildren. They all start the same: I once worked with this crazy man. His name was Alex.' Alex laughed, 'Come on, let's go and scare the shit out of some Dutchies.'

He didn't even bother knocking on the door, just walked right in and shone the torch at the head in the bed immediately in front of him. It was Blondie. He leaned down and pulled the sheet back. Blondie's eyes opened wide and he sat up with a start.

'*Wat ...?!*'

'Police. Get your feet on the floor. NOW!'

Blondie swung his feet out of bed and stood up.

'I didn't say stand up; I said get your feet on the floor. Sit down.'

Blondie's companion started to stir. Alex directed the torch beam at him. 'Stay exactly where you are until I tell you to do otherwise. Understand?'

'Yes, Sir.'

Alex shone the light directly into Blondie's eyes. 'So, where were you earlier tonight? In town?'

'Yes.'

'Both of you?'

'Yes.'

'Which bars?'

'Katrina's. Only Katrina's. What do you want?'

Alex bent down and stuck his face into Blondie's. 'The game is: *I* ask the questions, *YOU* supply the answers. Understand?'

Blondie nodded.

'You stole a painting from Katrina's.'

'No… no! We didn't steal anything.'

'That wasn't a question. That was a statement. I repeat, you stole a painting. Someone saw you do it. They also saw you remove the frame. You are a fucking thief. Where's the painting?'

'We didn't steal anything.'

'You're a liar! You were seen. Now, where is it? How did you get back to camp? Taxi?' *You clever bugger,* thought George.

'No, we drove here, a friend's car.'

'Where is it?'

'Parked outside.'

'Get dressed, let's go and take a look.'

'Could we have the light on, please?'

'George. The light.' George turned darkness into light. Blondie stared. Then he stood up and faced Alex.

'You're a Corporal!' he shouted, 'I am an officer. I will have you court-martialed. You cannot treat me like this.'

Alex leaned into his face again. '*I* am a policeman and *you* are a thief. Now, get dressed before I drag you out there in bare feet and pajamas.'

His colleague climbed out of bed and spoke to Blondie in Dutch. Alex didn't understand, but they both started to get dressed.

'Bring the car keys, let's go.'

All four headed out the front door. The Steward was still away deliberating. Alex and George followed the two Dutchmen to the Volkswagen. Blondie went to put the key in the lock when he saw the little button was up. He turned to Alex, 'I think I forgot to lock the car.'

'I'm now going to search the car in your presence, understand? If there is no painting there, we will search your room. If we do not find this painting anywhere, you may report me. If I find the painting, I will arrest you.'

'But you can't arrest me, I'm an officer, and you're a Corporal.'

'I repeat,' said Alex, 'you are a thief, and I'm a policeman.'

He leaned inside the car and searched as before, under the seats, under the dashboard. He popped the front bonnet – again. It was still empty. He stood back, as if in thought. Blondie had a smile on his face. 'George, could you go round to the other side, I'm going to lift the backseat out.' The smile on Blondie's face disappeared. They pulled the seat out and there in the well, just as Alex had replaced it, was the Air Force sweater. Alex removed it, laid it on the roof and unfolded it. There was the stolen painting.

Blondie had gone very pale.

Alex looked at him and pointed, '*You* are a thief.'

Blondie had the grace to hang his head. 'I'm sorry,' he mumbled, 'it was just a joke, a bit of fun.'

'You must have a very strange sense of humour in Holland. In England they put you in jail for stealing. Who did it? You? Him? Or both of you?'

Neither spoke. Then Blondie admitted, 'I did.'

'Right. Back inside. Both of you. I want your ID cards. In the morning I'm putting you both before your CO. At 08:00 I will be in front of the Officers' Mess. I will take both of you, together with my report, to your CO. He will deal with it. Any questions?' They both shook their heads.

The next day, at 16:00 in the afternoon a transport plane departed Sylt for Holland. Blondie and his mate, together with their kit, were on board.

Alex received a handshake and a commendation from the Dutch Commander.

Katrina received a huge bunch of flowers with a written apology, and of course, she got her painting back.

From his own CO Alex received a rather tame rollicking.

Something about exceeding his power of authority . . .

Chapter 26

Avenging Katrina

It was exactly 16:00 when the phone on Alex's desk rang. It had been a cold, grey day, with angry black clouds scudding across the sky, and rain –or snow– was sure to come. It was definitely cold enough, though in Alex's office it was hot. Too hot actually, with the radiators stuck on full blast, impossible to turn down, since some long-forgotten painter had sealed the screw-down tops with several layers of thick white paint. Alex had the door open and his No. 2 jacket hung on the back of his chair. Filling in long overdue traffic reports wasn't exactly his idea of fun, but the WO-man had insisted. It was either that or get his hair cut, and that was definitely a no-no. Another two weeks at least, maybe three if he was lucky. Alex was very particular about his hair; he liked it to be just a shade too long. He knew he could always get away with that. He leaned forward and picked up the phone.

'P&SS Detachment.'

'Alex?'

'Yep.'

'It's Kev.'

'Hi, Kev. How's tricks?'

'Usual shit. Boring as hell. I sometimes wonder who I upset to get stuck here!'

'Transfer.'

'Can't. I've tried twice. Keep getting turned down.'

'Must be your wonderful personality, Kev.'

'Yeah, maybe. Either that, or it's because I screwed the Flight's wife. I think he's got it in for me.' They both roared with laughter at the unintended pun. 'OK, Kev, tell me what's up.' Kevin roared with laughter again at the second unintended pun. 'Jeezes, Kev. What's got into you today?' Kevin burst out laughing again. 'Well done, Alex. That's three in a row. You win the jackpot, son. Now, let me see, what's the prize? I can let you have the Flight Sergeant's wife.' And off he went again.

'Kev . . . Kev! Kevin! Shut up! Will you?'

'Ooh, Alex, I love it when you're so masterful.' And he collapsed in laughter again.

'Kev, Kev . . . KEVIN, was there actually something you wanted? YOU rang me. Remember?'

Kevin slowly calmed down. 'Sorry, Alex. Listen, there's some Kraut driving a bloody great Merc, parked by the gate. He asked our *Dolmetscher* if he knew you. I told him, yeah, I know you, and you're on duty until 22:00. That OK?'

'What's his name?'

'No idea. He told me to tell you *"Kat"*, and he gave me two parcels.'

'Kat with a "K"?'

'Yeah, as in pussy. You been at it again, Alex?'

'I'm coming.'

'Gee. That was quick.'

Alex slammed down the phone, grabbed his jacket, snatched the keys for the duty vehicle off the hook and ran out the door, taking the steps two at a time. The Landrover fired first time and Alex pulled out from under the huge tree where he always parked and onto the cobbled road, turning a full 180 degrees, the rear wheels scrabbling to keep hold, then headed for the guardroom. As he reached the guardroom, he could just make out the rear number plate of a large black Mercedes before it turned left onto the main road and headed towards the motorway. NF. Nord Friesland. One of the new number plates that now included Sylt. His mind was racing: *Sylt... Katrina ... Kat!* Alex slammed the brakes on outside the guardroom, pulled up the handbrake and leapt out of the Landrover, leaving the door open, and ran into the guardroom.

'Jeezus! Where's the fire, Alex,' grinned Kev as he stood up.

'Where are the parcels, Kev?' Alex demanded. Kevin walked over to the table by the guardroom window, picked up the parcels and handed them over to Alex. Alex looked at the parcels. One felt solid. On one side it said "Mr Alex". The other wasn't really a parcel; it was a large brown office envelope filled with something that was very light. On the front, it was again addressed to Mr Alex. It was the same handwriting on both packages, but Alex didn't recognize it. 'OK, Kev. Describe the Kraut.' Kev thought. 'OK. Well, I definitely wouldn't like to meet him on a dark night. It wasn't that he was huge, or anything. It was his eyes. You can tell.'

'What can you tell?'

'That he's a hard bastard. A bit like you really, when you get pissed off.'

'Describe him, Kev. Tall? Short? Fat? Thin? Hair? Marks? You know the drill!'

'OK. Well, I would say he's about six foot two. Not heavy. Sort of trim. You know, like he keeps in shape. And he had a small scar on his nose, sort of V-shaped. His hair, well it was cropped. Silver, very smart.'

'Karl.'

'You know the guy?'

'Yes.'

'Funny friends you have, Alex.'

'He's not a friend. I just know him. He works for somebody I know.' Alex turned and walked out of the door, 'Thanks Kev.'

'Anytime, mate. Take care.'

Alex climbed in the Landrover and put the parcels gently on the front passenger seat. He had a bad feeling about this. He didn't know why, but it didn't feel right. It had been eight weeks since Alex had left Sylt. Eight weeks. And they'd agreed. No matter what they felt – it was for the best. No communication. No phone calls, no letters, nothing. Just memories. Memories were good. Memories were forever. They'd felt more in those four weeks together than many people feel in a lifetime. Alex thought about it every day. Being together. The walks on the beach, the pebbles she arranged in the sand which said "I love you" before the tide came and washed them all away. The crazy boat ride, the bonfires, the music, the soft lights of her apartment, the wonderful food and the incredible love-making that sometimes went on for hours. God, how he missed her. It hurt.

Alex put the Landrover in gear and swung back to the Detachment. He walked into his office and closed the door. Something was wrong. He knew it. She wouldn't send Karl 500 kms or more down the motorway to deliver parcels if everything was OK. He sat down at his desk and stared at the parcels. Finally, he pulled the solid one towards him and stared at the writing. He didn't recognize it and it certainly wasn't Kat's. He slid his knife blade under the flap of brown paper and through the tape that held it closed. Removing the brown paper he looked at the silver box it contained. That was also taped shut. In the bottom right hand corner in black Gothic print it read *Gallerie Mossmann.* Very classy. He remembered *Mossmann's.* Very upmarket. She'd bought a silver photo frame there, laughing and telling him with this she'd hold him forever. He slit the tape and opened the box. On top was a white envelope, sealed and addressed to Mr Alex. Underneath was the photo frame holding a picture of Kat. God, she looked beautiful. He remembered the scene. It was their last night together. She stood by the piano, resting her hand lightly on the keys and the Club photographer had taken several pictures of Kat singly, and finally of Alex. 'For posterity,' she had laughed. 'Now I have you for the rest of my life'. Across the bottom right hand corner she had written "For Alex, my only love! Now and forever - Kat" He opened the envelope. It contained one sheet of paper, written in German. He read:

Dear Mr Alex,

Please forgive me, I do not speak English. It is with great sadness that I write to tell you of the death of your much-loved friend Katrina. I am heartbroken. and I find it difficult to put on paper to you exactly what I feel. Simply emptiness and pain. I am sending Karl with this parcel because I trust him. Her photograph stood with yours on the piano in the lounge with a deep red rose in water always between them. She put a new rose there every day and spoke to your photo all the time as if you were here. This photo was intended for you. She loved you, Mr Alex, more than anything on this earth. Please, is there anything you can do? The man responsible is now walking free. The second packet contains newspaper cuttings that can tell you far better than I can just how she died. When some time has passed would you please call me. Below is written my home telephone number.
With great sadness,
Sofie

Alex was numb. He sat as if made of stone.

Then, suddenly, the tears began to roll down his cheeks – unbidden and unstoppable. Big, silent tears. He uttered not one sound. He tore open the envelope and laid several newspaper cuttings across the desk. *Sylter Tageblatt and Sylter Rundschau.* He read them again and again. Each word hammered in the pain. He learned how Kat had died.

The *Tageblatt* said that around 3 a.m. an American Military Policeman, off-duty and drunk, had tried to gain entry to Katrina's. The doorman had attempted to prevent him from entering but had been forced aside. The American had gone to the bar where he'd promptly fallen over a stool. Katrina had told Karl and Heinz, her two bodyguards, to throw him out. They got him as far as the door when he managed to break free and pull a gun from his waistband. Screaming obscenities he began firing wildly in all directions. One of the bullets hit Katrina in the head. She died instantly. When the gun was empty, he sat on the floor and cried. The paper reported that the man in question, a black 35 year old Master Sergeant by the name of Abe Miller, had been taken into custody by the German police.

Newspaper reports dated two days later said the Americans were petitioning for the transfer of Miller to their custody for trial.

One day later, the *Sylter Rundschau* carried a report, saying during the autopsy it had been found that Kat was roughly two months pregnant.

Alex stared. *Pregnant?* Kat was carrying his child . . . And now his child and Kat were dead. Killed by some drunken American! He couldn't concentrate. The words were going round and round. Nothing made sense anymore. He walked to the window, opened it wide and leaned out taking deep breaths of fresh cold air to clear his head. Finally, it worked. He returned to the table, put the reports in chronological order and read them all again.

The final *Tagesblatt* report, dated eight days after the shooting, said that after much diplomatic wrangling the Germans had handed Miller over to the US authorities who would be responsible for his trial. And yet Sofie said the man was walking free…Alex sat and thought.

What could he do?

From here? Nothing. He needed to be in Sylt.

He opened the door and walked into the corridor just as the WO-man was puffing his way along towards the exit.

'Oh, hello, Alex. Just off to the Mess. I'll be there for about an hour if anybody needs me.'

'Sir, I need to talk to you.'

'Can it keep till morning?'

'No, Sir.'

'That's two "Sirs" from you in two sentences. I've hardly had that many in all the time I've known you.'

'No, Sir.'

'Three! My God, it must be important. OK. My office. Now.'

'Yes, Sir.'

The WO-man looked at Alex, but he didn't speak. He just turned and puffed his way back whence he had come. Alex followed. 'OK, Alex. Sit down and tell me what it's all about.'

'I can't tell you what it's all about, Sir, but it's important and I need time off.'

'OK, Alex, you can stop calling me Sir now. Servility really doesn't suit you. What do you want?'

'I need time off. Five days minimum. One week max.'

'When?'

'Now.'

The WO-man said nothing, but sat there and eyed him through a cloud of smoke. The ash from his cigarette again fell down the front of his tunic. He didn't move but squinted at Alex when the smoke got into his eyes. Finally he said, 'I know you Alex; ask nothing, give nothing. They all say you're a hard man. Tell me, are you in trouble, son?

Alex blinked. *Son?* 'No, Sir.'

'The truth now, it stays in this room. Word of honour, are you in trouble?'

'No, Sir. I'm not.'

'OK. Good enough. You've got seven days. One week, starting tomorrow. Never mind the forms, just clear off. And Alex … don't let me down.'

'No, Sir.'

'For God's sake, Alex. Enough!'

'OK, Boss.'

'Now bugger off, and I'll see you in a week,' and through a cloud of smoke he waved Alex towards the door.

Alex went back to the Duty NCO's room and closed the door. He opened the key cabinet and took out two keys, each on the end of a red tag. He went to the shelf behind his desk and took down an empty box file. Then he walked across to the big grey safe that stood in the corner of the room. The weapons safe. In this safe, on the top two shelves, in purpose made racks, were forty Smith&Wesson revolvers. On the bottom shelves, also in racks, were eight Sten guns. Each revolver had a number painted on the underside of the butt. He took the end one, number 40, and put it inside the document case, closing it and then locking the safe door. He put the document case on his desk and the key to the gun safe back in the key cabinet. Then with the second key he opened the small green safe which held box upon box of ammunition for the weapons. He took two boxes of ammunition, twenty five shells in each box. He dropped them in his trouser pocket, returned the key to the cabinet and left the office.

He had no idea what he was going to do. He just knew he had to be in Sylt.

9:30 next morning Alex drove off the car carrier onto dry land. He drove out of the station and then stopped immediately in front of the phone cabin. He dropped two *Groschen* coins in and dialed the number written at the bottom of Sofie's letter.

'*Hallo.*'

'Sofie?'

'*Ja...?*'

'Alex here. I'm in Sylt. Where can we meet?'

'Alex! You're here! . . . Oh - I live in the Strandstrasse, right next door to the Nelly Lund family hotel. Do you know it?'

'Hmm. Sort of. Isn't that the street that runs parallel with the Friedrichstrasse, the main street?'

'Yes, Exactly! I live at number 12. The house has a separate garage, standing back a bit.'

'OK, Sofie, I'll be there in half an hour.'

Alex found the house easily enough. A car was parked outside in the street but the garage doors were wide open so he drove straight in. Sofie greeted him at the door with a big hug, tears streaming down her face. They went inside. She made coffee and they sat in the kitchen while she explained again what little she knew of the events of that terrible night. It added nothing really to what Alex had read in the papers, but Sofie astounded him by saying that the Americans weren't even keeping Miller locked up pending his trial, and that he was spending most evenings in the Pigalle, leaving about 11:30, and that Old Kurt, the taxi driver, picked him up at the *Alte Post* on the Bismarckstrasse, and took him back to Camp.

'Sofie, I need somewhere to rest and think. I have an idea, but I need to think it through.'

'Mister Alex, you can stay here. I have two empty rooms. Normally I live with my sister but she is visiting our mother in Hamburg and will not be back until Sunday evening. It is not a problem.'

'OK, Sofie, thanks. I'll go and sleep now if I may, and do you think you could go and close the garage doors? That way no-one will know I'm here. And please, stop calling me Mr Alex. It makes me feel uncomfortable. Just Alex will do.'

She gave him a timid smile, 'OK, Alex, *danke*. I'll show you to your room now and then I'll close up the garage.'

Alex slept the sleep of the dead; nine hours straight through. He showered and shaved, then went downstairs to find Sofie was out but had left him a note:

> *Alex, I've gone to Katrina's.*
> *Will be there until 2am.*
> *See you for breakfast. 9.00 OK?*
> *Food in fridge. Help yourself.*
> *S.*

Alex sat and ate, and while he ate he slowly developed his idea. By midnight he was back in bed, and slept like a baby – conscience clear – until eight next morning.

At breakfast he asked Sofie whether she had a car. 'Yes,' she replied, 'it's parked out front. My sister uses the garage, but with being at the club I come home anywhere between two and five. People are asleep, so I try to be quiet.'

'Right. Now, Westerland is usually wrapped up in bed, or at least all inside by ten, apart from the strip that is.'

Sofie laughed. 'Yes, we are very orthodox people, us Germans – very punctual in our habits. By ten pm the town is dead, apart from the strip, as you said.'

'Sofie, do you think you could take me into town this evening, about ten, and show me just where Old Kurt picks up Abe Miller? And, by the way, how well do you know Old Kurt? What's he like?'

'Yes, of course I'll take you into town. And Old Kurt, well, I've known him for years. Before the war he actually worked for my father – drove one of his lorries. Very late in the war his house was bombed in an American air raid. Kurt was badly injured, his son Helmut, on leave from the front, was killed, and it took two days to dig Gertrud out from the cellar under the house. She was unhurt, unbelievable really. The *Amis*? Mmm . . . let's just say they're not his favourite people.'

'And yet he picks up Abe Miller?'

'Alex, he has to survive. He's seventy, even older probably, and he's not in the best of health. He's lived fourteen years longer than anyone expected him to, and he takes Abe Miller to the Camp because no-one else will. So, he charges him double. It's his way of getting back.'

'But no-one else would take him?'

'No, everyone hates Abe Miller in this town, and because the police handed him back everyone hates the Americans as well. We are being dictated to, Alex, and we don't like it.'

At 10:15 that evening Sofie parked her car on the corner of the street and turned off the lights. 'That there is the exact spot where Kurt picks up Abe Miller. He's here five nights a week.

Never on Sunday and Monday. He's here Tuesday to Saturday, and somewhere between eleven and eleven fifteen Abe Miller will stagger down that street and climb into Kurt's taxi right there, opposite the *Alte Post.*'

'Sofie, do you think you could have a word with Kurt and ask him to be diplomatically ill tomorrow and not pick up Abe Miller?'

Sofie slowly looked across at Alex, and tears started to run down her cheeks.

'I know what you're going to do Alex,' she said, and then she leaned across and put her arms around him, and sobbed uncontrollably.

When they got back home Sofie immediately picked up the phone and dialled Kurt's number. His wife Gertrud answered. No, Kurt was not at home, he'd gone to pick up that *Arschloch* Abe Miller and take him back to camp. When Kurt returned, Sofie said, would she ask him to phone her immediately. Nothing to worry about. Just call her. It was important.

Kurt called just after midnight and spent the next few minutes mumphing about the Americans and their disgusting drunken habits, and about Abe Miller in particular. *'Voll wie 'ne Sau*! Huh! – drunk as the proverbial skunk, as usual. Sometimes I don't know how he finds the taxi. Still, at least he didn't vomit tonight. Yuk!'

Sofie explained what she wanted Kurt to do. Go to the doctor's in the morning, complain he didn't feel too well, something hurts him, then go home and stay there. Do not pick Abe Miller up tomorrow night. Kurt was quiet for some time while he digested this. Then he said, 'Sofie, I've known you all your life, I may be old, but I'm not senile. Be careful, this man is very dangerous, and what about the authorities?' He suddenly stopped, then continued, 'Sofie, do you have a visitor?'

Sofie paused, then gave a hesitant 'Yes.'

'The Policeman?'

'Yes.'

'Ah …, I thought about that many times, and what he would do when he found out.' He paused again, 'Sofie?'

'Yes?'

'Tell him he must be careful. This man is a drunken animal. And big. Very big. What do they feed them on in America? But tell him if he succeeds, he will have the thanks of the whole island. Tell him that. And tell him if he needs to lose himself, then he must come to me. There are still ways for a person to disappear, even so long after the war. We will help him, Sofie. If he needs it, we will help him. Tell him that.'

'I will, Kurt. Thank you.'

'And Sofie? After tonight, we never mention this again. Ever. You understand that?'

'Yes, Kurt, I understand. I thank you – we both thank you.' She put the phone down and burst into tears.

Next morning after breakfast, Sofie went out to the market and then to Katrina's. She had paperwork to do. Alex tried to keep calm but found himself pacing up and down, going round and round in circles, frequently washing his hands, and the number of times he urinated had reached double figures by mid-afternoon. He developed a pain in his neck at the base of the skull; it went up into his brain and burned like a poker. Above his heart he had a burning sensation that seemed as though it wanted to choke off his air supply. *God, if this is how he felt now, how would he feel later?* He found himself shaking. He swallowed three aspirin he'd found in the kitchen cabinet and went upstairs to lie on his bed. He promptly fell into a deep sleep.

Suddenly he felt someone gently shaking him, 'Alex. Alex, wake up! It's nine o'clock.' Alex was instantly alert. He felt refreshed; his brain was clear. He held out his arms; his hands weren't shaking. He felt good. He felt strong. He could do it…

Alex rose and showered, but he couldn't eat. Just a glass of water. He sat on the couch with Sofie and held her hands. 'Listen to me, Sofie. I want you to drop me on the corner of Wiesenstrasse, just before you get to the *Alte Friesenstube* at 10:30. That's one block away from where I need to be. When you've dropped me, go to Katrina's and behave as normal. I know it's difficult, but you must do it. At midnight I want you to park on the car park of the *Kurhaus*. Wait until quarter past. If I don't turn up go back to Katrina's. I will either see you or I won't see you. OK?'

She nodded, her eyes full of tears again.

At 10:25, Sofie's Volkswagen pulled up on the corner of Wiesenstrasse. Alex leaned across and kissed her gently on the cheek. He took her hands. 'Sofie, be calm. Go to Katrina's and remember: midnight on the car park. Wait fifteen minutes, if I don't show, go back to work. If I do, we go to your place. OK?'

She took a deep breath, 'OK.' She kissed him on the forehead. He then climbed out onto the pavement and watched as she drove away. He felt nervous, but not in the way he'd been earlier. He wanted this to happen. He walked slowly along the street and then turned into Bismarckstrasse. A hundred metres away he could see the street lamp opposite the *Alte Post* where Kurt usually parked. Alex settled back into a shop doorway and waited. Time seemed to stand still. Half an hour later he'd only been there five minutes. He tried to keep calm. He was on edge. He wanted it over. Ten forty five, ten fifty, eleven o'clock. Nothing. He stepped out of the doorway and walked slowly along the street, keeping close to the wall and keeping the street light on the opposite side of the road. Fifty metres from the corner he stopped and stepped into another doorway. He waited. Eleven oh five. Eleven ten. Then he heard them: footsteps. Uneven footsteps. Then a figure shambled into the light cast by the street lamp. Alex looked. A man. A big man. A black man. He was swaying as he stood. He pulled a pack of cigarettes from his pocket and flipped one towards his mouth. He missed and the cigarette fell to the ground. He swore. He took another out of the packet, put it in his mouth and lit it with a lighter. Swaying; all the time swaying. Alex stepped out of the doorway and walked out into the road towards him. *Forty metres.* He kept walking, making no effort to keep quiet. *Thirty metres.* Still the man had his back towards him. Then the man ceased swaying and seemed to listen. He lifted his head and turned. *Twenty metres.* He looked directly at Alex. He raised his right hand and drunkenly waved, 'Hi there.' *Ten metres…* Alex replied, 'Hello Abe.'

'Do I know you?' He peered at Alex. Recognition dawned. 'Yeah, I know you, you're that Brit cop. That time at the Pigalle. The riot.'

Close enough. Slowly Alex took his right hand out of his pocket, clicking the safety catch off as he brought up the revolver. He pointed it at Abe Miller's face. His hand was steady.

'Jeezes, man! What the fuck yer doin'!'

Alex didn't speak. He was totally calm – like ice. Then, he squeezed the trigger. Twice. Exactly as he'd been taught at Netheravon, in what seemed a lifetime ago, in another world. The noise was so great, Alex was sure the whole island would hear it. Abe Miller's face and head disintegrated, going backwards and upward in a great spume of red and white spray. Calmly, Alex clicked the safety catch back on, put the revolver in his pocket, turned, stepped back into the shadows and walked slowly toward his meeting with Sofie. Surprisingly he felt no reaction. Nothing. Neither elation nor fear. Simply a kind of flatness; an emptiness, a void. He'd killed a man. He'd avenged Katrina. Surely this wasn't how it was supposed to be. It meant no more to him than if he'd just swatted a fly.

Next day Alex drove slowly into the rail terminal to catch the morning train that would take him across the sea, back to the mainland. There were seven cars in the queue in front of him, and each car was being stopped by the police. Then Alex's turn came. The policeman held up his hand. Alex stopped and wound down his window. The policeman stepped in front of his car and looked at his number plate – GH 67B. He came towards Alex, 'British?'

'Yes.' Alex handed him his Warrant Card.

'Oh! A policeman.'

'Yep.'

'Going on leave?'

'No, been to visit a friend.'

'*Alles in Ordnung! Gute Fahrt,*' and with that he waved him forward.

Eight hours later, Alex was back in his own bed in Sundern.

He slept peacefully.

BACK AT SUNDERN

27- AWOL - Again!
28- X Marks the Spot
29- Brian, Absinthe and Mind that Fucking Tree!
30- The Ice Maiden and Bullshit, Absolute Bullshit!
31- Demob

Chapter 27

AWOL - again!

Against orders, Alex – in uniform – had climbed aboard a military train in Germany, then a boat from Holland, followed by two more trains, and travelled back home to the UK simply by showing his warrant card. He was, in effect, absent without leave. So far, he'd been absent for four days, then . . . Sunday, 6 pm. Alex lifted the phone and sent the following telegram via the operator:

> O.C.
> No 1 Provost & Security Services Detachment
> RAF Sundern
> BFPO 39
> Germany
> Getting married Tuesday.
> Returning Wednesday.
> See you Thursday.
> Alex

Monday morning the news swept through the camp like wildfire. The WAAFs, without exception, were incensed. Dina announced that she was going to kill Alex, but only after she'd castrated him with a blunt knife. Many offered to help. Alex also received a telegram from OC No 1 P&SS Det.:

> Congratulations.
> Delighted with news. Look forward your return home.
> Everyone.

No mention of being arrested and slung in the nick on return.

Thursday afternoon a Landrover picked Alex up from Gütersloh railway station and took him straight to the detachment. The WO-man was waiting. 'My office, Alex.' Alex followed the cloud of smoke. 'Close the door, Alex, and sit down.' He indicated a chair in front of his desk.

'First. Sincere congratulations are in order. Everybody wishes you well. The CO is at Two TAF, but he's included in that. Second. You nearly gave me a heart attack. When I heard what had happened I took a gamble and told the Boss that Friday I'd sanctioned a week's emergency leave. Problems at home, that sort of thing. When your telegram arrived the boss called me in. He waved the telegram in the air. *"Is this the end of the problem, or the start of a new one for young Alex?"* The WO-man parodied the CO waving his arms in the air. *"That's all,"* he said, and then he sent a telegram off to you.' The WO-man eyed Alex and went on, 'Hope you won't have problems with that young lassie here. All the WAAFs are against you which, I suppose makes quite a change in that department. By the way, you're on duty at 22:00. Thought it would keep you out of mischief, at least for tonight. Get Paddy to run you to the billet and get some shuteye. He can pick you up again tonight for duty.'

Alex stood up, 'Thanks for—'

The WO-man held up his hand. 'Not necessary, Alex; just go and get some rest.'

Chapter 28

X Marks the Spot

By 22:00 that evening Alex sat behind his desk, absently sipping a cup of coffee. He'd slept like a log - only a few hours, but a cool shower took away any remnants of drowsiness, and he felt good. Ready to tackle the world again…

At 22:05 the phone rang. Alex picked it up, 'P&SS Detachment.'

'Why?'

'Hello, Dee.'

'Why…? Why'd you do it, Alex? Why?'

'It was necessary, Dee. Had to be.'

'We need to talk, Alex. We can't leave it like this.'

'I'm married now, Dee. There's nothing to say. That's it.'

'I'm coming over.'

'The Detachment's locked. I can't let you in. Anybody sees you in here and tomorrow morning they'll hang me.'

'Listen, Alex. All calls for the Detachment come through the PBX. Jenny will monitor the lines. Anything comes in, she'll know. Lock the Detachment and I'll open up the PBX door. We talk tonight and I promise I'll never bother you again. You know I keep my word, Alex.'

Alex paused, then made up his mind. 'OK. I'm coming.'

They talked, back and forth, back and forth, till two in the morning. Alex stood up. 'Look, Dee. It's getting us nowhere. I'm married, that's it. I need to go.'

Dina started to cry.

'Unlock the door, Dee.'

She unlocked the corridor door and Alex walked out. Dina followed him and locked the door behind her. Then she ran the length of corridor and leaned against the locked Detachment door. She stared back at Alex, tears rolling down her cheeks, but then, through her tears, she smiled.

'I love you, you know,' she whispered.

First she kicked off her shoes. Then her tie, followed by her shirt; she literally ripped it off, buttons bouncing off the tiles. Next, her skirt joined the heap and she leaned back against the door.

'I want to say goodbye properly, Alex. Just once more. Once more to last me forever.' Then she removed her bra and let it fall to the ground. 'Alex, please.' Finally she stepped out of her panties. 'Alex, please . . . make love to me.'

Alex, ever the gentleman, obliged.

Next morning, the NCO i/c PBX wanted to know who was responsible for painting a bright red "X" outside the police detachment's connecting door.

There were rumours, which were never confirmed, but each time Alex visited the NCOs' side of the NAAFI, the jukebox across the communal bar and in the ORs' side sprang to life with Connie Francis's rendition of "Frankie" – *Once I was your sweetheart, now I'm just a friend.*

Also, someone had gained access to the NCOs' bar and put up a sign, again painted in red, which loudly proclaimed:

ALEX IS AN ASSHOLE

Chapter 29

Brian, Absinthe and Mind that Fucking Tree

The following Monday evening Brian banged on Alex's door, 'Open up, Alex, it's party time!' Alex opened up to find Brian standing there with a bottle of something in his hand and a silly grin on his face. 'Party time, Alex. We need to celebrate your marriage!'

'By the look on your face you started some time ago.'

Brian held up the bottle, 'Absinthe. Ever had any?'

'No.'

'I'm told it'll blow the top of your head off.'

'Wonderful. You know where the glasses are.'

For the next two hours they yarned and steadily emptied the bottle, while the world was steadily becoming a foggier, less defined place. Suddenly there was a loud banging about downstairs and a voice called, 'Alex, you up there?'

Alex stood up – the room spun. He grabbed hold of the table and proclaimed, 'Jeezes, I'm pissed!'

'Makes two of us, then!' Brian stood up and promptly fell over.

'Alex!'

'Coming!'

He struggled to get Brian, who was now quietly giggling away to himself, upright. He propped him against the wardrobe. 'Bri, can you hear me?' Brian continued to giggle.

'Look, stand there and try not to fall over, OK?'

Silence.

'OK, Bri?'

A mumble.

Alex opened the door, went to the top of the stairs and looked down. Jock and Taffy were inside the front door.

'Bloody hell, Alex! You're pissed!' said Jock as he looked up at the now swaying Alex. 'You're duty driver tonight. You're on in half an hour!'

'Bollocks to that! I'm not letting him drive me tonight. He's pissed as a newt,' said Taff.

At that moment, Brian staggered out of the room, stood swaying at the top of the stairs next to Alex, peered at the two downstairs, raised his hand in greeting, took one step forward and walked straight out into space. He hit the third or fourth step with a thump and then slid the rest of the way downstairs. He lay at the bottom and didn't move.

'Alex! Stay where you are!' shouted Jock, 'Don't want you down here as well.'

Taffy bent over the inert figure of Brian. 'Well, at least he's still breathing. Hope he's not broken his back. I think we should leave him and call the medics.'

'Can't do that, Taff; he'd be in all sorts of shit. Let's try and move him,' said Jock.

'OK. You lift his shoulders. I'll try his legs.' They moved him, all of six inches. A dead weight. Brian grunted, then mumbled something unintelligible to himself. Then he farted. 'Better . . .' he said quite clearly, and promptly went straight back to sleep.

'I reckon he's OK,' said Jock. 'Totally pissed, but OK. Problem is we're never going to get him up the stairs.'

'Why don't we strip his bed and make it up again down here, in the corridor? Nobody's likely to come in. Only Bri and Alex live here.'

So, blankets and pillows were thrown downstairs. Brian was then somehow dragged into his new bed, silly grin still on his face, and he slept the night away on the corridor floor, oblivious to everything.

'Alex,' said Jock. 'Climb in bed and sleep it off. I'd do your shift myself, but I've been on all day and I'm knackered. Taff here's banned and can't drive until he gets his licence back. Just go to bed.'

'Problem is, if I do that and the boss finds out he'll chop my bloody legs off.'

'Yes, and what happens if you have a prang?' interrupted Taff.

'Oh, Ye of little faith.'

'Alex, you're pissed. You can't even stand straight. I'm not going out with you.'

'OK. I'll drop you off at married quarters, but if I don't check out and the boss finds out, I'm in the shit. Drive us up to the Detachment, Jock, and get the keys to the duty Volks off Paddy – tell him I'm outside talking to Taff – then put the Landrover away and I'll take the Volks out. And keep your mouth shut.'

Jock did as asked and then headed for home.

Alex and Taff sat in the Volks with the windows wound down, and while Alex fumbled with the key trying to find the ignition, the rain poured in.

'Can't find the hole.'

'Never known you have trouble before. Maybe it needs a bit of fur around it!'

For some reason Alex found this incredibly funny and collapsed in laughter. Taffy took the key from him and put it in the ignition. 'OK. All done. You ready, Alex?'

'Where's the road, Taff?'

'Christ! You serious?'

Alex collapsed in laughter again. Then he turned the key, nimbly popped it into first, and promptly stalled the engine.

'This really is not a good idea, Alex.'

'OK. I'll take you home.'

'Alex, if you take me home and then you have a prang on your own I'm in the shit for letting you go out.'

'And if I have a prang and you're with me, then we're both in the shit anyway. Which shit do you prefer, Taff?'

'Alex, just let's go. That way,' he said, pointing right. Alex drove slowly towards the camp exit and gave the blue light a twirl so that the German guard would lift the barrier.

'I'm shutting these windows, the rain's pissing in!'

'Don't do that Taff! We'll mist up and then we can see bugger-all! You know what these Volkses are like.'

Taffy wound his window up anyway. They passed through the barrier and Alex accelerated. 'Turn left at the top of the road, Alex.'

'Can't see sweet-bugger-all through the windscreen!' said Alex, as he leaned forward to clear it with the back of his glove.

'Mind the fucking tree!' screamed Taffy, and he leaned forward across Alex, jerking the steering wheel to the left.

'What fucking tree?'

Taffy hauled up the hand brake. The Volks stalled.

'That fucking tree!' shouted Taffy, jabbing a thumb in the direction of the offending obstacle. 'The tree at the top of the fucking road. It's been there longer than you have! It's always been there! Jeezes, Alex! You're totally pissed!'

'I'm hungry.'

'What?!'

'I'm hungry. Your missus make me my sandwiches tonight?'

'Alex! We're sitting in the middle of the fucking road, not going anywhere, and you're *hungry*?'

'Can't see a thing, Taff. We're all misted up.'

'Look, Alex. Take this thing out of gear, start up and park over there on the grass verge.'

Silence.

Taff knocked the car out of gear, then he turned the ignition. The Volks fired. He directed the air towards the windscreen, full blast. They sat there not speaking, while the windscreen slowly cleared. 'OK, Alex. Park it on the grass verge over there. Think you can do that?'

'…'course I can!'

They jerked across the main road and parked on the verge. Taffy pulled on the hand brake and turned off the engine.

'Alex, you're pissed, totally pissed. I've never seen you like this before.'

'Never been married before.'

'Is that what it was? Soon be a bloody wake if you keep driving like this!'

'Bri wanted to celebrate…'

'Yeah, well, Bri's not duty driver. You are! And you're bloody kaylied!'

'What's the missus made for me tonight, Taff?'

'No idea!'

'Gimme a sandwich, Taff. Any coffee? And let's sit here for a bit.'

'Alex! We're a hundred yards from the camp gate, plus we're on the main road. What if the Old Man drives by and sees us. What then?'

'We could have a picnic.'

'Alex, you're mad! Stark staring bloody mad!'

'You're the fourth person to tell me that since I got back last Thursday.'

'Who's told you then?'

'The WO-man, Dina, Brian and now you.'

Taffy handed Alex a sandwich and poured him a cup of coffee from a flask. 'Must be something in it then! Now, stuff that in your face and shut up for five minutes!'

'Hmmm. Tuna. Love tuna. Love your missus. But she's married to you.'

'Stow it, Alex. Just sit still, shut up and eat!'

Alex ate his sandwich. Then he ate Taffy's, plus he drank all the coffee. 'Need a winkle, Taff,' and with that he opened the car door, stepped out into the pouring rain, walked to the front of the Volkswagen and in the full glare of the headlights proceeded to pinkle all down his left leg and across his shoes before, at last, getting the trajectory right and projecting an arc up and finally down into the roadside ditch. He climbed back in the car, totally soaked.

Taffy sniffed. 'Jeez, Alex, you stink! You pissed all down your trousers and over your shoes.'

'We used to do that when we were kids.'

'What?!'

'Squeeze the end of our willie so that it blows up like a balloon in the middle and then let go, and see who can wee the highest up the wall.'

'Well, tonight you lost 'cause you pissed all over yourself. Look, Alex, we need to move it, you know? You all right to drive? How'd you feel now?'

'I feel wonderful, Taff, wonderful! I've eaten all your sandwiches, drank all your coffee. I can see at least two of everything – except the road, of course. I can't see that at all.'

Taffy turned the key in the ignition and put the blowers full on the windscreen. 'Fit to drive, Alex? Seriously now. Are you OK?'

'I doubt it, but never mind. Where would you like to go on this wet and windy night?'

'Aren't we supposed to go to Rheda?'

'I don't know.'

'What do the docs say?'

'Nothing. I never filled them in.'

'You mean we've got no docs? No authorisation?'

'Taffy, I'll do it when we get back. I know what, how'd you fancy a trip down Kassel way?'

'But that's a couple of hundred kilometres away, there and back!'

'So? We'll tootle along there, then turn off and drop in at Borgentreich on the way back, get the duty cook to do us a fry-up, have a chinwag with whoever's in the guardroom and then toddle off back here. We could be in bed by five.'

Taffy looked across at Alex and slowly shook his head in utter disbelief. 'Do you know what? . . . You're certifiable!'

'I know, but it's much better than being a boring, old Welsh fart!' and with that he clicked the car into first, released the handbrake and spun the wheels away from the verge. 'Borgy, here we come!'

They drove in relative silence for the next hour. Alex peering through the windscreen and seeing practically nothing, while at the same time fighting the inclination to fall asleep. The further they went, the harder the rain. It was coming down in sheets. Soon after departing, Taffy fell asleep and started to snore. He snored for the next forty five minutes. Alex suddenly turned the siren on. Taffy shot up. 'What's up? What's up?!'

'Early morning call. Why should you sleep while I drive?'

'Where are we?'

'No idea. Can't see a thing. It's like the black hole of Calcutta out there. Lucky there's no traffic.'

'What time is it?'

'Just gone midnight; another half hour and we'll be there,' Alex replied. He accelerated and that's when he saw the bend. He immediately touched the brake. Mistake! The car's back end swung round. Alex turned into the skid; nothing happened. Foot off the accelerator, the Volks continued to spin. Round once, round twice. Then the car hit the side of the road and slid across the grass verge on the opposite side of the road where it slammed sideways into a stone wall. The engine died. They sat there stunned; no-one spoke. Taffy with his mouth wide open and with his hands pressed firmly against the dashboard. Alex grimly holding on to the steering wheel. 'Well, I guess we've landed, Taff. ...You OK?' Taffy nodded. 'Are you hurt anywhere?' Taffy shook his head, then slowly turned and looked at Alex. 'They'll lock us up and throw the key away. You know that, don't you?'

'Why are you always such a pessimist, Taffy?'

'Pessimist? You've just written off a car, we've got no docs to authorise our being here, and you're pissed as a newt!'

'*Was* pissed as a newt, Taff. *Was*! Now I'm stone cold sober, believe me. Sit tight while I see if I can drive this thing off the grass so we can look at the damage.' He started up and drove gingerly off the soaking grass verge and back onto the road. They both climbed out to inspect the damage.

'Blimey, Alex, the whole side's smashed in!'

Alex took a closer look. 'OK. Front bumper U/S. Front wing caved in. Passenger door dented. Back wing likewise. Could be worse.'

Taffy looked at him, eyes wide open in surprise. 'How?'

'Well, we could be dead.'

Shaking his head in disbelief, Taffy only managed to mutter, 'Now what?'

'Well, it drives. So I guess the best thing is to get it to Borgentreich and let somebody take a look at it.'

'Alex, it's gone midnight. Everybody's in bed!'

'Then we'll just have to get them up, won't we? Come on, hop in, we'll head for Borgy.'

Alex did a three-point turn and then headed off back down the road in the general direction of Borgentreich.

'Got a problem, Taff. I hold the wheel straight and the car goes right. If I want to go straight on I have to hold the wheel to the left. It drives like a crab. I'm going to have to take it very slowly. We'll be there in half an hour.'

Fifty minutes later they pulled up before the camp barrier. Nobody there. Alex put the blue light on and sounded the hooter. Two blasts. A head peered out of the guardroom window, saw the Volks and came to lift the barrier. Alex drove through and parked in front of the guardroom.

'Hi, Geordie, how's tricks?' asked Alex.

'Oh, it's you Alex. What are you doing down this way?'

'Thought we'd have an early breakfast.'

Taffy just looked at him, saying nothing.

'Got a bit of a problem Geordie.' Alex showed him the side of the car.

'I'm impressed!'

Taffy looked at him in disbelief. *Another nutter.*

'Have you got a mechanic you can lean on Geordie?'

'What? Now?' He looked at his watch.

'Yes, now. I need somebody to look at this car and see just how bad it is. The thing drives like a crab.'

'I've actually got two mechanics who started jankers today. One week. Both pissed in town.'

'Know them?'

'Alex! On this camp I know everybody!'

'Where's the Jerry guard for the barrier?'

'Asleep in one of the cells.'

Alex laughed. 'I see you run a tight ship!'

'He's a good guy. There's nothing to do after midnight.'

'Wake him up and send him to get those two mechanics back here, pronto.'

'I'll do it, Alex; less fuss. No arguments. You watch the shop. I'll be ten minutes.'

The Volks was inspected and then test-driven.

'You've got a major problem,' said the first mechanic. 'What's your name?' Alex asked.

'Geordie.' 'Jeezes – not another one!' The two Geordies grinned at each other.

'OK, tell.'

'There's no real chassis on these vehicles,' explained Geordie, 'and on this one the underneath is twisted.'

'And?'

'Write-off.'

'You're joking!'

'Nope.'

Alex stood and thought. Taffy was slumped on a stool in the corner, biting his nails. He didn't say anything; just sat staring at the floor.

'OK, Geordie. Can you and your mate here hammer out these dents and then spray this side to match the rest of the car?' Everybody just stared at Alex.

'You really *are* mad, you know.' This now from Taff in the corner.

Alex held up his hand. 'Can you do it, yes or no?'

The two mechanics looked at each other. 'Yes,' said Geordie.

'How long?'

Geordie thought. 'Three, three and a half hours, give or take.'

'OK. Do it. Geordie here will remove you from the jankers sheet, and I'm sure he'll look favourably on you if you get pissed again.' He looked at guardroom Geordie, who nodded. 'Oh, and by the way, when you've done it, mouth shut, OK? I mean it – mouth shut!'

Both mechanics nodded.

'Right. Off you go. Taffy, cookhouse. Time for breakfast!'

At 05.40 the car was delivered back to the guardroom. It shone; not a mark to be seen.

'Try not to touch the body, the paint's not quite dry.'

'At least it's not raining. Thanks fellas. See you Geordie.' Geordie nodded.

'Taffy, in the car. Let's go. Need to be back well before eight.'

The car looked beautiful. But it still drove like a crab.

'How do we explain this, Alex?'

'No idea. Let me think.'

They drove in silence all the way back to Sundern, and then straight to the MT section. 07:50. They both climbed out of the car.

'What now, Alex?'

'We wait for Mac.'

On cue, the man himself strolled in.

'Hi Alex, Taff. *Alles klar?*' Mac loved to exercise his German.

Alex explained the problem and handed the keys to Mac, who took the Volks for a drive round camp. 'Write-off,' he said when he arrived back, 'Bugger of a job.'

'Got a sledgehammer, Mac?'

'Sure,' he pointed.

Alex walked over and picked up the sledgehammer, walked back to the Volks and promptly swung it into the front wing. Once, twice, three times. He kept going until it was well and truly smashed in. The rear wing was treated the same way, then the front passenger door was dented and scratched.

Taffy looked on speechless, sheer terror written on his face. Mac just stood there grinning. 'I take it you know exactly what you're doing?' he asked with a chuckle.

'Yes, but you haven't seen me doing it.'

Mac stuck his hands in his pockets and shrugged, still chuckling. Alex took the docs out of the car and tossed the keys to Mac. 'One accident-damaged car delivered to you by me. That's all you need to know.'

Mac nodded. Alex stood and thought. 'Mac, you got a driver who can take Taff home?'

'Sure.'

'Taff, go home. See a Kraut doctor and get a sick note.'

'What!?' Taff croaked.

'Do it! You've got the runs, stomach upset, anything. I don't care but get a note for at least three days. I'll get the docs filled in plus I'll do an accident report and draw the diagram. Now then, you remember where we had the accident?' He looked at Taff, who just nodded. 'OK. 50 metres before that bend a road joins it from the left. It's a T-junction.' Taffy nodded again. 'Right. A black Karmann Ghia came belting out of that road and didn't stop at the stop sign. I braked to avoid running into him and we went into a spin. Exactly as it happened. Black. Karmann. Ghia. And *no* idea of number! You got that?'

Taffy nodded open-mouthed, not taking his eyes off Alex.

'That's all you need to remember, OK?'

'We'll never get away with it!'

'Want to bet?'

Taffy turned away and walked over to the MT office to wait for his driver. Mac came closer to Alex. 'I could change the front tyres. Got some duds here. You know, worn tread. A note in the report to that effect might help. What do you think?'

'Do it, Mac. Poor grip on a night like that. Just the job. Lucky not to be killed.' Alex waved to Taff. 'I'm off for a kip now. I'll call it in this afternoon. You visit the doc, OK?'

As if in a trance, Taffy lifted his hand and nodded. Not a word passed his lips.

Alex headed for the billet.

Chapter 30

The Ice Maiden and Bullshit, absolute bullshit!

Two days later, Alex sat behind one of the desks in the duty NCO's room drinking coffee and reading a month-old magazine. Ten o'clock, and he was standing in for Charlie while he nipped to the NAAFI shop. He'd already been down town and sorted out a shunt. Flight Looi's wife from Gütersloh had hit an old man on a bike while doing the school run. A broken wrist and lots of tears.

'I didn't see him, I really didn't see him. I'm so sorry. Tell him, tell him I'm sorry. It was my fault.'

Alex sorted it all out. Told the wife to lock the car and leave it, then delivered the child to school and ran the wife back to married quarters at Marienfeld.

'What's your name?'

'Alex.'

'Mine's Lisa.'

'I know.' She looked at him.

'It's on the accident report.'

'Oh, yes. Of course. I'd forgotten. Look, are you in a hurry? I could make us a cup of coffee or something. You've been very kind, taking Liz to school and running me home. Do you give this service to everyone?' She moved closer.

Alex's antenna started to glow. He took a step back.

'Not everybody, Lisa. Depends on the circumstances. A cup of coffee would be nice, but I've got to fly. Need to be back at the Detachment by ten. Things to do and all that.'

'Will I see you again? Will I be charged, or anything like that?'

Alex ignored the first question and concentrated on the second as he made his way toward the front door. 'Shouldn't think so, but it's really up to the German police. I'll see what I can do. Maybe a caution, maybe a small fine. No idea, really, but don't worry about it, OK?' Alex opened the front door and walked out into the garden. 'Bye, Lisa. Take care.'

She blew him a kiss. 'Bye, Alex.'

Alex climbed into the Landrover, waved and drove away. At the beginning, he'd been surprised. Now he no longer was. There were always ladies looking for a little excitement while hubby was away playing war games with NATO. And a white hat was always an attraction.

Charlie told him that Taffy's wife had been in to see the WO-man. He'd got a stomach bug or something like that. Diarrhoea, vomiting. The doc had apparently said four days off. The WO-man had told her he should take a week. Alex smiled to himself. *Great!* No sooner had he settled himself behind the desk than Hella walked in with his coffee. 'Saw you drive up, Alex darling; thought you'd be ready for a cup.'

'Thanks Hella, you're a doll.' She blew him a kiss and walked off. She knew he was watching her bottom, so she gave it an exaggerated twitch as she reached the door. She laughed to herself but didn't look back. Alex gazed after her. He liked Hella. In fact, it was more than that. In the beginning she'd called him *Schatzi* until Alex told her he was nobody's *bloody little treasure* and he didn't like it. She'd looked at him quite calmly and said that in that case she'd call him Darling. *Alex, darling*, she'd cooed. He hated it even more than *Schatzi*, and she knew it – and that's why she did it.

He'd been there about three months when she walked in one morning and announced as usual: 'Coffee time, Alex darling.' Alex was alone. She put the coffee on the desk and instead of turning and leaving the room she asked, 'Alex darling, what do you think of me?' Alex stared at her.

'Cat got your tongue, Alex? Not shy, are you?'

Alex thought. Then he answered. 'No. But I'm not sure what you want.'

'The truth, Alex. From you, always the truth.'

Alex cleared his throat. He felt nervous and his mouth was suddenly dry. He took a sip of coffee and stared up at Hella. She was tall, almost as tall as he was. Maybe five ten, and she had beautiful long blond hair and the clearest, brightest blue eyes. She was gorgeous. Alex cleared his throat again. 'Well, I think you're beautiful. I think you're smart – both clever and smart, and dress smart, and I think …' He stopped. What else could he say? That he felt like screwing her? Which he did. As did everyone else in the Detachment.

She was talking to him. He looked up. 'Sorry. I missed that.'

'What do they say about me, Alex? I know that they call me behind my back "The Ice Lady" or "The Ice Maiden". They think I'm a lesbian. Do *you* think I'm a lesbian, Alex?'

'Err, no …' *Where is this going?* He was losing it.

'Would you like to go out for a drink with me, Alex?'

Alex's knees started to tremble under the desk.

'Would you, Alex?'

'Yes.' *Hell, why not? Nothing ventured and all that.*

'Let's see, when are you next free, Alex?' She walked to the Detachment roster and ran a finger down it. 'You work too hard, you know.'

'It's what I do.'

‘You’re free on Wednesday evening, Alex. Wednesday is a quiet day in town. We could go to *Zum Wiesengrund.*’ She stopped. ‘No. I have a better idea. You will come to my apartment and I will cook dinner. Would you like that, Alex?’

Alex had trouble finding his voice. ‘Yes, sounds good,’ he answered as nonchalantly as possible. It came out something like a croak. Nobody, but nobody, had ever come on to him like this; so openly, so blatantly. He realised he’d got an erection. God, he hoped he didn’t have to stand up.

‘Good! Wednesday evening then. I will meet you in *Steiner’s* – that is your place, isn’t it? – at seven pm. We will have a drink – one drink – Alex, and then we will go to my apartment for dinner. You will not be disappointed, I promise.’ She walked towards the door, turned and added, ‘I am a very good cook,’ then smiled and walked across the corridor to her own office.

And, as Alex now reminded himself, never would he forget that Wednesday night with Hella. Dinner had gone well. Hella was indeed a superb cook. Then they moved to a sofa, and after Hella had poured them each a glass of wine, her story began to unfold.

She had been born in Munich in August 1932 and tonight was her twenty-sixth birthday. Her father had been a high-ranking NAZI official and her mother, who came from Bavaria, had met and fallen in love with him on a trip to Berlin in the summer of 1931. Her father had been married – he already had three daughters – but her mother had been devoted to him and so she had stayed. At the beginning times had been hard, but as the NAZI party had steadily risen to power, her father had also risen through the ranks.

By 1937 Hella and her mother had been installed in a beautiful apartment on the *Unter den Linden* in Berlin. Her father had kept his two families separate, although his wife had known that Hella and her mother existed. From 1938 onwards he had always been a member of Hitler's closest entourage. 'And,' she added, 'in September 1938 he was at that now-famous meeting in Munich, with your Mr Neville Chamberlain. Peace for our time indeed. That man was a fool!'

Throughout the early Forties, the family had had the best of everything, but then in September 1943, Hella, at the age of eleven, had been sent to live with an aunt – her father's sister – in Gütersloh. The aunt had married into the famous Wolf family who were highly respected locally, and who were reputable and nationally acclaimed wire rope manufacturers. Her father had been a far-seeing man, unlike some of his peers, and had believed that for Germany the war was now lost. He had papers prepared which showed that Hella was now the daughter of Aunt Ilse. Ilse's husband had been killed in a bombing raid on Peenemünde. Hella had remained with her aunt until her death two years previously. 'Not a very noble death. She fell under a train at Gütersloh railway station.'

'What happened to your real mother?'

'She was killed in a bombing raid on Berlin.'

'And your father?'

'He stayed with Hitler until almost the very end. Then he got out and tried to make it to Switzerland. He had false papers. However, the Allies had photographs of everyone they were looking for and he was caught. My father was, after all, quite famous.'

Alex looked at her, right eyebrow raised in question. 'What happened?'

'They sentenced him to death at Nuremberg. But,' and here she smiled, 'like Uncle Hermann he was able to cheat the hangman. He died at a time of his own choosing.'

Alex did not speak. She looked at him, 'Are you shocked, Alex?'

'No. Why?'

'Most people would bc.'

'We can't choose our parents, Hella. But why did you tell me all this?'

'Because I had to tell somebody, Alex, and I chose you. I chose you because I trust you. Will you keep my secret, Alex? Always?'

Alex nodded.

'Right. You've heard that part of my life, now I'll tell you the rest. My aunt put me in a private school, Schloss Heesen, some sixty kilometres from here on the way to Dortmund. I used to come home at weekends. I loved it there. I never believed I would, but I did. And it was there that I discovered I preferred girls rather than boys . . . if you know what I mean.'

Alex nodded again, not trusting himself to speak. All he knew was that by now he had a gigantic erection and he hoped she wouldn't notice. He held his wine glass with two hands in his lap and tried to concentrate on something else. It was impossible. He could smell her, not her perfume, but her womanly smell. It was beautiful. He tried not to think about it.

'More wine, Alex?' She smiled at him, then stood up and fetched the bottle from the cooler on the dining table. She stood in front of him and slowly filled his glass to the brim. 'Why don't you take a sip, Alex?'

Slowly he raised the glass to his lips, trying not to spill a drop. She stood there watching him, smiling, their eyes locked into one another. Alex took a sip. He could feel his heart thumping hard in his chest. Hella bent down, briefly brushed her hand tenderly over his hair and then kissed him gently on his left cheek. For a moment he closed his eyes. Her smell was almost overwhelming. Then she straightened up. Softly she said, 'So you see, Alex, they are right, your friends. I *am* a lesbian. They call me the Ice Maiden. But that's where they are wrong. I have passion. I just don't show it.' Then she added, 'Do you know what they call you behind your back, Alex?'

Alex shook his head, still not trusting himself to speak. His mouth felt dry.

She went on, 'When they are being polite they call you the Ice Man, because you too never show your feelings. No matter how dirty the job, you never show emotion. You just do it. But I know you have feelings, Alex. I believe you have passion.' Her eyes never left his; her voice almost beseeching. She reached out and took his hand. 'Tonight the Ice Man and the Ice Maiden are going to make magic. And Alex,' she hesitated, her eyes burning into his, 'in that sense I really am a maiden, because I have never made love with a man in my life.'

Alex held her gaze, took a breath, and gently squeezed her hand. He smiled at her and slowly stood. She looked down at him – a surprised smile on her face – then locking her eyes with his, 'Don't be afraid, Alex. I'm not fragile and I won't break.'

They made love continuously throughout the night. Sometimes soft and gentle; sometimes hard and wild. She became hysterical when Alex told her about Renate and all the things you could do with a willie he'd learned when he was fifteen. In the grey light of dawn she lay in his arms and cried. Quiet, gentle sobs, and as the tears rolled down onto his chest he held her tight and kissed her hair. 'Hush,' he said, 'don't cry. You'll be alright.'

'I'm crying Alex, because it never can be. I am what I am, and us being together forever would be a disaster. When you're young Alex you wish with all your heart for a night like this, a wonderful, magical night of love. Well, I've had it, we've had it, Alex. And I thank you; it was beautiful.' She sat up and looked at him; tears were drying on his cheeks. She kissed his eyes. 'I love you, Alex, but it can't be. You know that?'

He nodded.

Then she glanced down and smiled yet again. 'I see – the night isn't over yet. What a wonderful way to start a new day!'

His daydreams were suddenly shattered as Sergeant Meredith, Head of Traffic, came storming into the office and slammed a handful of papers on the desk in front of Alex, making the cup and saucer rattle and Alex's coffee overflow.

'Bullshit!' he shouted. 'ABSOLUTE BULLSHIT!'

'And a good morning to you, too. I take it you have a problem?'

Spittle was working its way from the corner of his mouth down to his chin. Somebody was obviously very pissed off. 'I feel honoured; pray tell.'

'This report you put in to Bill. It's all lies! It's simply not possible for an accident to happen the way you described it and cause all that damage to a Volkswagen. I know that stretch of the road. For a start there is no road that joins it. There is no T-junction!'

Gotcha, thought Alex, and *Thank You, Corporal Kendall from Police Training school, Netheravon,* who had told them If you ever have to lie, build the lie on facts and then KISS – Keep It Simple, Stupid! He'd done exactly that.

'Sergeant Meredith, if you'd like to take a run out to that spot, you'll find that not only is there a T-junction where I say there is, but if you care to examine the stone wall I guarantee you'll still find green paint from the Volkswagen there. And, now that we have dry weather, I'm sure you'll be able to see the actual skid marks on the road. Just what is this bullshit you were on about?'

'This report stinks.'

'Why, because I wrote it? Go out and look for yourself. Everything will check out.'

'Something's wrong here, I can feel it. And if I don't get it from you, then I'll get it from your mate when he comes back from sick leave!'

'You won't, because there's nothing to get and you know it. That report is genuine!'

At that moment there was a knock on the open door and the CO walked in. 'Excuse me, gentlemen, am I interrupting anything? Sergeant? Alex?' He looked from one to the other. Alex looked at Sergeant Meredith. The Sergeant in turn, looked at the CO. 'No, Sir, just discussing an accident report,' he said.

'Right. Alex, I have to go to Celle. Be away for two days. Do you think you could run a patrol by the house a couple of times each night? You know how it is.'

'No problem, Sir. Do you want us to knock the door and say hello?'

'That would be nice. Thank you, Alex,' and with that he turned and left the room.

Sgt Meredith turned to Alex. 'How is it,' he stormed, 'that the CO calls you Alex? He calls me Sergeant Meredith. He calls the WO-man Mr Smith, he calls everyone else by their rank, and yet he calls you Alex? WHY?'

Alex shrugged. 'It's my name.'

'Everyone calls you Alex, dammit! Even the German cleaning ladies call you Mister Alex, and that interpreter of ours practically bows before he speaks to you!'

'Just the way it is, Sarge.' Then tongue-in-cheek, 'Would you perhaps like me to call you Malcolm?'

'My name isn't bloody Malcolm! It's Michael!' he shouted and glared at Alex. He stopped. Alex was grinning. Meredith realised he'd been had. 'One day you'll go too far. You break all the rules. You get away with bloody murder in this place. You don't conform, dammit, and yet nobody – I repeat, *nobody* – including the CO, does anything about it. Why? WHY!?'

Alex looked at him. Meredith was dark red with fury.

'OK. You really want to know?' he replied, trying hard to hang on to his temper.

Meredith glared at him. 'Yes! I bloody well do!'

'Right! I'll tell you. This morning you wandered in at nine o'clock. I'd already been here since before eight and taken care of one traffic accident downtown. You will go home at five and I'll still be here until maybe ten. If there's a ruckus in town and somebody's wielding a broken bottle or glass, who do the German police ask for? *"Herr Alex".* If the guardroom rings with a problem, what do they say? "Is Alex there?" He continued, 'Take *your* section; traffic. If there's an accident, either downtown or anywhere in our area, the first thing the German traffic police say when they ring in is *"Herr Alex, bitte".* Why don't they ask for you? Have you ever even been to an accident while you've been here? I've never seen you. They know I work the traffic and keep it moving, even though strictly speaking, it's their job. I help the medics look after the injured, but I'm not a doctor or nurse. I help pull bodies from the wreckage, but I don't work for the fucking undertaker. Last week I pulled two crushed and severed legs from a car when the engine came back under the dashboard and landed in some poor bastard's lap. Last month I held a young lad in my arms who'd come off his motorbike and smashed in the side of his head against a tree. Part of his brain was scrambled and one eye was hanging out. He should've been dead, but he wasn't.

He made strange, whimpering noises and cried for his mother. It took him almost ten minutes to die, and he bled to death all over me. I wouldn't let the medics take him. That way he died with me and not on his own in the back of some sodding ambulance. I've had three new uniforms in the last eighteen months, and all because people have either bled or vomited all over me before they died in my arms… Want me to go on?' Alex stopped and looked at him.

Meredith shook his head and looked at the floor. He'd gone pale. Alex continued in a more gentle tone, 'And that, Sergeant Meredith, is part of the reason why people call me Alex.'

Meredith nodded – his mind clearly elsewhere.

'And now, Michael, if I were you, I'd sod off and file that report.'

Meredith looked across at Alex, eyes open wide with surprise. 'You just called me Michael!'

'So I did.'

'I think you also told me to sod off…'

'Slip of the tongue, Michael.'

He looked at Alex, smiled and nodded. Then he picked up the papers and silently left the room. Alex let out a huge sigh. His coffee was cold. He wandered across to Hella's office; the door was open. 'Do you think I could have a fresh one, Hella?' he asked, offering up the cup.

'I heard it all, you know.'

Alex looked at her and nodded.

'Come on in, Alex-darling, and close the door.'

She put the cup on her desk, walked up to Alex, put her arms round his neck and kissed him gently on the lips. He held her tight. She felt him slump. He buried his face into her hair and slowly exhaled. He was mentally drained. This felt so good. She smelled of fresh apples.

'Alex. Darling Alex. I know I have no right to ask, but you know that I love you even though I can never show it. I also believe that you love me, but perhaps differently. Am I right?' Alex nodded. 'Tonight I want you to come home with me. Will you do that, Alex?'

Alex whispered yes into her hair. She felt wet on her face. She held him tight and turned the key in the door, locking it. She turned back to him and looked him in the eyes. 'Only with me, Alex. Only with me can you show your feelings.'

She stood back and looked at him, wiping the silent tears from his cheeks with her fingers. 'I will never ask about your new wife, Alex, but have you ever been in love? Really in love? I mean, before?'

He looked at her and nodded. 'Yes,' he whispered.

'What is her name?'

He closed his eyes for a moment. 'She's dead. A drunken American cop shot her. Her name was Katrina.'

She looked at him, eyes questioning, a frown on her face. 'And the cop, Alex? What happened to him?'

Alex hesitated and thought for a moment. Finally, he said: 'He's dead.'

She looked at him, her eyes piercing into his. He could physically feel the love flow from her. 'When must you work again?'

'Day after tomorrow.'

'Then tonight, Alex, I would like you to tell me all about Katrina. You carry too much pain, Alex. You must let it out. Will you do that?' Alex nodded again. It was all he seemed capable of at the moment. She spoke softly again, 'Tonight and tomorrow are for us, Alex. Just for you and me. No world will exist outside our walls. Just the two of us, there for each other. Trust me, Alex. Trust me like I trust you.'

‘I trust you, Hella. Thank you.’

She stepped back slightly, then moved closer again and punched him gently on the chest, a playful smile on her lips. ‘Think nothing of it, my love. Tonight - if you let me, I’ll make you forget the world outside. I’ll take your pain away. Just you and me, only the two of us.’ She looked at him quizzically, ‘Well?’

He put his arm around her, pulling her closer, smiled back at her and murmured, ‘I like.’

Chapter 31

Demob!

Friday 26th February 1960 was the day that changed Alex's world. Forever. The previous day he'd had his final meeting with the CO. Smudger was there, of course – he was always there – as usual wheezing and puffing through the cigarette smoke. Somehow, he seemed like a father to Alex. Alex had one month to go before his four years were up. They'd been badgering him for the past three months to sign on, to do the 22. They promised the world. He didn't want the world. He wanted practicalities.

In the end they'd hammered it out; it had been agreed. The Boss put it to the AOC Provost, who also agreed. The AOC put it to whoever AOCs put these things to. Again, it was agreed. Alex would sign the forms. He'd go the whole way. In return, Alex would get his third. Then he would do P1 Advanced and Technical Police Training. After that he would return to Sundern – unheard of! – *and* he would head up Anti-Vice. Nose clean for three years and he would make Flight. Another three years, an unavoidable admin course, and he'd make Warrant Officer.

He'd be twenty nine.

He sat at his table in *Steiner's* looking out at the railway station. He glanced at his watch; 20:30. He'd got plenty of time. Eat a *Kotelett*, swallow a beer and then later drive over to married quarters to pick up Taffy. Taffy's wife always made sandwiches for Alex. *Maybe a run over to Bielefeld,* he thought; *sit and chat with the Redcaps for a bit. Then maybe scare the shit out of a few pongoes in the Out of Bounds. Back here by three, then bed. A nice steady evening . . .*

Heini delivered his breaded Kotelett, fried egg and sliced gherkin on top, with a pile of potato salad at the side. Just how he liked it. *'Bier, Heini. Bitte'*

'Sofort!'

Alex tucked into the homemade potato salad; best in the world bar none. The beer was placed next to his plate. '*Danke, Heini.*'

He looked up. It wasn't Heini!

'Good evening, Alex.'

There were two of them. The fat one who'd brought his beer, looked a bit like Smudger actually, and the other one looked like, well, he looked a real hard nut. Crew cut, chiseled features and cold, cold eyes. The fat one spoke. 'Mind if we sit down?' Alex waved his knife towards the two empty chairs. They sat. Crew Cut next to the window and Fat One opposite Alex. They got straight to the point. 'We know all about it, Alex,' said Fat One.

Alex carried on eating, but his heart was suddenly beating faster. Fat One sat and waited for a minute, 'Sylt,' he said. 'We know.' Alex's throat constricted. It was suddenly difficult to swallow. He carried on chewing, saying nothing.

'Cat got your tongue, Alex?' Fat One again. 'Sorry about the pun.' Alex continued chewing, swallowed and took two long gulps of beer. 'Listen. If you two want to play games, there's a Kindergarten round the corner. Sod off.'

'That's what we like about you Alex, cool under pressure. Never give anything away. Underneath, I bet you're pissing your pants.' Alex looked him in the eyes.

'Fuck it, Alex. Drop the hard man stuff! We know! Sylt. You. Katrina. The Yank. We know what happened!'

'Sod off.'

'OK, Alex. The attitude is admirable, but the games are over. I'll spell it out. Sylt, you and Katrina had an affair.'

'It wasn't an affair!' Alex stared at him with sheer hatred.

'OK. You and Katrina fell in love. She got pregnant. A drunken Yank shot her. You went back and shot the Yank. End of story. In a nutshell.'

Alex said nothing. 'We can prove it.'

'What do you want?'

'You!'

'Come again?'

'We want you. But not in the way of hands behind your back and read you your rights.' He handed Alex a card. He studied it.

Technology Transfer Services Ltd.
John Hardcastle
General Manager

'You're John Hardcastle?' asked Alex.

'For today, yes.'

'And you want me to work for Technology Transfer? Is that right?'

'Sort of, we're offering you a job. Let's say your country needs you.'

'Jeezes, you're a couple of spooks!'

'Sort of.'

'What the hell do you want with me?'

'Well,' said Fat One, 'you have certain skills that we rather admire. And one should always exercise one's skills, don't you think?'

‘And if I don’t accept this offer?’

‘Oh… I should think at least twenty years, wouldn’t you?’ He looked at Crew Cut, who nodded on cue. ‘Turn it over.’ Alex turned the card. On the back was a telephone number. ‘Tomorrow is your party, right?’ Alex nodded. ‘OK, you will not be signing any forms. Your CO has been advised there’s a change of heart. You’ll leave here next week and go to Innsworth. You’ll go through demob in the normal way. You don’t talk to anybody. Understood? On your last day you ring this number. You’ll be picked up. Any questions?’

‘Would you answer them?’

‘Probably not.’

‘Finished?’

‘Yes.’

‘Then sod off.’

On 22nd March 1960, at precisely 2:40 in the afternoon Alex walked through the main gate at RAF Innsworth.

A car – and Fat Man – were there to meet him.

BOOK III

CONSEQUENCES

Alex touched many lives and in turn was touched by many in his life. The result of these encounters had consequences for all – friends and foes alike. Or, as Alex's mentor, Alan Lake, aka Crew Cut or Psycho, put it bluntly and dispassionately:

"Friends are a luxury you cannot afford; they will be the death of you, or you of them."

32- Gerry

33- Big Bill

34- Brian

35- Charlie

36- Dina

37- Sgt. Mike Meredith

38- Hella

39- Debbie

40- The Fat Man

41- Crew Cut

Chapter 32

Gerry

In November 1959, Gerry began dating Jenny, the WAAF who had monitored the incoming calls on the night of Dina and Alex's final meeting.

In January 1960, after much arm twisting by Alex, Gerry finally took his driving test and passed.

In August 1960 Gerry and Jen returned to the UK for a huge family wedding. They put off a real honeymoon and decided to take a skiing holiday during the winter instead.

On 5th January 1961 they drove down to St. Martin in Austria where they had a wonderful three week holiday – "Great snow, sun and sex" as Jen had said in a postcard to her sister.

On 26th January they set off for Sundern, glowing with health and in high spirits. From St. Martin it was only a few kilometres to the German border. Once across they headed for Schneizlreuth and then turned north. Just outside Siegsdorf, on the road to Traunstein, they hit a patch of black ice on an exposed bend. The car spun out of control, turned once, turned twice and then – oh so gently – spun into a ditch and rolled over.

Jen climbed out of the car, completely unscathed. She couldn't move Gerry. A motorist travelling behind fetched the police from Traunstein while his wife stayed with Jen.

The medics pronounced Gerry dead at the scene of the accident. He was unmarked, but his neck was broken.

Chapter 33

Big Bill

In the autumn of 1959, Big Bill confided to Alex that he loathed the work he was doing. He didn't like imposing rules on people, he hated breaking up bar room brawls –he always seemed to get hurt – he detested intervening in family disputes, and he dreaded going out to traffic accidents. Alex tried to talk Bill round but it always came back to the same thing: when it was time to be posted back to the UK, he was going to remuster.

'As what?' Alex had asked him.

'A cook,' Big Bill had replied.

Now nobody, but nobody in their right mind remusters from Provost to go work in a kitchen!

'You're bloody mad!' said Alex.

'Hark who's talking,' came back the reply.

For Alex's going-away party in February 1960, Big Bill took over the Malcolm Club and did all the catering. The quality of the dishes served up surprised everyone. Bill obviously had serious talent in this line of work.

In April 1960, Big Bill finally remustered as a Chef and returned to the UK for training. Here he met, and later married, a young Irish girl who was on the same course. Bill started to work his way up the ladder and in 1967 his son Declan was born. His wife left the Air Force.

In 1982, Bill took his pension, left the Air Force and headed for Dublin to work in the family restaurant.

Bill retired with the rank of Warrant Officer and had for the preceding twelve years represented the RAF in many major catering exhibitions and contests where he had walked away with numerous cups, medals and certificates.

Big Bill, now aged 74, still puts in a full day at the restaurant which he owns with Declan. They were awarded their second Michelin Star in 2002.

Chapter 34

Brian

Alex arrived at Sundern a couple of weeks after Brian, in the late spring of 1958, and from the very beginning they got on together like a house on fire. They were both tidy by nature, enjoyed each other's company whenever their work roster allowed it but, strangely enough, in all their time at Sundern they only ever worked together on a couple of occasions. For all their common traits, their interests couldn't have been more different. While Alex's attention mainly focused on work, work, and more work with a little light entertainment thrown in from time to time, such as fostering his friendships with the fairer sex, Brian was heavily into rugby football. Rugby ruled and, oh, having a pint or two with the boys from the rugby football team - as often as they could possibly swing it! Sludge was the tipple. Since a Saturday night party followed by a Sunday morning game of rugby does not exactly gel, comments such as "I only vomited once during the game today" came as no surprise to Alex. And even though they forever seemed to be on opposite work shifts, a strong bond and liking for each other developed, but they did not live in each other's pockets.

In January 1959 Alex bought himself a very nice second-hand Mercedes 180 from a German doctor who'd decided it was time to upgrade. The deal was arranged by Mac who, as well as running the MT section, had his fingers firmly stuck in many different pies. You needed or wanted something? First try Mac! This particular deal involved the doctor handing the car over to Alex, no payment down, and then so much per month for two years. Incredible!

Mac also arranged transfer of ownership, organised the insurance policy plus he conjured up a signwriter – Yes, a signwriter! – to hand-paint Alex's numberplates - GH67B. "GH" for Gütersloh while the B after the number identified the British Forces stationed in Germany. All vehicles owned by members of the occupying allied forces in Germany had their own distinctive registration plates, regardless of their nationality

Naturally, it was agreed, all maintenance would be carried out by Mac in the MT section, after hours of course, and at greatly reduced rates. Wonderful arrangement! That car always ran like a dream and was Alex's pride and joy. When Alex left Sundern in February 1960, it was Jock who bought the car and took on the remaining payments. Mac, as usual, arranged everything.

Shortly after the Adolf Hitler birthday incident Alex decided to take a few days off and drive down to Paris; he asked Brian if he'd like to come. 'Of course I'd like to come, but I've got no money.' This, at the time, was *"situation normale"* as the French would say, for everyone.

'Where do we stay?'

'Sleep in the car'.

'What about food?'

'I'll fix it.'

'Petrol?'

'No problem.'

'OK, I'm coming.'

Alex's first trip was to the cookhouse where he had a little chat with the Boss-man to explain that he needed sufficient rations for two people for five days. What was forthcoming would have fed five people for a week. Who said emergency rations are crap? They lived like kings. Ready-to-eat beef stew, pork stew and lamb stew. Chocolate and biscuits by the ton. Tea, coffee, lemonade. Baked beans with this, baked beans with that. They had four big boxes of the stuff in the boot of the Merc.

One day to get down there and then the sights. The Eiffel Tower and Montmartre, the Louvre and Montmartre, followed by Versailles and Montmartre. Three days of sightseeing, three nights of Montmartre. And all on the cheap, of necessity!

Sleep? A few hours grabbed in the car wherever they could find parking. Then, turn around and head back east.

A stop off in the Alsace, which was bathed in brilliant sunshine. Alex parked the car in a quiet country road. They grabbed two blankets from the boot, stripped off and slept for six hours straight on the grass verge! They awoke looking – and feeling – like two boiled lobsters.

A quick trip to the nearest town where they only had sufficient money to buy one beer apiece and a single pickled egg, which they shared. But what fun!

Towards the end of 1959 Brian met, and promptly fell in love with, Margery, a WRAF NCO who at that time worked in PBX. She later remustered to the RAF Police. Brian advised Alex of his new-found love.

'Idiot!' was the unromantic response.

*

In the military, when people are moved on to a new posting, old relationships tend to fall by the wayside. Brian went to visit

Alex once, in the UK, in the summer of 1960. Then he went and married Margery. And then he went and got himself posted to Malta. Alex and Brian drifted apart, but they never forgot each other.

Over the years, Alex often talked about Brian with his family, and each Christmas they would all raise a glass in a toast to Brian, "wherever he may be". Likewise, Brian's growing family learned about Alex.

In December 1998, Alex spent ten days in the UK. He visited Brian's home town and tried to find him. He was unsuccessful, but over the years he kept searching. Finally, in August 2010, persistence paid off. Alex discovered Brian's address. He had returned to the town of his birth. Alex told Emm: 'I've found him!'

They decided not to contact him immediately but to make a surprise visit. One month later, in September of that year they flew to the UK and literally walked in on him at a local pub where he and Marge were preparing to have dinner with friends who were visiting from South Africa. The surprise visit turned out to be a huge success.

On 4th June 2012, the Queen's Diamond Jubilee, Brian and Marge celebrated 52 years of marriage.

And, Brian and Alex now speak together at least once a week.

Chapter 35

Charlie

Charlie left Sundern for demob via RAF Innsworth in January 1960, exactly one month before Alex. In March 1960 he arrived in South Africa where he was enrolled into the South African police force. He was stationed in Johannesburg. In June 1960 his wife Anne and daughter Julie flew out to join him. The family prospered. They had two more children, boys, David and Jonathan, and Charlie steadily worked his way through the ranks. His non-squeamishness when dealing with blacks seemed to go down well with his superiors, and for Charlie it seemed there was a never-ending supply of the indigenous population on which to vent his spleen.

In May 1976 Charlie reached the rank of Superintendent. His command now stretched outside Johannesburg and included the black township of Soweto.

The South African government, through the Bantu Education Department, had decided to enforce a long forgotten law requiring all blacks undergoing secondary education to be taught in Afrikaans rather than English. Students and teachers alike resented this; Afrikaans was, after all, the language of the oppressors. Teachers who refused to teach Afrikaans were fired. Students who refused to write papers in Afrikaans were expelled and where there were mass protests at schools; these schools were simply closed down. Charlie was in his element.

Then things changed dramatically.

On 16th June 1976 a protest march was organised in Soweto, the size of which took the police and army by surprise – more than 20,000 students turned up for the march. At first the march was peaceful, but then somebody made a fateful decision and the police began to fire round after round of teargas into the marchers. Panic broke out among the students and they ran in all directions trying to get away from the searing fumes. Many ran towards the police. The police opened fire. Several students fell. The march turned into a rampage as people tried to flee and police continued to fire into the crowd, indiscriminately killing and wounding.

Charlie was in an armoured Landrover with three other policemen to the rear of the main police lines. Some students, seeing how the police were firing into the crowd, changed tactics. Instead of trying to escape, many of them turned on the police and attacked them. The police continued to fire into the crowd but increasing numbers of marchers turned to attacking them and, by sheer weight of numbers, eventually broke through the main police line. The police turned and fled, hoping to regroup further to the rear. The police, and then the demonstrators, swept past Charlie's Landrover, leaving him stranded in the ever-growing mass of black humanity. At first, the Landrover was ignored but then somebody from inside the Landrover opened fire through one of the slits in the armour made for just such a purpose. The crowd stopped and turned on the Landrover. They rocked it from side to side and finally tipped it over. The crowd attacked the Landrover with anything they could get hold of – rocks, sticks, iron bars, machetes – until they finally broke open one of the side doors. The firing coming from inside the Landrover had ceased. The four occupants were dragged out – three black policemen and Charlie. The nearest members of the crowd attacked them and beat them to the ground. Then suddenly, as quickly as it had started, the beatings stopped. Somebody was making the crowd stand back – it was a woman. Eventually they formed a circle and at the centre of that circle stood Charlie, beaten and bloody, but still able to stand.

The woman gave instructions and four youths went forward and secured his arms and legs. He was thrown to the ground. The woman gave further orders and from within the crowd a jerry can was brought to her. She poured the entire contents of the jerry can over Charlie's head and upper torso and then threw the empty canister down beside him.

Petrol.

Then the woman lit the match.

A news crew in a helicopter was overhead filming. That night the whole of South Africa – and much of the world – watched as Charlie screamed his way to the Great Hereafter.

*

Charlie's manner of death should not be confused with what is now commonly known as "necklacing". In South Africa necklacing is said to have originated in the Eastern Cape on 23 March 1985 following the shooting and killing by police of 21 people.

The residents of the community attacked the home of a local community counsellor, believing him to be a police informer and necklaced the counsellor and his three sons.

They killed the wrong family.

The term "necklacing" means taking a rubber tyre, soaking it in petrol and then forcing it over the head and shoulders of the victim. The tyre is then set alight. The burning of the body in this way signifies both contempt and hatred for the victim.

Chapter 36

Dina

Alex's marriage in November 1959 devastated Dina but she was a fighter, and to the outside world she remained the person she'd always been: bright, bubbly and beautiful - not a care in the world! Although many people asked questions she never once divulged the secret of what had happened on that final evening with Alex – the evening where "X" marked the spot.

In March 1960, one month following Alex's departure, she asked for, and received, a posting back to the UK. Sundern had become a living hell. Everywhere she went she saw Alex in her mind and it felt as if she was being driven crazy. Her friends ran him down but she refused to play the game, and in the end she wouldn't hear a word said against him.

Her posting was to RAF Wilmslow in Cheshire and she hated it from the moment she arrived. She took her discharge in June 1962 and returned home to London.

She was 23 and she still missed Alex. Finally, in November of that year she found a job waiting tables at a night club in Soho and continued to do this for the next two years.

Dina had always had a good singing voice and had frequently entertained people with her impromptu renditions of Connie Francis songs in the NAAFI at both Sundern and Wilmslow. One night in November 1964 she was messing about at the microphone in the club before opening time. As usual she was taking off Connie Francis. Unknown to her, the owner of the club was sitting in the darkness behind the bar having a quiet drink. What he heard from Dina made him go cold.

Two days later Dina gave a private show to the owner and some of his friends. As a result of this Dina's days of serving tables were over.

She travelled the club circuit in London and the South for the next four years until someone suggested she enter the Hughie Green talent contest "Opportunity Knocks".

In 1968 she did just this and proceeded through several heats of the show, winning each one, until she arrived for the televised finale. Here she had the great misfortune to come up against Mary Hopkin who rapidly became the nation's sweetheart, and who went on to represent the UK in the 1970 Eurovision Song Contest.

Dina, while not the winner, went on to make two records and also went on the road appearing on the same bill as many famous groups of the time, including the Rolling Stones.

In the Spring of 1969, while on tour in Manchester, she met a doctor, twenty years her senior and a widower. They married just before Christmas of the same year.

April 1971 saw the arrival of a daughter, Rose, and in March the following year a son, Tristan, entered the world. Dina was 33, happy and at peace with the world.

In March of that year they moved to a new practice in Nottingham. In October 1986 Dina's husband Brian was diagnosed as being in the final stages of liver cancer. He died on Christmas Day the same year.

In March 1993 Dina placed an advertisement in the Sunday Times personal column, asking for anyone who had any knowledge of Alex from 1960 – 1993 to please get in touch with her. She had no replies, but someone in authority saw the advertisement and alerted Alex.

Alex was in Bulgaria.

Chapter 37

Sgt. Michael Meredith

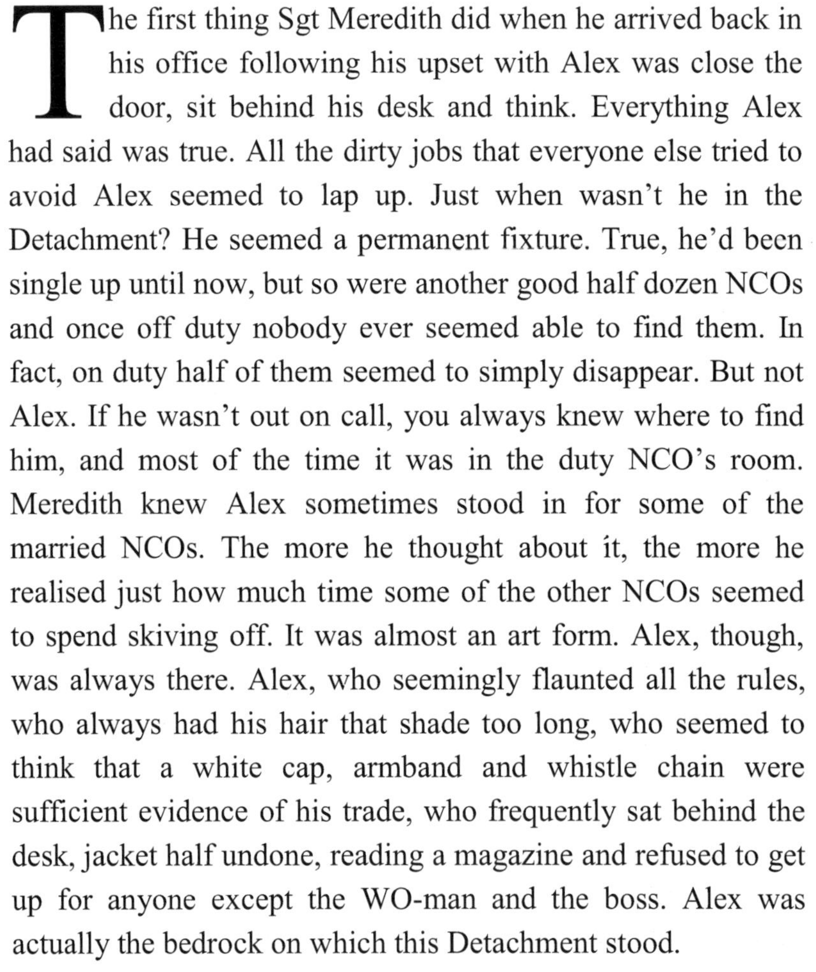

The first thing Sgt Meredith did when he arrived back in his office following his upset with Alex was close the door, sit behind his desk and think. Everything Alex had said was true. All the dirty jobs that everyone else tried to avoid Alex seemed to lap up. Just when wasn't he in the Detachment? He seemed a permanent fixture. True, he'd been single up until now, but so were another good half dozen NCOs and once off duty nobody ever seemed able to find them. In fact, on duty half of them seemed to simply disappear. But not Alex. If he wasn't out on call, you always knew where to find him, and most of the time it was in the duty NCO's room. Meredith knew Alex sometimes stood in for some of the married NCOs. The more he thought about it, the more he realised just how much time some of the other NCOs seemed to spend skiving off. It was almost an art form. Alex, though, was always there. Alex, who seemingly flaunted all the rules, who always had his hair that shade too long, who seemed to think that a white cap, armband and whistle chain were sufficient evidence of his trade, who frequently sat behind the desk, jacket half undone, reading a magazine and refused to get up for anyone except the WO-man and the boss. Alex was actually the bedrock on which this Detachment stood.

He made his decision, reached across and removed a rubber stamp from its holder, inked it and then firmly pressed it down in the top right hand corner of the file containing Alex's accident report – the one not thirty minutes previously he'd described as absolute bullshit! CASE CLOSED

He leaned forward and picked up the internal phone, then dialed 9 for the duty NCO's room. A voice answered, 'Alex'.

'Alex, I have a question.'

'Fire away, Mike.'

Meredith hesitated; he'd called him Mike. He knew it was ridiculous but he felt himself glow. Alex had actually called him Mike! 'Alex, the next time you get a call out to an accident do you think I could come with you?'

Alex didn't hesitate. 'Sure, Mike.'

'It's right what you said about me, you know. I go through reports, interview people after the event, draw graphs and bar charts, work out statistics, but since I've been here I've never actually been out to an accident. I've never seen or dealt with situations at the scene. I'd like to learn and I'd like you to teach me.' There – he'd said it!

'Mike, it will be a pleasure. Next time there's a call out I'll take you along. Let's hope it's nice and messy!' And with a laugh he replaced the phone.

Mike was commissioned in September 1963. He remained an RAF Policeman until he retired with the rank of Squadron Leader in November 1980. He then moved back to his home town where he opened a small driving school.

He saw Dina's Sunday Times advertisement in March 1993, but did not contact her. He felt there was no point since he'd had no knowledge of Alex's whereabouts for over 30 years, and even if he had known he wouldn't have wanted to be the one to possibly open Pandora's Box. He remembered Alex's disappearing trick, only to reappear one week later newly married. He smiled to himself as he remembered the rumours surrounding the red cross painted directly in front of the locked police Detachment door. *I bet they did it, you know. I bet they did it!* And he chuckled to himself. *Just like Alex!*

Subconsciously, Dina's advert kept gnawing away at his mind, and in September 1993 ex-Squadron Leader Mike Meredith placed an advert in all UK Sunday newspapers. It cost him a small fortune. Be worth it, though, he thought, if only...

On Monday, 6th September 1993, Alex boarded a Bulgarian Airlines Sofia to Brussels flight and helped himself to an English language newspaper from a stack in an overhead luggage compartment at the front of the plane. He was 30,000 feet somewhere over the former Yugoslavia when he came across Mike's advert. He laid the newspaper on the empty seat next to him, dropped his seat back to recline and closed his eyes. He sat motionless for a good ten minutes. Then he opened his eyes, returned his seat to upright and searched through the goodies pack in the pouch on the back of the seat in front of him. He extracted a postcard showing a Bulgarian Airlines Boeing and an envelope.

He wrote slowly and precisely, telling Mike he'd seen his ad and that he was well but could not at this time give him any further details. He ended *"Now I know where you are, we'll meet."*

On Saturday 8th January 1994 Alex rang Mike's front door bell. Their joy at seeing each other again was made obvious by the huge smiles on both their faces.

Alex broke a few rules by telling Mike something of his work over the past thirty odd years. Mike listened spellbound.

On leaving, Alex gave Mike a Post Office Box number in Brussels to which he could write. The letter would be retrieved from the PO Box, Alex explained, and forwarded to him by Diplomatic Bag. Wherever he was in the world they could communicate.

Alex would use the reverse method; by Bag to Brussels where his letter would be retrieved, stamped and popped in the Belgian mail.

They never met or spoke to each other again but they communicated regularly – Mike writing every week, until his sudden and totally unexpected death at the age of 70 in August 1995.

Chapter 38

Hella

Hella never forgot the time or date: 7:26am on 5th April 1960. It happened again the next day, and the day after that. Hella visited old Dr Dixius on Hohenzollernstrasse. Tests, more tests and finally the results. 'Hella, my dear, you are in perfect health. You are also pregnant. Approximately six weeks.' He peered at her over the top of his half-moon glasses. 'Is that good news or bad, my dear?'

Hella sat there and took it in.

In her heart of hearts she'd known it would be like this for the past three days, but the official verdict still rocked her. She slowly looked up at the doctor. Good news or bad … Exactly which was it? Pregnancy? She'd never even considered it. She was after all a lesbian – or was she? She hadn't been with anyone else from the very first time she'd been with Alex and that seemed a lifetime ago. When was it exactly?

She thought back to that first evening when she'd deliberately set out to seduce Alex, her 26th birthday, almost two years ago. God, was it really that long? She and Alex had made love on only four occasions, but after that first night with him she'd never been interested in anyone else, male or female. Good news or bad? She was having Alex's child. That had to be good. But Alex had gone and she'd never seen him again. They'd agreed. Nothing could come of it in the future, after all Alex was now married and even if she wanted to contact him she wouldn't know where to start looking. Alex didn't even know where he was going. On their last night together in March, and immediately before his departure to the UK, Alex had told her more about Katrina, about the unborn child, about Abe Murray and about the two people who'd contacted him in *Steiners*. He'd called them "spooks". He was being blackmailed, of that she was sure. By his own government. Did governments really do things like that to their own people? She had found it hard to believe, but of course she did finally believe it because it was Alex who'd told her – and Alex wouldn't lie to her, would he? No. Of course not! So, having Alex's child was good news - the greatest! But not being able to contact him, ever, would be terrible . . . She looked directly at the doctor, 'Doctor Dixius, it's the best news a girl could ever hope to hear.'

From the doctor's surgery she went straight to work where she gave notice that she would be leaving at the end of May – family problems. No, she would not be leaving the area.

Hella took stock of her situation.

Money. She didn't need it.

Well before his death, her father had seen to it that she would want for nothing. She had also received money and a family property in Munich when her mother had been killed in the air raid on Berlin, and then when her aunt died she inherited the apartment in which she had lived. She was she told herself, extremely well set up for life.

The problem was, of course, that the child would be without a father. Alex. Well, she would be both mother and father. After all, there were many children in Germany who had to grow up with only one parent, or indeed, without either. She thought. If it was a boy she'd call him Alex after his father. If it was a girl, she'd call her Alexandra, also after her father.

She'd made the hardest decision. She'd have the child, bring it up herself and never try to find Alex or interfere in his life.

Alex Junior finally struggled into this world following fourteen hours of intense labour during which he, head down and ready to exit, had apparently done the impossible and turned himself round and tried to go back to where he'd been resting in warmth and comfort for the past nine months. He finally entered, left foot first, and leaving Hella completely exhausted, at 4:00pm on a very bleak and cold 4th December 1960. 'Just like your father,' Hella muttered to herself, still feeling drowsy from the batterings of the past fourteen hours, 'always has to do things his way.'

For Alex Jr. life could not come fast enough. At six months he pulled himself upright and stood swaying by Hella's chair, making gurgling noises and pointing at what she was eating – blue cheese on crackers. She put a small piece on her finger and fed it to him, thinking he'd spit it out. He loved it and wanted more.

By his first birthday he was staggering around the apartment kicking a football in front of him. He had blonde hair and blue eyes like his mother, but the shape of his cheekbones were his father's, and he had this knack of being able to raise his right eyebrow independently of the left. Again, typical Alex. "The quizzical look", Hella had called it.

As the boy grew, Hella had tried to tell him about his father. It was then that she realised that she knew very little about Alex. All she knew was what had happened to him while he was in Germany. She knew his surname. She knew where he had been born and that was really it. How could you love someone so much when you knew practically nothing about him? His past? His family? She didn't even have a photograph.

*

The day had started normally enough, well maybe it hadn't. She'd got up at 7, prepared breakfast and then gone to wake Alex Jr. His room was empty, bed not slept in. It jolted her for a moment, until she'd remembered that yesterday Alex Jr. had left for his first summer camp. One week with the school to Prien on the *Chiemsee*, not too far from where she'd grown up. How time flies, she'd thought. He'll be eight at the end of the year. Not only that, in three days' time it would be her own birthday and she'd be 36. It would be the first time Alex Jr. had not been present for her birthday since he'd been born.

The weather that day had been hot, too hot. Dusk was just beginning to fall and Hella was sitting on the balcony, which overlooked the front garden, idly turning the pages of a magazine. She first noticed the woman as she hesitantly pushed open the front gate and then made her way to the entrance of the apartment block. The intercom in Hella's hallway buzzed.

'*Wer ist da, bitte*?'

'Are you Hella?' a voice asked.

'Who are you?' Hella replied.

'Please! Are you Hella?' There was more urgency in the voice now.

'Yes, I'm Hella.'

'Alex sent me.'

It didn't register at first. Then she thought she'd misunderstood. She just stood there. She started shaking; then more violently. She was vaguely aware of the buzzer sounding continuously somewhere in the background. She was in a daze.

She pressed the button to release the downstairs entrance hall door. She opened her own front door. She fell, rather than sat, in the armchair. She was aware of a hesitant knocking at the door, which slowly began to open. The woman stood there.

'May I,' she indicated, 'come in?'

Hella pulled herself together and stood up. 'Please,' she said as she walked towards her. 'I am Hella. Who are you?'

'My name is Ilse Beckmann.'

Hella shook her head, 'I'm sorry. That means nothing to me.'

'Of course not. But if I tell you I am the daughter of Professor Werner Beckmann?' She looked at Hella and raised her eyebrows. Slowly it dawned on Hella.

'You mean the physicist Werner Beckmann?' West German television and newspapers had been full of stories relating to Werner Beckmann's sensational escape across the border wire separating East and West Germany only two weeks ago. An atomic scientist of world renown, his somewhat dramatic defection had been a major coup for the West. Hella looked at Ilse, the hair on the back of her neck started to rise; suddenly she was covered in goosebumps.

'. . . Alex?'

Ilse nodded, 'Yes, Alex.'

'Tell me.' Hella led Ilse into the living room. 'Please sit down. Would you like a drink? It's very hot today. I have fresh lemonade, made just this afternoon.' Ilse nodded, 'Thank you.'

They settled into the armchairs across from one another. Ilse looked at Hella, who was leaning forward in her chair, nervously playing with her glass. 'Let me put your mind at rest, Hella. Alex has been hurt but he is well, and if you'll allow me, I would like to start this story at the beginning.'

Hella nodded.

'Just over two years ago,' Ilse began, 'my father applied for permission for our family; that is my mother, father and myself, to visit my aunt – my mother's sister – who lives in Dortmund. Permission was refused, but permission was given for my mother and me to go. They often do that, allowing one or two members of the family to travel, but refusing permission for other members; in this way they can manipulate us. They believe we will not go and never come back because they can put pressure on the remaining members of the family. My father was the head of a team carrying out research into various aspects of nuclear fission. I don't understand any of it, it's far too complicated, but he is – was – highly respected and travelled regularly, on his own of course, or with other team members to the Soviet Union and Czechoslovakia. My father had come up with a plan, a very simple plan, when you think about it. He told my mother and me that we should go to Hamburg, ostensibly on holiday, but that we should not return. He reasoned, and it turned out to be correct, that he would not be harmed or harassed as he was too important to the research team. When we arrived in Hamburg he told us to apply for political asylum. He expected no problems here and again he was right. I was then to fly to England and contact a professor at the University of Manchester and ask him to get in touch with the British authorities on my father's behalf, saying that he wanted to leave the country – defect if you like. Such a horrible word, don't you think?' She carried on, not waiting for a reply.

'My father told me not to contact the British Embassy in Bonn, or any West German institution. West Germany, he said – and certainly all government institutions – was riddled with Stasi informers. Once I had been in contact with the British authorities and I was back in West Germany, I was to write a letter to an address in Dresden – the content of the letter was irrelevant – and I was to commence the letter "Dear Uncle" and sign it "Eva". If the British authorities were interested in helping him I was to draw a line under the name Eva. If they were not, then I was to put nothing. The authorities were interested and I sent the letter signed with the name Eva underlined.'

Ilse paused and took a sip of her lemonade, before going on. 'In Dresden the letter was removed from its envelope, put in a second envelope and somehow appeared in his pigeon hole at the research centre. I was able to get information to him in this manner over the next 18 months. Four weeks ago my father met Alex. He went home from work one day and there was Alex sitting in my father's armchair in the living room reading a magazine; he almost frightened my father to death. Alex was going to travel with my father to Berlin and bring him out through a tunnel. After two days, Alex apparently received news to say the escape route was compromised and that he should get himself out. He talked it over with my father and said if my father was prepared to take the risk he would get them both over the border somewhere else. My father agreed. Alex then disappeared for three days.' Ilse put the glass to her lips again.

'My father had given up on seeing him again but suddenly he was back. They would leave, said Alex, in two days' time, Saturday morning. That way he would not be missed at work. Saturday morning Alex apparently caught a bus to the railway station where he stole a car. He then returned and picked up my father and they drove to another town, I don't know where, but they spent a most uncomfortable night sleeping in the car on a hospital car park. Next morning they headed for another town, and again I don't know where, neither Alex nor my father would say, but Alex left the car on the railway station car park. He removed the number plates and dropped them through a drain grating. They were now only about five kilometres from the border. They set out across country and arrived within one kilometre of the border at about midnight.'

Ilse took another sip before continuing, 'Alex then went to check out the border on his own and left my father behind a hedge in a field for about two hours. He was terrified but had to trust Alex. What else could he do? The place where Alex had chosen to cross was the very spot that he'd apparently visited on his 21st birthday. It had struck him at the time how easy it would be to get across there. No wall, only single strands of wire and fairly widely spaced VOPO observation towers. He came back for my father and they then headed for the wire. They crawled the last half kilometre. My father said it was agony and he was petrified that someone would see them. They sat and watched for half an hour. Nothing. Not a sound. They could see a cigarette glow from one of the observation posts, but that was all. Finally, at about 4am they crawled towards the wire. Alex cut the bottom strand of the wire and well, the rest you know. A dog running loose on the West German side heard the wire go and came to see what was there, just inquisitive really, saw Alex and my father and started barking. One of the VOPOs in the nearest tower shone a torch at the wire – they didn't even have a searchlight – saw movement, and opened fire at the wire. Luckily he strafed the area and didn't fire everything into one spot. He killed the dog, which was actually still on the western side, and Alex was hit in the leg. By great good fortune he totally missed my father, who was able to drag Alex into a clump of bushes about fifty metres from the wire. The firing alerted the West German border patrol who found my father and Alex, and promptly delivered them to the nearest hospital. Alex was not badly hurt and is now hobbling around with a stick. A model patient he is not. He wants out. My father is now in England, but he made me go and visit Alex. Alex is desperate to see you and he asked me to come. Under the circumstances it's the very least I could do. He thought for some reason you may not want to see him. What shall I tell him?'

'Tell him to come,' replied Hella. 'Oh, please do tell him to come!'

Hella found it impossible to sleep that night and it had nothing to do with the all-pervading sticky heat that seemed to swamp most of mainland Europe. It was Alex. No contact for eight years and now this. But nothing mattered anymore. Alex was here in Germany, he was hurt and he needed her, that's all she needed to know. As daylight pushed away the darkness, she finally fell into a fitful sleep.

Time seemed to stand still for the next two days. Hella found herself repeatedly checking her watch to find that only a few minutes had passed since she'd done exactly the same thing. She couldn't settle, she couldn't sit still. Up-down, up-down. Out onto the balcony and back again. Ilse had refused to give any more information about Alex to Hella. She wouldn't even say which hospital he was in. She simply said she was following instructions. Alex's instructions.

The third day was Hella's birthday, 26th August. Today she was 36. She felt miserable. Today of all days she should be happy. Alex Junior was away and halfway through his school camping trip. And Alex? Well, where was Alex? Eight years and nothing. Now he was here – somewhere – and he'd been hurt.

*

She missed the taxi when it finally arrived but was alerted by the persistent buzzing of the entrance hall phone. She was shaking as she picked up the handset. 'Yes?' And then, after eight long years, she heard it, something she thought she would never again hear in her life: Alex's voice. He was talking to her… What was he saying? 'Sorry, what did—'

'I said, "Would you please press that little black button in the bottom right hand corner, or are you going to make me stand out here all day?"

She pressed the button, opened her front door and flew down the stairs to meet him.

* _ *

The story of Hella, which included the first of many meetings with Emm in 1983 and continued until 1996, was part of the material stolen in Sofia, with the exception of the following:

Alex Jr. found his mother when he arrived next day. She lay in bed and appeared to be asleep, the corners of her mouth lifted gently, as though smiling at some inner thought. Photographs were spread around the bed. Alex and Emm were due to arrive from Bulgaria in two days' time to celebrate her birthday.

'It was the excitement,' the doctor told him, 'just too much for her heart to take.'

Hella died on 24th August 1996, two days before her 64th birthday. At her own wish Hella was cremated. Alex and Emm were present. The plaque commemorating her life in the Garden of Remembrance reads:

Hier auf Erden fand ich Liebe

(Here on earth I found love)

Chapter 39

Debbie

Towards the end of March Debbie knew in her heart she was pregnant. One week later tests confirmed it. She greeted Derek with the news on his return from exercise in Italy. 'Who's been a clever boy, then?'

He regarded her blankly. 'Come again?'

She faced him with a huge grin on her face, 'We're pregnant! You're going to be a Daddy!' She noted the stunned look that suddenly appeared on his face. She could almost hear the brain working – *When? How?* She took the advantage. 'It must have been that humdinger we had before you went up to Finland!'

The concentration was still on his face as he frantically tried to remember any humdinger he'd had during the past twelve –no, maybe eighteen– months. Blank. A total blank.

She attacked again. 'Surely you remember that night, I think it was three, maybe four days before the flight to Finland. I know you were pretty tanked up – well, we both were – but it sure worked for me. Anyway,' she tapped her tummy, 'you scored a bulls-eye! We're pregnant. Well done, Daddy!' She went over to him, put her arms around his neck and gave him a squeeze. The response was negligible. She kept at it. 'Come on! Surely you can do better than that? Give me a squeeze. A big one, while you still can!' she laughed. He squeezed, half-heartedly. *A daddy . . . Shit*!

*

Debbie arrived "Stateside", as she called it, mid June 1959. Following two weeks leave Derek reported for duty at Davis-Monthan Air Force Base, Arizona.

The first shock was when he failed his aircrew medical and was assigned to temporary clerical duties within the squadron.

The second shock was when, three months later, he failed again. In-depth examinations revealed the presence of stones in both kidneys, together with a cyst on the liver. He was placed on light duty, put on a strict dietary regime, ordered to participate in supervised physical training classes and forbidden to touch alcohol.

Derek struggled.

Debbie bloomed.

At three months, she looked radiant. Health positively oozed from every pore, and she had so much energy. Incredible!

She'd always had a passing interest in photography and in September 1959, now six months pregnant, she signed up for a twelve month photography course, run on base and sponsored by Kodak. Her course was rudely interrupted when, on 12th December, she was rushed to the base medical centre where she promptly delivered a 6lbs 2oz Derek Junior into the world.

She hugged him, she kissed him and she whispered, 'Right on time. Well done, little man!' Then she studied him more closely and couldn't find a single feature that resembled Derek. She giggled to herself… *Of course not, silly.* On the other hand – *My God!* – was she going to have a problem! One look at the eyebrows and cheekbones and it would be obvious, even to Derek, who the father was. Five dollars to each of the shift nurses solved the situation.

On his arrival at the ward, Derek was greeted with, 'What a beautiful baby! You can see at a glance who the father is. He looks just like you!' And so it went on. Derek looked, studied, but failed to find any resemblance to himself. Still, the nurses must know, mustn't they? After all they deliver babies every day! Derek Junior was accepted.

In March 1960, Derek collapsed at work in agony. He was rushed to hospital where his right kidney was removed together with a growth the size of a chicken egg.

In July Debbie filled in the forms and sent off for her desperately desired papers.

Four weeks later she read the letter of rejection.

Back in April 1946 a spot check on Debbie's handbag had revealed a package containing eight slices of smoked bacon, four eggs and a one pound packet of coffee. Debbie, who was eighteen and at the time worked in the kitchen of the Officers' Mess at the US Air Force base in Kassel, was dismissed. No charges were brought.

Debbie was devastated. Everything she'd done over the past three years had been geared towards obtaining those papers. They represented "Freedom". Now she would stay in chains. She needed to break free. To be her own person. To be independent of Derek, of everybody. To be responsible for making her own decisions.

She needed work.

For the next week she scoured the newspapers for job offers, something she could do at home and still be able to care for Derek Jr. Fortunately, all he seemed to do at the moment was drink her milk, burp, sleep, fill his nappy, then start all over again. She smiled to herself; he was a wonderful baby. *Thank you, Alex, and ... Thank you, Derek, too*! In the second week of her search she noticed an ad placed by the Earl Silas Tupper people. They were looking for ladies willing to host parties at home to sell their now famous magical "burping box”. Plastic food containers so named because when the lid was closed it “burped”, sealing off the air.

Debbie’s Tupperware parties became the talk of the base. Not only did she sell the plastic boxes, she also recruited other wives to host parties. Derek complained loudly and strongly about his house always being full of those “damn giggling women”, but in December the complaints stopped when Debbie quietly pointed out that her income was now greater than his.

Freedom . . . ? Almost!

It was also in December that Debbie won the Eastman Kodak “Amateur Photographer of the Year” Award. Photographic equipment and a hefty cheque followed. She took a rental on a shop just off the main shopping street in Tucson. Redecorated and laid out as a portrait studio, she called it “Debbie’s”.

Portrait photographs of wives and children from the base kept her afloat, helped by the Kodak award. She canvassed magazines and newspapers for freelance work. Slowly she put together a portfolio. The work came in. For the next two years, she worked all hours of the day and night. Her bank balance grew, but she felt tired.

Freedom? No. She was a slave to work.

In January 1964 she dropped Tupperware. She no longer needed it. Derek was still involved in squadron clerical work. There was no hope of ever flying again, and he’d already decided that next summer he’d take his pension. He’d have completed 25 years of service. Meanwhile, he’d had no more health scares and he’d finally stopped drinking.

Life was pretty good.

Debbie took a mortgage to buy the property she’d been renting; then she remodelled it. She’d won several photographic awards and she could now pick and choose which commission to accept and which to reject. She put together a portfolio of models, all unknown, who'd answered her ads placed in several newspapers. This was sent off to established agencies, manufacturers of ladies' clothing, swimwear, lingerie, ski-wear. The list was endless. Debbie had a way with cameras; the work gradually started to come in. Then she turned to children's wear with the same results.

By 1968, "Debbie's" was a household name among clothing manufacturers and mail order companies. She now owned a warehouse, which she converted into a specialised photographic studio. Eight photographers worked for her along with another six technical staff and six clerical staff. Derek was among the clerical staff, and as he put it, he cooked the books. Freedom? Perhaps.

Derek Jr. seemed to grow by the day. A handsome boy, now nearly nine. Debbie often wondered how Derek didn't spot the resemblance to his biological father. Meanwhile, Derek had turned into a good and caring father, always there to see him onto the school bus in the morning, and always there to meet him when he arrived home at the end of the day. Debbie always seemed to be working.

March 1973 saw Debbie move the business and her family, lock, stock and barrel, to Los Angeles. A birthday treat, she called it. She was now 46. During the past eighteen months she'd been making more and more trips to LA and Hollywood, where two of her models that she'd originally supplied as extras were beginning to make a name for themselves in films. She'd spent the past year analysing the film industry. She was particularly interested in any gripes she heard; people who felt hard done to and why, and the industry's needs. She felt that, in addition to her present businesses, which after all could be run from anywhere, there was an opportunity to be had in Tinseltown.

She intended to take it.

She formed a separate company, *"Debs – Agent to the Stars"* and starting with her two original models she targeted those who expressed discontent with the roles they were getting and, perhaps more importantly, those they were not getting. She convinced them, one by one, to leave their present agency and come to her. Then she went to work on repackaging, remodelling and rebuilding confidences and egos that had been bruised. Then she went to work on the Studios.

It was a long, hard grind, but at the end of three years there wasn't a Studio head or executive of note who hadn't duelled with Debbie. The agency now grew steadily. She hired lawyers and PR people skilled in the arts and skulduggery of the movie world. She slept little, but seemed to thrive on it. Derek had long ceased to complain about the fact that Debbie was never home and Derek Jr. refused point blank to take any instructions from his mother.

Debbie ploughed on. She was terrified that if she stopped or slowed up the whole monstrous package she had created, would come tumbling down.

1978 saw her stable of stars bring home 2 awards, Best Supporting Actress, and Best Newcomer. After the ceremony she returned home with Derek who complained of feeling more tired than normal.

Debbie wanted to talk.

Derek wanted to sleep.

She poured herself a Campari soda while Derek went to his bedroom to change. Five minutes later he returned in pajamas and dressing gown. 'I think tonight was very special for you,' he said, 'and I'd like to join you in just one drink to celebrate your success. You deserve it, Little Dora from Kassel, now the toast of Hollywood. You've done well.'

'I've done it for the family, Derek.' He looked up at her, as she handed him his drink. It was his first in … how long? Fourteen years! And she didn't even comment when he asked for it. He took a sip and immediately screwed up his face. 'Yuk, that's horrible! I don't know how you can drink that stuff! And no, you didn't do it for the family, Debbie. You did it for *you*. Everything that we have, you did for you. For Dora. You had to get out from under and for some reason prove yourself. I was the first stepping stone, your passage out and to the States. I knew it when I married you but I didn't care. "Why not?" I thought. "Let's give it a whirl!" Anyway, in those days, if we weren't flying, we were drunk. Who cared about the future? Everybody thought we'd soon be at war with the Sovs; still might be yet, the way some things are going. The point is though, you've succeeded. You've made it beyond anything you could possibly have dreamed of. I certainly never thought we'd have anything like this.' He put his glass, still full, on the side table and stood up, rubbing his chest. 'Indigestion. Getting it a lot lately. I'll just get the Maalox,' and he headed towards the bathroom. He returned crunching two tablets, 'Be better in a minute.'

'Maybe you should get a check-up at the doctor's. Just to make sure?' He shook his head. 'Thank you, but no thank you. I've had enough of them to last me a lifetime after we moved back here from Germany. Doctors I can do without. One last thing, though. Derek Junior is joining the Air Force.'

He paused and looked at her, 'He's unhappy at university, I've more or less brought him up while you went out to earn a crust. Then we bought the loaf and now we own the whole damn factory, several factories in fact. So, he's heard all the stories, not once, but a hundred times, and I guess he just wants in. Says there's nothing here for him.' He shrugged, 'What can we do? He's turned eighteen. I said I'd talk to you, soften the blow, sort of thing. He doesn't dislike you. As he said to me: "She's never here to dislike". So, I guess, he's all grown up and wants to see the world.'

She nodded and took a sip of her Campari. 'Aircrew?'

Derek laughed, 'Hell no! He wants to be a cop. Can you believe that? A cop! I guess I must have told him too many cop stories.'

She smiled across at him, 'But you don't know any cop stories.'

'Maybe not. But I still remember the stories that English cop, Alex, used to tell us: "Freedom! Fuck the world!" and all that stuff. You used to be big on freedom until you went and made all that money and made yourself a prisoner of your own success. What price freedom now, Debbie?'

'Do you hate me, Derek?'

'Hell no! Why should I hate you?' He waved his arm around the room. 'What's to hate about all this? It cost us, but did we have it in the first place? I guess not!' He rubbed his chest again. 'Damned indigestion. I'm going to bed. You here in the morning?' He stood up.

'Yes, I can be if you want me to be. No need to leave until mid-afternoon. Anything special?'

He hesitated, 'I'd like to – now, how do I put this? – I'd like to reminisce. Talk about the old days. Kassel. The Top Three Club. The flights I made all over Europe with the crew… and Alex, of course. Mustn't forget Alex, must we?' He crunched on two more Maalox as he headed for his room. At the doorway he paused, turned and blew her a kiss. 'Night, Debbie. Sweet dreams, and … congratulations, I mean it.' He went into his room and gently closed the door behind him.

Debbie slowly exhaled. Her heart was lodged somewhere at the bottom of her throat, threatening to choke her. He knew, of course. He must do, to say things in such a way… But he'd also said he didn't hate her. He liked the luxury. Maybe he'd made a trade-off with himself. Tomorrow she'd find out. She looked at her watch; change that: today she'd find out.

Now, for a few hours' sleep.

She knew he was dead the moment she entered the room.

There was something different, stiller, perhaps. There was also a strange smell. Acrid, acid – she couldn't tell what it was. She walked across and opened the curtains. Then she turned and looked at Derek. The bedclothes were down around his waist and he lay on his back, hand on his chest and mouth slightly open. His lips were blue and so, she noticed, were the tips of his fingers. He seemed peaceful, and somehow younger, the lines had disappeared from his forehead and around his eyes. She stood for a moment and looked down at him. Nothing. So many years and then… nothing. No tears. No feelings. Just nothing. Is this what she'd become; a person totally devoid of feelings? Just where had it all gone wrong? But then, even from the beginning, had it ever really been right?

'Goodbye, Derek, sleep well,' she whispered, as she quietly closed the door and went to call the doctor.

Almost twelve months had flown by before she realised that Derek's passing had hardly made a ripple in the waters of her life. Sure, there really was no-one home when she finally arrived there, usually well past midnight every day, but then both Derek and Derek Junior were normally in bed well before then.

From Derek Junior she'd heard nothing. Immediately following the funeral he'd gone. She'd been at the office and when she returned home, there'd just been the note. "I'm joining the Air Force, just like my Daddy", he'd written. And then he'd signed it, "With love, your son Derek" No "Junior", she noted. Well … Derek was the man in the family now, such as it was. He'd even put three kisses after his name, and finally he'd added a postscript in different coloured ink. "I do love you, you know. Thanks for my life". She'd puzzled over that for a long time, but came to no conclusion.

Now, eleven months on, she'd heard nothing. Not a card, not a phone call, nothing. She also realized with something of a shock that she'd never really sat and thought about him. Was she really that hard? That distant? That cold? Truth be told, she was. That's how people saw her. She survived – and won – in a man's world. *To hell with it!* she thought.

Over the next few years her empire continued to grow. She'd never taken up with another man. Oh, the offers had been there, and one or two had tried it on, but she'd gently rebuffed them all. Why did she need a man? In fact, why did she need anybody? She'd more than proved herself. People needed her more than she needed them. And sex? That had died a death long before Derek did. She sat and daydreamed.

The best sex she'd had in her entire life had been with Alex. It wasn't just sex. That first night in the kitchen in Kassel, she'd waved her hand and said "improvise". She laughed inwardly. Oh, how they'd improvised. If only the kitchen could talk, what a tale it would tell. Animal lust. Sheer animal lust… After that it had changed. The lust was still there, but she also felt love – no, that's not right – she also felt loved, and in turn she gave love. *Dear Alex*, she thought, *I wonder where you are now*? Would she like to see him again? The answer was in her mind even before she'd completed the question. An emphatic "Yes". *One day,* she said to herself, *one day, I'm going to find you, Alex. One day – but not now...*

*

The letter landed on her desk one hot July morning. She looked at the envelope, it was typed. She turned it over, no return address. It was marked "Personal" in the top left hand corner. The postage stamp was German. It was franked 14-07-1988. She slid her letter opener under the seal and peered inside. A photograph and another small white envelope. She lifted out the photo and stared. Icy fingers ran along her spine; the hairs in her neck stood up. No! It can't be. It just can't be . . . *Alex!*

She shook her head, trying to clear the thoughts that seemed to overwhelm her. *No, no... It's not Alex... It's Derek!* She noticed she was shaking. In his uniform, topped by his white hat, he was the spitting image of his father. She laid the photograph down, put her head in her arms on the desk and burst into tears.

Back in her apartment that evening, she poured another Campari Soda, her third in less than an hour. She was terrified; afraid to open the letter. She had no idea what it might say, but it was now ten years since she'd last seen Derek, well, she just— *Get a grip*, she told herself. *This isn't like you . . . Open the letter!*

She sat in her favourite armchair, the one facing the fireplace and reached for her glasses. She hated them. Hated them so much that no-one even knew she needed them. She wore them at home only. Her little secret. She read the letter through quickly, once. Then again, more slowly. And then a third time, pausing to re-read and digest a particular sentence. She removed her glasses and lay back in her chair.

So, Derek was married. A German girl called Ursula. She was pregnant – just. The baby was apparently due around the third week in February next year. Ursula had insisted that Derek tell his mother. She also insisted that his mother should know they would be returning to the States at the end of October. Could they come and visit?

God! Debbie closed her eyes and sighed. In three months they'd be here. Ten years of nothing, and then all of a sudden everything! A wife, a child and coming home . . . And, "PS: I love you, Mom". The tears rolled quietly down her cheeks. She rose and walked a little unsteadily to the drinks cabinet. Should she or shouldn't she? She felt a little tipsy. Been a long time. *To hell with it!* She poured herself another Campari – number four – but since she was the only one counting, no sweat. Funny, Derek used to say that. "No sweat," he'd say, "No sweat!" She smiled at the thought. Slowly she walked across the room and stood gazing out of the huge picture windows. Los Angeles lay spread out before her, lights all a-twinkling. *Beautiful... how beautiful*, she thought. She raised her glass towards the city and made a silent toast: *To you, Alex, wherever you are... for the love that you gave me. To you Derek, for silently accepting everything I did. To you, my handsome son, for being who you are... and to you, Ursula, for bringing him home. You must be one tough cookie!*

*

She'd spent the best part of an hour sitting in her chair, doing nothing. Well, she wasn't exactly doing nothing, she was thinking. No, not thinking, deliberating. She wasn't usually this indecisive, but then this decision wasn't like all those others she had to make on a daily basis. This was personal. Real personal. She'd tried twice before and they'd failed. Why would this time be any different? Maybe they'd fail this time as well. OK, so if they did, they did. But she had to try.

In three weeks it would be her 81st birthday. Her thoughts kept wandering to the past. More than twenty years had gone by since Derek had returned home. How time flies, she thought, and we barely realize it. We only know when we start to look at it in "episodes" – so many episodes in my life! What about Alex? He'd be 70 on the same day – if he was still around. Nonsense! Of course he's still around. People like him don't die at 70. Well, at least she hoped not. It was unfinished business. That's how she had to look at it. Unfinished business. Decision made, she picked up the phone.

*

She studied the man who now sat in front of her. Big, black and handsome was an easy way to describe him. A little over sixty, she guessed from what she'd been told, but he looked the best part of ten years younger. What was it that doctor woman had said? *Sixty is the new fifty*! Well, looking at this one, she'd be spot on.

He'd come highly recommended had Ed Burke. Worked freelance for the studios, all of them. "The best," they'd said. "Can do anything. Makes the impossible possible." Ex CIA, ex this, ex that. You got a problem?

Ed'll fix it.

She fixed him with a stare. 'They say you're the best.'

He inclined his head slightly. 'Thank you, Ma'am.'

'*I* didn't say you're the best; *they* did.' She waved her right arm around, without indicating who exactly – them! He'd heard she could be crotchety. Seemed they were right! 'Well, thank you anyway, Ma'am.' He smiled. What beautiful teeth. And the smile went to his eyes, not false. She liked him. 'I want you to find somebody for me. Somebody I want found and somebody other people don't want found.' He nodded. Obviously a man of few words. She pointed to two buff coloured files that lay on the coffee table beside her chair. 'I want you to take those files with you and read them. Read them and study them in depth. They're from two people like yourself who tried to do what I'm asking you to do, and failed. I don't want you to fail. This person seems not to exist, at least officially. Maybe he doesn't even know that. I want you to listen carefully to what I'm going to tell you and then I want you to go out and find him.'

'May I record?'

She nodded, as he pulled a small Sony cassette recorder from his briefcase, switched it on and placed it on the table next to her.

She started at the beginning, the time she first noticed Alex as he walked into the Top Three Club in Kassel, back in February 1959. She told him everything, leaving nothing out. Even the kitchen sink would have had the grace to blush. Not Ed Burke. He didn't even blink. Then she pointed to the files. 'The bottom one is 1998. The top one is 2003. They say the same thing. Alex does not exist. I know different. He was born 12th March 1938. His birthday's the same as mine. There's no birth certificate. His father was in a Scottish Highland Regiment. This regiment has no such record. He was in the Royal Air Force Police. The Royal Air Force has no record of him. I even have his number; they say this number was never issued. I could go on. It's a waste of time. It's all in these files. Read them.'

She paused for breath. She calmed herself, she was becoming agitated. Then she carried on. 'Both investigators said the same thing. If this man existed – and he did – these records were removed for a reason, and there is only one lot of people with the power to do it.' Ed Burke nodded in agreement. 'The government. For some reason they wanted no trace. That suggests he must have worked for them in some way – not a normal way, not a permanent way – but in a way that made it possible to deny him. It suggests he worked alone and it suggests he did jobs they didn't want traced back. Dirty jobs, illegal jobs.'

'Mr Burke,' she continued, 'I haven't told you why I want him found. Now I will. The last time we saw each other was 12th March 1959, our joint birthdays. We spent most of the morning making love.' She paused and smiled, as though seeing something that only she was party to. Then she went on, 'Our love-making produced a son. Our son produced a daughter. I want Alex to know he has a son and a granddaughter while there is still time. Find him, Mr Burke. Money is not a problem. Time may well be!'

She stood up and held out her hand, indicating that this meeting was now over.

At the end of one week Ed Burke and his team reached the same conclusion as the previous investigators. Alex did not exist, no documents anywhere, nothing, and yet they knew he did.

Day eight: At 10:00am UK time, Ed placed a call to the Royal Air Force Association at its headquarters in Leicester, England. In L.A. it was 2:00am. Did they, he asked, have anyone on their books by the name of Alex Gordon. Politely, but firmly, it was explained to Ed that this type of information could not be divulged. He changed tack. Could he send a letter to the Association, containing a second letter in the name of Alex Gordon. If Alex was a member, could they send it on. If not, would they return it. After checking, the answer came back that, 'Yes, we could do this,' and, 'Oh, Mr Burke, are you aware that the Royal Air Force Police now have their own association?'

Ed wasn't aware.

Would he like the number?

You bet!

*

Alex received the two letters separately, but on the same day, at his home in Greece. They were identical. In short, Debbie Curtis, widow of the late Derek Curtis, now resident in Los Angeles, wished to contact Alex on an urgent private matter. Contact could be arranged by calling the writer at the number listed above.

Alex checked his watch. Nearly 11:00am. That made it 1:00am in LA. He went into the garden where Emm was eating breakfast by the pool. *Strawberries again*, he noted. *We'll look like strawberries by the end of the summer!*

Without comment Alex dropped the letters on the table next to her.

'Telephone,' she pointed towards the house.

'Could be a can of worms.'

'Then we'll go fishing.'

Alex smiled. She knew him too well. Nearly thirty years together, what did he expect?

'Debbie. That name rings a bell. Isn't that the lady you knew back in Kassel? German, but married to an American? You, as usual, were doing things you shouldn't.'

Alex nodded. She knew all his "ladies". It had been necessary. A cleansing of the soul, perhaps. She was the only person in the world who knew of his double, sometimes triple existence. She was his rock. Even people like Alex needed a rock. He watched her nibbling on a strawberry while she filled in yet another crossword puzzle, clearly enjoying the unseasonably hot morning. She loved strawberries; winter, summer, morning, noon, night. She never tired of them. And she loved crosswords; did them in four languages. Brilliant mind!

He thought back to when they'd first met.

He'd been on a road trip round Europe, five countries, five embassies, nine days. He'd met her at a hotel just outside Brussels, getting ready to move to Germany in less than a week, and having a farewell dinner with her hairdresser.

He was smitten.

Luckily, so was she.

The move never took place and one week later she joined him on a four-day visit to the British Embassy in Paris. They'd been together ever since. She was 23 - almost 19 years younger than Alex.

In less than a year she was crossing borders with him – sometimes without papers. "Fun", she called it. She'd been with him in Burundi, Rwanda, Congo and the Ivory Coast. Nobody looks at a couple, he'd told her. It had meant lying to family and friends. That was hard.

Then there was the time they'd crossed from West to East Germany. For some reason the guard commander had got upset with Alex. He'd ranted and raved and finally he'd pulled his pistol and stuck it in Alex's chest. She'd yanked Alex backwards and stood in front of him and screamed at the border guard: 'How dare you stick a gun in my husband's chest!' She snatched her passport off the desk, opened it and pushed it in the guard's face. 'That,' she said, 'is a diplomatic passport! Now stamp it and let us go! We're trying to enter your bloody country, not leave it! And,' she added in fury, 'do you want me to give birth all over your filthy floor?!' The guard was so surprised he stamped both passports and even held the door open and saluted as she climbed back in the car.

As they drove away, she squeezed Alex's leg. 'God, I'm shaking. I nearly wet myself back there. That was close.' She was wearing a maternity dress and patted the bulge. She looked seven or eight months pregnant. The bulge contained 200,000 West German Marks and the passports were false.

She was just 24.

In 1993, when Serbia was blockaded by the West, she talked a Serbian official at the embassy in Sofia into convincing Belgrade to issue visas for the family. Alex, Emm and the two boys. Instead of the boys flying to their school in Switzerland, they travelled by car.

Window dressing.

11 Serbian militia checkpoints between the Bulgarian border and Belgrade. That was hard on the nerves. Belgrade: the gunrunners, the black marketeers, the blockade busters, every slime-ball you could possibly imagine. The pinhole cameras, taking down car and lorry numbers. Filling up with supposedly unobtainable fuel and then on into Hungary, Austria, Germany, and via Liechtenstein to the final destination in Switzerland. Turn around and head back. Floods in Switzerland. Snow and fog in the Alps. Last car train across the border into Italy. The viaduct that collapsed, killing so many people. Meeting up with their contact in Milan. Then on to meet dear old Adriaan – one of the few genuine friends they

had – in Lecco on Lake Como, not even five minutes late! A wonderful evening… Turn around yet again and head back into Germany; another meeting. Then into Austria and Hungary; the border jammed with refugees as they tried to enter Serbia. The plainclothes Serbian police at the Bulgarian border, openly stealing anything of value from their own countrymen before allowing them to cross into Bulgaria. Animals. "Now, that was something!" was how she described it. Definitely not for the faint hearted.

And then, that time sitting on a sunny hillside overlooking the railway siding outside Petrich in Bulgaria, with the children, pretending to have a picnic while watching a Greek goods train emptying thousands of litres of fuel into Bulgarian and Serbian tankers. When full, they immediately hightailed it to Kosovo and then into Serbia proper. Taking photographs and noting number plates. The armed guards, the black painted helicopter that buzzed them, no registration numbers, the downdraught from the rotor blades covering them and their picnic with dust. The two guards in the helicopter, sunglasses and Kalashnikovs, gesturing for them to leave. Apocalypse Now? All it needed was The Ride of the Valkiries from the tannoys. Alex pointed to the diplomatic number plates on the Landrover. Sunglasses-Number-One spoke into a microphone, waited for what seemed an eternity, then finally saluted and the helicopter veered away.

It was the dust in the strawberries that upset her . . .

Alex retrieved the letters and headed back to the house. 'I'll call. Should be able to upset someone this time of night.'

It was now well into the early hours in L.A. It was still his favourite pastime, baiting Americans. The phone across the Atlantic trilled twice. 'Ed Burke.'

'My God, don't you have a bed to go to?'

For a moment there was silence. Then, 'Who's this, please?'

'I believe you're looking for me.'

'Please, who's calling?'

'You wrote two letters. I have both.'

Silence, and then, 'Mr Gordon?' He sounded incredulous.

'You may call me Alex. Everyone else does.'

'I'm rather surprised, that's all. People have been looking for you on and off for years. Without success, I may add.'

'I decided to come out of the woodwork. My wife thinks I'm too old to play childish games. Time to settle down, play with grandchildren, that sort of childish game. Less stress, no health warnings, live longer. Tell me Mr Burke, how do you play with a nineteen year old granddaughter who doesn't even know you?' Silence.

Alex broke it. 'So, how's Debbie?'

'She's very well, a bit cantankerous now and then, but, well, you know…' he trailed off.

'Age, you mean.'

'I suppose.'

'Ed, I've been cantankerous all my life, and I'm still only 70. Well, will be tomorrow. Your timing was good. Debbie and I share the same birthday. She tell you?'

'She did, and the timing was not planned. Accidental, really. May I ask where you are?' Alex burst out laughing.

'God, you're difficult. I meant–'

Alex interrupted. 'I know what you meant, Ed. Just playing. I'm in Greece.'

'As in: You live there?'

'Me and another nine million or so. A wonderful place to be. Half the country's work-shy. The Albanians, Bulgarians,

Serbs, Gypsies – and don't forget the odd Chinese or North African – they do the manual work. The Greeks sit on the pavements and drink coffee all day long. Suits me.'

'A melting pot.'

'A time bomb, Ed. One day the bubble will burst and we'll all be in the crap.'

'Can you give me an address, Alex?'

'Nope, but I'll give you a number. Can you write?'

Ed burst out laughing. 'I really do want to meet you.'

'You're at the end of a very long queue, Ed… Ready?'

After he'd read out the number, there was silence. Then, 'What sort of number is this, Alex?'

'A phone number.'

'But I've never seen anything like it; there's no country code, it's, well, it's strange!'

'Ed, you can ring that number anytime from now until midnight Thursday evening. That's midnight Greek time on 13th March. The only person who will answer is me. OK? After that time the number will change. Understand?'

'OK, Alex. I'll be in touch.'

Alex disconnected and waited. Thirty seconds later the phone rang. Alex picked up the receiver. 'Go to sleep, Ed. It's time for strawberries.' He replaced the receiver. How he loved tickling Americans!

It was almost 24 hours to the minute when the phone buzzed and the light on the red receiver began to flash. He reached for the phone and settled back in his chair. Then he pressed the button, the light went out. Down the phone line he heard only silence. He waited. Then a chuckle. 'We playing games, Alex?'

He didn't know what he'd been expecting, but somehow she sounded, well… frail!

‘We used to be good at games.’

‘Long time ago, Alex.’

‘Happy Birthday, Debs.’

‘Happy Birthday, Alex. Do you know, nobody’s called me Debs in nearly fifty years. I called one of my companies *DEBS.*’

‘One? How many do you have?’

‘Exactly? Not too sure. Double figures, anyway.’

‘So, you succeeded then.’

‘Depends how you define success, Alex. It cost. Money I got, friends I don’t.’

‘Freedom? You always wanted freedom.’

‘Freedom is relative, Alex. It’s all in the head. Nobody has freedom, only obligations and responsibilities. As the kids say today: Life sucks.’

‘You really believe that?’

‘I guess not – well, maybe sometimes. Then I get real and go build another company. Before you know it, another lifetime gone. Anyway, tell me things, talk to me, Alex. You married?’

‘Yes.’

‘How long?’

‘Long time, met her nearly thirty years ago.’

‘Kids?’

‘Two boys. Both at university.’

‘That it?’

‘No. I’ve got a daughter and granddaughter. Not here, England.’ He cleared his throat.

‘And?’

‘Well, I’ve got another son. A Colonel in the German army. Not widely publicized.’

‘Wife know?’

'Yes.'

'Rest of family?'

'No.'

'Well, now I know… You sitting down, Alex?'

'Sure.'

'You comfortable?'

'Yes, why?'

'Let me recap. You got three sons and one daughter, right?'

'Yes.'

'Wrong, Alex. You got four sons and one daughter.'

Silence.

'You still there, Alex?'

'Tell me.'

'We have a son, Alex. Remember March 12, 1959? Well, D-day was 12 December 1959. His name's Derek, and five years ago he completed twenty one years as an Air Force Policeman. Just like his daddy. His real daddy that is.'

Alex stumbled for words, 'Why didn't you tell me?'

'How could I? I was married. I needed to get to the Promised Land. I told Derek it was his. Deep down, he never believed it. The night before he died he said next day he wanted to reminisce, and he mentioned you.'

'What about your son Derek?'

'*Our* son Derek. Well, I'm not sure. I think he feels something isn't right. Derek –my Derek– spoke to him about you, even told him some of your jokes, but I really don't know. I tried to find you before. Twice. They said you didn't exist. Your choice, Alex?'

'No.'

'Thought not. Anyway, I wanted you to know. You've also got a granddaughter – Annie. Film actress. Doing very well. Nearly twenty three. You mind if I tell them, Alex?'

'I guess not.'

'Is that a yes?'

Silence. Then they burst out laughing simultaneously. 'You remember.'

'Alex, I've never forgotten. Not one damn thing have I forgotten' She paused, then giggled.

'Fancy a bit of telephone sex?'

'Debbie!!'

'What? You become a prude all of a sudden? Never mind. It'd probably kill me anyway. Going to tell your wife?'

'Yes.'

'Any problem?'

'No.'

'Good. Listen, Alex. Can we talk again? Lots to say and no-one to say it to.'

'Sure, Debs. Listen, that Ed Burke, he any good?'

'He found you.'

'No, he didn't find me. I rejoined society. I'm public again. It was deliberate.'

'This good or bad?'

'Don't know yet, Debs.'

'You be careful; you're not twenty one anymore.'

'As my wife regularly reminds me.'

'Debs, ask Ed to call me before tomorrow night, he knows why. I want to send him something. If he doesn't know what to do with it, tell him to find somebody who does. Then we can talk.'

He could almost hear her thinking. Finally she said, 'I think I understand, Alex. Now you go and enjoy your birthday. My best to your wife.'

He stayed where he was for a few moments, taking it all in. A son, a granddaughter, Derek dead and Debbie seemingly mega rich. Quite something. Oh, well, time he lay it out for his wife.

He walked into the garden. She was lapping the pool. Sixty every morning, regardless of the weather. Roughly a kilometre. He sat in a chair and watched how she swam. Effortlessly, would probably cover it. Finally, she stopped. One heave of the arms and she was out. Steps unnecessary.

He knew what was coming; it never varied. She did it to annoy him – well, not annoy, irritate. Grinning, as usual, she walked up behind him, plonked a kiss on top of his head and at the same time draped her wet arms around his neck, dripping water all over his crisply ironed shirt. Light blue began to darken. Sometimes he'd swear, sometimes he'd throw her back in the pool. She had been known to pull him in with her, fully clothed. It was a game, a ritual.

He stood up. She ran laughing to the other side of the pool. 'Not today, Emm. We need to talk.' He had a variety of names for her. "Emm" meant serious stuff. He pointed to the chair next to him, then took his soaking shirt off and hung it on the back of his chair. Be dry in ten minutes in this sun. He poured himself a black coffee from the Thermos while she stood and towelled herself dry. Finally she sat down and looked across at him.

'Debbie?' He nodded and took a sip of his coffee.

'Problem?'

'No. It appears I have a son, or rather Debbie and I have a son. His name's Derek, like his dad who's now dead, and he also has a daughter, a film actress called Annie. Twenty two, doing well. Debbie's mega rich. No problem, just wanted to find me, tell me and ask if she could tell them. She's 81. I think it's an age-thing. Before I die, and all that.'

Emm was grinning. 'And when was Derek born?'

December 12, 1959.'

She laughed out loud. 'Ah! Your birthday treat. Well, you certainly had a memorable twenty-first! East German border, produced Derek, and, not forgetting, breakfast by Pete.'

He looked at her. 'Good Lord, you remember that? You've got a memory like an elephant.'

She stuck her tongue out at him. 'I'll take that as a compliment. Now then lover boy; let's do a count, just for fun. As I remember it, in February and March you were having it off with Debbie. In the summer it was Katrina. September and October it was Dina. November you got married and celebrated by having a farewell session with the aforementioned Dina. And of course we mustn't forget Hella, whom you seemed to fit in whenever you had time to spare. I'm impressed. I don't know how you ever found time to go out and arrest anyone. 1959 was obviously a vintage year for you, even by your exacting standards.'

'So, everything is cool, as the kids say?'

'Why wouldn't it be? Your extra-marital activities ended with me. *But*...if they didn't, a call to your very ex-friend Gorby would mean that running around dick-less would be the least of your problems. Capisce?'

She stood up. 'I'm going for a shower. Coming?' She was taunting him. 'See if you can emulate your twenty-first at seventy... or, is it *All Passion Spent*?'

He laughed. 'Something like that, and anyway, I've done my five kilometres. That's enough exercise for today.'

She turned and walked towards the house and he was watching, just like she knew he would. Halfway she stopped, glanced back over her shoulder and wiggled her bottom at him. 'Coward,' she said, 'Change your mind, you know where I am.'

'Raincheck!'

'No way! This is a once only super-duper special seventieth birthday offer which expires in fifteen minutes.'

Oh, well, why not? he thought to himself. *Could be dead by tomorrow! Then again, if it's THAT super-duper, I could be dead in half an hour!*

Always a risk-taker, he heaved himself up from the chair.

She giggled and ran…

Chapter 40

The Fat Man

The Fat Man had a name. Godfrey. That was his real name. He also had a second name. Sutton. That was not his real name. When Godfrey was first asked to choose a cover name under which to work it bothered him. He was afraid he might not know who he was or, forget who he was supposed to be. He asked if he could continue to be known as Godfrey. His employers finally relented, and Godfrey remained Godfrey. The second name was a different matter. After several sleepless nights, Godfrey had a brainwave. Could he, he asked his employers, be known as Godfrey Sutton? 'Certainly,' they replied, 'but why?'

It turned out that Godfrey had been born in Sutton Coldfield and he was fairly sure that, come what may, he would always remember his place of birth.

'Even under torture?' they'd asked.

Godfrey blanched.

'Only joking,' they'd assured him. After all Godfrey was a boffin.

Godfrey also had a specialty. The Wall. The *Innerdeutshe Grenze,* the *Deutsch-Deutsche Grenze* or the *Zonengrenze.* The name was irrelevant. Godfrey knew it all. All 1381 kilometres of it. He could draw it in his sleep.

The experts will tell you the wall was impregnable because it was guarded by some 48,000 NVA troops. That it had three metre high electric fences topped with razor wire. That it had landmines, dogs and ditches. All true. But, that it was impregnable? Not true.

Godfrey knew all its secrets. Godfrey knew how to get in, and then how to get out again. He knew how to get under, over, through and around it.

The East Germans thought it was impregnable.

Godfrey knew it was not.

When The Wall was built, modified and later improved yet again, the East Germans built stretches of wall that were deliberately insecure, but to the untrained eye were simply a continuation or part of the wall. The mines that were laid were fake, the fence was not electrified and at certain points it was possible to move between two given watchtowers and not be observed. There were no cameras. And all this was deliberate. There were twenty seven such places – one every fifty kilometres, or so. But why? For almost thirty eight years it allowed the East Germans to successfully infiltrate their agents into the West and later extract them again. They thought no-one knew. They were wrong. Godfrey knew. And for over twenty years he used these “special places”, as he called them, against their original designers. He told Alex.

Alex told no-one.

Between 1962 and 1983, and with Godfrey’s meticulous planning, Alex crossed and re-crossed this supposedly impregnable wall a total of eighteen times. Nine times in, nine times out. The one time Alex ignored Godfrey’s advice to abort he ended up getting hurt.

The strain, the pressures, the tremendous responsibilities weighed heavily on Godfrey. When Alex was hurt, Godfrey disappeared for three days. No-one could find him. When he eventually reappeared, bleary-eyed and hung over, they sent him off on two weeks' sick leave. The damage was done, however, and Mr Smirnoff became his constant companion.

To Alex, Godfrey had replaced Old Smudger as a father figure. Depression set in towards the end of 1980. He went on many cures, all to no avail. The end finally came on Saturday 26th February 1983 in the shape of one bottle of Smirnoff and two bottles of pills – twenty three years to the day that he'd first met Alex in *Steiner's*, back in Gütersloh.

It was Alex who found him, as Godfrey had known he would.

The meeting had been prearranged – they always were. *Alex will take care of everything* ... was one of his last thoughts.

And Alex did.

Meaning no disrespect, but as a sign of true affection, Alex had placed a bottle of Smirnoff in Godfrey's left arm and a glass in his right hand.

Alex never crossed *The Wall* again.

Chapter 41

Crew Cut/Psycho

... Psycho looked deep into Alex's eyes, 'For you,' he said, 'there is no going back. This is your life. If you want to survive remember this,

"Friends are a luxury you cannot afford
They will be the death of you, or you of them."

And then the games began.
Holland, Belgium, France, Italy, Luxembourg, West Germany, East Germany, Ivory Coast, Burundi, Rwanda, Congo, Bulgaria, Serbia, Kosovo, Bosnia, Croatia and Greece.
There is no such thing as a friendly place.
Alex remembered The Rule. He broke it once and survived.
He found his rock.
Emm.
Psycho also broke The Rule. A honey trap.
He died.
Such is the nature of The Games...

-

Timewise, Crew Cut played a minor role in Alex's life – three months – but the knowledge he imparted proved crucial in terms of Alex's wellbeing and ability to survive in extremely hostile and difficult situations and still complete a mission successfully.

Following his departure from Innsworth in March 1960, Alex spent the next two months living in a crofter's cottage in the Highlands of Scotland. Crew Cut was his constant companion – his mentor, his tutor, his guide and his guard. As Alex put it: 'We would eat together, work together, sleep together and shit together. Never once did he let me out of his sight. Never once did I see him smile. He was an automaton. Slowly I began to hate him.'

Following Scotland the pair moved to Wales for a further month where, '… the bastard made me run up and down mountains every day, seven days a week, for the next four weeks. At times I wanted to die rather than face it all again the next day, the day after and the day after that. The really annoying thing was that he did it with me – everything. And of course, he was better than me. He was like a machine. By now, I really hated him. I wanted to kill him, and he knew it. In my mind I changed his name from Crew Cut to Psycho, because that's what he was – a controlled psycho, a freak. I'd never met anyone like him in my life and I've never met anyone like him since, - and believe me, I've met some real weirdoes over the past fifty years.'

Alex paused and looked at me. 'Do you know what his name was? Alan. Alan Lake! And he came from Stoke-on-Trent. Can you imagine? Stoke-on-Trent! I thought the only thing they produced in Stoke-on-Trent was pottery, but no, they produced Alan Lake, and nobody's ever heard of him. Sad really. . . After three months of living in each other's pockets it came to the parting of the ways. We shook hands – he didn't even smile then – he just told me to keep my nose clean and remember what I'd been taught. Might save your life one day, he said. It did. I owe him. I never met him again and didn't hear anything about him until 1987, I think it was. It seems

Alan had finally broken the rules – and paid for it with his life. Alan worked the Balkans and somewhere along the way he met a Romanian girl by the name of Mihaela. Mihaela Miculescu. What exactly happened I don't know, but on this occasion he'd crossed over into Romania to see her. Idiot! Completely unauthorized and against the rules! They were of course waiting for him – *Securitate* or DIE, that is. A classic honey trap and Alan, of all people, walked right into it.'

Alex then turned to me and asked: 'Do you know what man's Achilles heel is?'

I shook my head, not wanting to break into his train of thought. This was Alex in full flow; a rare occasion!

'It's his dick. Man thinks with his dick. Always has, always will. The honey trap has been around since creation and still we fall in the pot. Temptation. We can't resist it. The most stupid thing on this planet is man.' He paused. 'Anyway, I'm getting carried away. Back to Alan.'

Then he looked at me again, '… and don't tell my wife I said that. She's been saying it for years. Wouldn't do to let her know she's right. I'd never live it down! Now, back to Alan… So, these bastards were waiting for him. They thought he'd just put up his hands and surrender. They were wrong. Alan apparently managed to draw his pistol and got off a couple of shots, then he ran for it. The meeting took place in Giurgiu. That's on the Romanian side of the border and on the Danube. Across the other side is Bulgaria. This was January, freezing cold and lots of snow everywhere. Anyway, Alan made it to the river, but there was no way he could get across the bridge to the other side. So, what did he do? He jumped in the freezing cold water. In January! Ice everywhere! The Danube is some two kilometres wide there because of some scattered islets diverting the flow of the water. Can you imagine just how scared he must have been …? No, of course you can't. He started swimming. The bloody Romanians opened fire, and that was the last they saw of him. The Bulgarian border guards on the other side of the river heard the gunfire and started running round like headless chickens, shining their lights in the water. Somebody with a bit of brain finally unhooked a police launch and started searching their side of the river. They searched back and forth for over one hour; nothing. Then, they returned to the jetty and guess what? There was Alan, arm jammed through a metal mooring ring, floating face up against the jetty. Eyes closed; they thought he was dead. They dragged him out of the water and found he'd got two bullet holes in his back but was still alive, just. They stuck him in an ambulance and hightailed it to hospital. Into the theatre, onto the operating table, and you know what? The old bugger opened his eyes, saw where he was – and get this – he smiled. He actually smiled! Then he closed his eyes and died. Two bullets and hypothermia. Even Psycho couldn't survive that combination. So, that was the end of Alan – Crew Cut, Psycho or whatever you care to call him.'

He glanced across at me. 'That was the end of Alan, but it's not the end of the story. Want to hear what happened?'

I nodded, enthralled. *Did these things really happen in life?* Alex continued. 'Five years later, in 1992, Christmas day I think it was, the Bulgarian border police found the body of a woman floating in the Danube. She'd been secured to a metal mooring ring on the jetty at Russe by a rope tied to her right arm. She was fully clothed and a handbag was attached to her body by a strap that ran over her left shoulder. Documents in the handbag identified her as Mihaela Miculescu and somebody had put two bullets through her head.' He paused. 'Beautiful! Beautiful, beautiful! Poetic justice, don't you think?' and with that Alex got up and left, leaving me with more questions than before.

It was two days before I worked up the courage to ask the question that had been persistently nagging at my brain since that last interview with Alex.

I hadn't dared ask him in case he gave me the answer I didn't want to hear and, truth be told, I'm a little afraid of Alex. He has that effect on people. Alex had left for Holland that morning. It seemed now or never.

I was sitting in the living room with Emm, trying to read through my notes. My interview sessions with Alex were over –he'd made that clear– yet I still had one question burning in my mind. My brain refused to let me concentrate. The television was on, playing quietly in the background. Neither of us was watching. I cleared my throat nervously. Emm looked up from the magazine she was reading and smiled across at me. 'You want to ask me something, don't you? Something you can't ask Alex.'

God! She can even read my mind!

'I've felt it, ever since Alex left this morning. You're on edge and can't relax. You can always ask. Just remember, it doesn't mean I'll always tell.'

I cleared my throat again. I just hoped I wouldn't start to stutter; it happens sometimes when I'm nervous. And now I was very nervous. I began. 'Can you tell me where Alex was in 1992?' There, it was out!

The smile didn't change. 'Alex was in Bulgaria, we both were. We lived there for nearly six years. Why?'

'Well, it was something Alex said.' … *Come on, don't chicken out now!*

'What did Alex say?'

'Can you remember where you were at Christmas?'

She frowned. 'Of course! We were at the Sheraton. We lived there for a year, and I remember that particular Christmas very well. It started to snow at exactly midnight. Our suite looked out over Sveta Nedelya Square. All the lights were on and with the snow falling, it was as beautiful as any Christmas card.'

She laughed, reliving the moment.

'It was a beautiful scene, that is until the old Russian water bowsers came along with snow ploughs attached to their fronts, and started to clear away the snow. Then it was back to reality.'

I remembered Alex's words: *Temptation. We can't resist it.* 'Was Alex with you the whole of Christmas?' There, it was out!

She hesitated, looked at me rather thoughtfully, and then, still smiling, but somehow more serious, said, 'He didn't do it, you know.'

'W-what?' It came out like a croak.

'That which you somehow think he might have done.'

'How do you know?' *Dammit!* I was going to start stuttering next.

'*I* would know!' This came out so forcefully that I sat back in my chair with a start.

'I'm sorry. But to answer your question: No, Alex wasn't with us for the whole of Christmas. He went away on the twenty third and returned just as the snow started to fall.' She turned the full smile on me again. 'At the time, we thought it was rather poetic. And, to save you asking the question, no, I don't know where he was. I learned many years ago not to ask questions of Alex. If, and when, he wants me to know something then he will tell me. But—' And she was still smiling at me. 'I know all the stories. I've lived with Alex for nearly thirty years. I'm his safety valve. Everybody, including Alex, needs one. And, whatever it is you think he may have done, you're wrong. Does that answer your question?'

'Yes,' I replied rather weakly.

But, of course . . . it didn't.

Printed in Great Britain
by Amazon